TIME ENOUGH
LATER

Praise for Time Enough Later

"Miss Kylie Tennant has rather a weakness for practical young women
and shiftless middle-aged men. In *Time Enough Later* she once again
tells, with racy humour and point, the adventures of such a female. Miss
Tennant's young women are quite frankly adorable, and Bessie Drew
is no exception to this rule; indeed, I'm inclined to give her very high
marks for sheer entertainment value. Child of a Sydney slum, she attaches
herself with firm ferocity to a ne'er-do-well lodger of her mother's, who
owes everyone money, including his landlady. But Bessie, who is gifted
with a little imagination, sees in him a way to better things, in spite of the
bitter opposition and contempt of her family, and clings on. Somehow
the experience is not all that she hoped for, but on the credit side not
nearly so bad as it might have been, for Bessie has that delightful self-
reliance and warmth of character with which Miss Tennant so richly
endows her heroines. The scene is Sydney. Maurice Wainwright, the
middle-aged philanderer, who takes himself so seriously as an inventor of
genius, is also an exceedingly accomplished photographer. And though he
hates the commercial side of this particular line, he manages to persuade
a rather shady business man to set him up in a studio. Bessie tags along as
receptionist, charwoman and general handyman. Her family are outraged
and indignant, but she defies them all. Eventually Maurice falls in love
with her. There is a grandly comic party thrown at his studio, which
Miss Tennant does superbly. Bessie is self-appointed chucker-out; at the
climax affairs get a little out of hand, however, so she deserts Maurice
and goes off home for the night. But at the party she makes friends with
an eccentric woman scientist, who has a shack in the country. Bessie
and Wainwright go down to this place for a week-end. They find the
scientist away, and the place hardly conducive to illicit love. They become
engaged, however, but it is the country with all its simple earthly joys
which has taken real possession of the girl's heart. Quite a number of
complications, including another devoted male, and the fact that she has
got herself engaged to the fantastic Maurice, have to be sorted out before
Bessie can give herself up to the fullest joys of the simple life. At times
this lively narrative descends to the level of roaring farce; but Bessie, in
spite of dingy perils and desperate moments, keeps her common sense,
high spirits and generosity, and stays a darling to the end."

John Hampson, The Spectator

TIME ENOUGH LATER

by

KYLIE TENNANT

SANDNESS
MICHAEL WALMER
2020

CHAPTER I

I

THE Drew family had assembled for tea with tempers as pleasant as garlic at a wedding. A bone of contention in the Drew household was always picked bare, being brought out at every meal and worried over with snarls and snappings. This particular disagreement had lasted for several days, and the Drews were now heartily sick of it. When big Bill Drew looked up from his second cup of tea and said ominously : " Don't think I've forgotten about it just because I've said nothing," there was a unanimous howl from his family : " For Crisake, shut up ! "

" There's a way to talk to your father ! "

Hitching his heavy frame back so that his chair balanced on two legs, Bill Drew glanced deliberately from his eldest son to his second son, his eldest daughter, and then at his wife.

" Where's Bessie ? " he demanded.

No one replied.

" If I find," Drew continued, " that she's coddling that Wainwright fellow again, I'll skin her." He turned to his wife. " Any stew left, Amy ? "

" You know there ain't," his wife retorted. " What d'you mean saying : ' Any stew left ? ' like that ? What do you think I am anyway ? A cafeteria ? You had your three helpings, didn't you ? You had more'n any of us."

" A man comes home from his work and expects to get at least a square feed. 'Tisn't as though I didn't give you the money. What you do with it beats *me*. Never a decent meal." These were only the preliminaries and no one took any notice. " I suppose you've done nothing all day, if the truth was known, but feed the coot in the back room."

"Shush! He'll hear you."

"What do I care? You drag him out of the gutter to live on me. Call that taking in boarders? Having that smarmy-faced lizard living on us? I ain't forgotten what I said this mornin'. You got to tell him to go."

"It's your place to tell him. I don't see why I should do everything," Mrs. Drew protested. She was a small, stringy woman with a piercing voice. "How was I to know the man wouldn't pay? He comes here lordly as can be and walks in as if he owns the place. Getting me out of bed at one o'clock in the morning to let him in!"

"*You* let 'im come here, and *you* got to get rid of 'im."

"I don't see that," Mrs. Drew complained shrilly. "That's like you all over. Sit there telling me what to do. Oh yes! You can do that all right. But," her voice rose dramatically, "have I ever known you do one mortal thing in this place when I was trying to make ends meet? Taking in a boarder for the back room, and a nicely spoken one too, and you may talk about bringin' in your money regular, but how far does it go? And when I work my fingers off scraping and scratching for a few extra pennies, do you do anything but sneer and jeer and sit there like a fat old bull whale? No...." Mrs. Drew paused breathless with indignation. "No, you do *not*."

"Oh, cut it out, Mum." George, the elder son, moodily stirred his tea. "Dad's bad enough without you starting."

"Well, why don't you pick on *him*? Why turn on me as though I began it? I'll admit," Mrs. Drew conceded handsomely, "that the man's got to go. I'll admit that. I'll even admit I might of made a mistake takin' him. But you know you can't be too fussy and he . . ."

" All right," George snarled. " Don't go over it all again."

" Who's going over it all again ? What are you picking on me for ? You always was like that, George. Stick up for your father every time. It's not as though he's ever done anything for you. Anything you've ever had I've had to pinch and scrape for, ever since you was a tiny little child, and now, when I expect you to show a little help and consideration . . ." George's mother stopped for breath.

" All right," George growled. " If you're all so blasted well scared of the chap, I'll tell him to get out myself."

This was so unexpected that it produced a momentary silence. For George to offer to do anything at all was epic. His efforts were usually directed towards getting things done for him.

" George, the hero of Archer Street," his sister Beryl observed.

George turned on her. " Will you shut your mouth ? I don't see you've any reason to put your spoke in. If I wasn't so sick of hearin' you all yapping about him, I wouldn't take the job on. It's none of my business. I didn't let the room to him, did I ? "

" Don't go over it all again," Beryl snapped. She was fidgeting about the room with one eye on the clock and the other on her father. Her mouth fidgeted too. It was a petulant red mouth which she distorted into all kinds of little pouts and curls. She was a sharp, pretty little girl, able to hold her own with any of the two hundred employees of the store where she worked behind the lace counter. At the moment she was regarding George and her father very much as though they were two old ladies fussing over a bit of lace.

" Go on, George," she said nastily. " Let's see you throw him out."

" Why pick on George ? " Herbert chimed in, grinning. Herbert was still at school, but he always defended George and took a malicious delight in annoying his sisters. " The bloke's Bessie's affair. Bet you anything you like she's in there falling all over him at this minute."

" Bessie ! " Mrs. Drew shrilled.

" Coming."

" There," Mrs. Drew said, relieved. " She's upstairs in her room. She's not with Mr. Wainwright at all. Go on, George."

George got to his feet reluctantly. He was a weedy, lanky youth with a shock of black hair that stood in wisps straight up from his forehead. George worked in his uncle's garage, but his real interest in life was greyhounds.

" Maurice Wainwright ! " he exclaimed, twisting his mouth in a way startlingly like Beryl's. " What a name ! Don't suppose it's his own anyway. Oh, well ! Here goes ! "

Beryl followed him to the door.

" Where're *you* going ? " her sire demanded, roused.

" Out."

" Out ! You're always out. But where the hell you going ? That's what I want to know."

Beryl's mouth straightened into a thin line. " I'm going out."

Her father's face flushed. His somewhat bloodshot eyes bulged.

" You cheeky little devil," he roared. " Take that ! "

Beryl, with the aplomb of a prize-fighter, jerked her head out of the way just in time.

" I'll teach you," her parent breathed fiercely. " I'll teach you to talk back at me."

" You let the girl alone," Mrs. Drew screamed. " You let her alone."

But Beryl had streaked to the door. " I hate you," she informed her father deliberately. " I hate the very sight of you. And I'm going out of this house to get away from you."

" Then you don't come back," her parent stormed. " You can sleep in the street for all I care. Get out of here and stay out." Breathing heavily he relapsed into his chair. " That's the kind of family I've got. No respect. No bloody respect at all."

" And a fine father you are to talk that way," Mrs. Drew retorted. " How do you expect me to bring them up decent with you in the house swearing and cursing and bullying and roaring from morning till night ? "

" You," said her spouse, liberally buttering a piece of bread, " are enough to make an angel spit blood."

He was not in the least disturbed by the dramatic exit of his daughter. He had lost count of the number of times Beryl had left for the pictures in just such a manner and returned tranquilly at the usual hour.

" George is taking his time," he remarked, gulping a large bite.

" Gawd ! Haven't you had enough to eat ? Always your stomach ! There ain't nothing with you but wanting food. And butter one and eight a pound, and you've got about a pound of it on your bread."

" A man's got to *eat*, hasn't he ? "

George slouched in from the hall.

" Well ? " his father growled. " Did you see him ? "

" I saw him all right."

" Well ? "

" He says he's sick. Says he wants a doctor."

" What does he think this is ? A blasted rest 'ome ? "

" He looks pretty crook. It wouldn't be much good if he died on us, would it ? "

" The thing is to get him out of the house. Never mind the dyin' part. We can't pay for doctors, and he ain't likely to pay himself. Who does he think is goin' for doctors anyway ? You ? "

" Not me," said George firmly. " Bessie's just gone."

Mr. Drew's blood-pressure again mounted in a steady purple to his brow. " What ! " he roared.

" She was upstairs getting her coat on when I went in to see him." George leant reflectively on the doorway. " He does look pretty bad."

" There's not one of you any good," his father raged. " So that's what Bessie's up to ! Wait till she gets back and I'll knock her head off."

He flung himself down into the chair again muttering, and presently, still rumbling under his breath, dragged forward the loaf and began to saw off a hunk of crust.

" And put less butter on it this time," Mrs. Drew snapped from the sink where she was collecting the dishes for washing-up. She turned to George. " I suppose if the man's as sick as all that there's nothing to be done about it."

" I s'pose not," George said gloomily.

" That's just it," his parent growled. " He's done it on purpose. You can't tell me. He's that sort. Anything to get out of paying the rent."

II

Archer Street, Redfern, just missed being a slum by a narrow margin. It had not made up its mind whether it was a busy industrial thoroughfare or a quiet stretch of working-men's terraces. A depressing squalor, a respectable squalor, afflicted it ; this was compounded of soot from the machine shops, the smells of a brewery and a patent medicine factory, a lack of interest on the part of landlords, and the noise of trams from the street corner. The brewery was in the opposite direction to the patent medicine establishment, and Archer Street between them was a battle-ground, dominated sometimes by the odour of hops and at other times by the more mysterious herbs

6

of the rival business. Residents were reconciled to the pungency of the air by the cheapness of the rents.

It was a street where doctors seldom visited. The sick of Archer Street never called a doctor while they could stagger to the out-patients' department of the hospital or to a chemist's shop. The doctor who was dragged to 71 Archer Street by the determined Bessie was young and inexperienced. He was by no means reassured by the voice that rumbled menacingly down the narrow hall.

" Bloody doctors," announced the voice from the kitchen. " Bloody blood-suckers."

" In here." The girl opened the door furthest along the hall. " I've brought the doctor, Mr. Wainwright," she told the patient.

" Thank you, kid," the patient whispered. " You can clear off now." His tone was that of one graciously releasing the children from school.

There was nothing very prepossessing about the sick man. He lay in a disordered heap of bedclothes looking like a Victorian illustration of Death in the Workhouse. His face seemed to partake of the grey shabbiness of the cotton sheets with a growth of beard over it like a scrubby dark blanket. The bones of his face projected through this covering much as the iron bedstead jutted from the thin bedclothes. He had wrapped around his neck a woollen muffler, the kind of woollen muffler that old ladies knit and give as a present. Despite the incredible stuffiness of the room the man was shivering. The doctor strode over and opened the window.

" I hate fresh air," the patient croaked haughtily. " It's the one thing I have in common with . . . with . . ." he waved his hand feebly, " this place."

" What's the trouble ? " the doctor asked briskly. In any film he would have stepped into the part of the brilliant young surgeon who carves up the Woman He Loves like a piece of steak. Actually his brisk manner

7

covered an uneasy lack of confidence in himself.

" I caught a cold," the man on the bed wheezed. " I can't get my breath. If you can give me something . . . relieve the pain. I must see a man to-morrow . . . business." He shut his eyes exhausted.

" You'll have to forget business for a while," the doctor said, after he had made his almost unnecessary examination. " You have bronchitis."

" I can't possibly," the man said, opening his eyes. " I can't possibly . . . be sick."

The doctor scribbled hastily. " Get this made up tonight. I suppose you have someone to send to the chemist ? I mean — you don't sound as though you belong here."

" These people," the patient shook his head, " very proletarian. Crude type."

" You must have care and attention. Common humanity would surely prompt them to . . ."

" Humanity ! " the patient replied with sudden energy. " As well expect a sonata from chopsticks."

The doctor smiled. " How about the girl who came for me ? "

" Bessie ? A good kid. Oh, I'll manage." He weakly waved one large square white hand and let it fall. " But it's just my luck. Just as I'm arranging to build up a business again. . . ."

" What is your business ? " The doctor was interested.

" I'm a photographer. Lost all my money . . . law suit. That damn lawyer broke me. Had a good case . . ." he gasped. " And now . . . just as I have a chance of getting on my feet . . ."

" Don't talk any more."

" Can't pay you . . . you know," the patient gasped apologetically. " But when finance adjusts itself . . ."

" Don't worry," the doctor reassured him. " I'll call back to-morrow to see how you're getting on."

8

There was no need for him to call back, but there was something about the patient that interested him. Never in his life, the doctor thought, had he seen a more startling-looking person. The man looked like a devil, a very sick and frightened devil, with piercing black eyes, a big hooked nose and high domed bald brow. Everything about him was incongruous, a ridiculous mixture of absurdity and dignity.

" I know what it is," the doctor said aloud. " You look like someone in disguise."

The man on the bed was not in the least offended. He could not have reached his forties without hearing many comments on his peculiar appearance. He smiled, and as he smiled the doctor noted how shocking his red mouth looked in a shabby setting of grey skin and black bristles.

" It is not a business asset," the patient gasped. " Should have been an actor if I'd had the memory."

The doctor turned in the doorway. " I'm pleased to have met you, Mr. Wainwright," he said impulsively. " The chemist and I have a working arrangement. Don't bother about paying him."

That was the effect Maurice Wainwright had on people. You either hated the sight of him or he could have your liver for breakfast.

On his way out the doctor knocked sharply on the kitchen door. The voice was still rumbling, but it was a much more satisfied, after-dinner rumble.

" Could I speak to you a minute ? "

" Yeah. How is 'e ? "

" In a very serious condition. He will need care and nursing."

" Well, you'd better take him out of here. He won't pay you, I can tell you that. Been 'ere three weeks and never paid a penny. Not a penny, has 'e, Amy ? "

" I can't help that. He will need someone to look

after him." The doctor turned to Mrs. Drew. " As far as food is concerned, nothing heavy. Broth, custards, lightly boiled eggs — things like that. He needs building up." He turned to the girl Bessie. " See that he puts that thermogene across his chest. Give him the inhalant twice a day. He will need more blankets, and if he throws them off, keep tucking them round him. Keep the window open and the room warm. Take the prescription down to the chemist and give him this note. I think that's about all."

In the kitchen a stupefied silence reigned.

" Blasted hide," George muttered, rousing himself.

" Well, I suppose we can't just let him die on us," Mrs. Drew snapped defiantly. " There wouldn't be much chance of ever lettin' the room again with all the neighbours tellin' people somebody died in it."

III

It was Bessie's busy night. She had to wait at the chemist's shop for the medicine, and it was nearly nine o'clock when she finally entered the patient's room with a draping of blankets over her shoulder.

" What's that you have ? " The patient started to cough as he spoke.

" Blankets. The doctor said you were to have them." They came from Bessie's bed. " Here, drink your medicine and don't talk."

" I want you to do something for me, kid. Get me a pencil, will you ? There's one in my vest pocket at the foot of the bed."

" Don't talk. I'll find it."

Competently she searched his pockets like a young wardress. There was something sturdy and dependable about Bessie. She had a habit of standing with her feet planted apart as though to repel the buffets of some

hostile force. She was not at all pretty ; but she had
vigour, the cool impudence and humour of youth, and
was as unselfconscious and independent as a butcher-boy.
Of her one accomplishment her family had in vain striven
to cure her. Bessie whistled. She had been taught to
whistle by an eccentric and drunken uncle who whistled
for a living outside hotels. Every time the Drew family
heard Bessie whistling, it acted as a reminder of her disgraceful Uncle Jeffery and brought down the parental
wrath upon her. She could not whistle in the biscuit
factory where she worked. So she whistled by stealth.
It was over her whistling that she had made friends with
the lodger one Saturday morning when she was practising
down at the end of the yard.

Bessie watched him now maternally as he scribbled
on a bit of crumpled paper. He was talking as he wrote
and coughing as he talked.

"You know Surry Hills, don't you ? Get off at the ice-
works and go down Stretcher Street, and it's the third
house down. Got that ? " He spoke carefully as he
would to a child. " Go along to the third house and
knock. If no one answers, stand out on the footpath
and shout ' Ernie ' as loud as you can. Got that ?
Ernie's sure to be there. Give him the note and tell him
Maurice Wainwright says to come with you and bring
The Book. Got that ? " He sank back with his eyes shut.

Bessie meditated. " I'll get into a row. It's late."

Maurice Wainwright opened his eyes again and regarded her with patient weariness.

" Run along, Bessie," he murmured, " like a good girl.
You'll find some coppers for your fare on the dressing-
table."

He gave one of his characteristic waves of the hand
as though, with other annoyances, he would brush her
words like so many mosquitoes from the air.

Bessie hesitated a minute, rearranged the bedclothes,

removed the medicine glass to the dressing-table, then went cautiously on tiptoe towards the back door. There was a drizzle of rain falling, but if she fetched her coat from the front hall, she could be detected. Even now someone might call from the kitchen. Never did an escaping convict exercise more caution. Once outside the gate she began to run. She could run like a black-fellow, with a free, speedy lope. It would be quicker, she reflected, to run to Surry Hills ; but since she had her fare, she might as well use the tram.

It was a Friday night shopping crowd, bumping and swaying and hot. Bessie gave up her seat to an old lady and wriggled as close to the door as she could, sniffing with her quaint snub nose at the smell of streets and people, asphalt and rain. It would be good to go into a park and see the rain coming down in the dark ; but in Redfern walking by yourself in parks was likely to lead to unpleasant consequences. Mr. Wainwright, she remembered with pleasure, had promised to take her out for a day in the bush when he felt better. It was a pity he was so hard up. She knew all about his business, and the quarrel with the lawyer, and the trouble over his case in court. She, Bessie, could fight for herself ; but a man like Mr. Wainwright was, well, just like a man. Not sensible. Bessie had a hearty contempt for men. George and Herbert and her father and Uncle Jeff who had died in a " home ".

" They kid themselves," Bessie said to herself. Take Dad, for instance. Driving a truck for a furniture ware-house was not much of a job ; but for all his roaring, he would never have the chance of another. He was just kidding himself that he meant something by roaring at his family. She, Bessie, did not kid herself.

She swung her muscular young frame off the footboard before the tram slowed down at the ice-works, and began to search for Stretcher Street.

" Sure you don't mean Fletcher Street ? " the police-man asked, licking his thumb as he laboriously turned the pages of his little directory. " There isn't any Stretcher Street, but Fletcher Street's just over the road."

It was a mean street of tall houses much like Archer Street : one of those back streets that remain the same century after century. The houses rose from the footpath in a wall without a scrap of green or a porch to mark them as dwellings. Mr. Wainwright had said the third house. But which side ? Bessie gave it up. She stood in the middle of the street and called up all her courage.

" Ernie ! " she shouted desperately. There was no response. Bessie shut her eyes and drew in a deep breath. She let out a howl like a timber wolf :

" Err . . . nie ! "

A lighted window was flung up irritably. There was a clink at her feet, and, groping on the pavement, her fingers closed on a door-key. She stood relieved but per-plexed. The charm seemed to have worked ; but what was she supposed to do with the door-key ? She drew in another supply of air.

" Err . . . nie ! "

A head was thrust out the window and an angry voice roared : " I threw it down. What's wrong with you ? "

The window slammed down again.

Bessie reasoned that a door-key must mean going into a house. She would go into the house door below the window and trace the voice to its source, surely the mysterious Ernie himself. The key fitted the front door ; she opened it, groped her way through the dark hall to the stairs and began to mount. On the first landing she stopped afraid. There was someone there ; someone crouching and whispering in the corner of the landing. With an inarticulate cry Bessie rushed up the remaining stairs and beat on the door under which the light shone.

It gave way before her and she found herself flung gasping into the room.

"There's someone there!" she gulped. "There's someone on the landing!"

The owner of the room was typing at a table by the window. He took Bessie in with one stern glance from her shabby shoes to her disordered hair.

"What of it?" he asked sharply.

He was a loosely built, grey-haired man with eyebrows that did not match. One eyebrow, permanently crooked, lifted towards his grey hair in cynical disapproval. The other eyebrow remained normal but bushy. He had no collar on. It hung with his tie over the back of his chair.

Bessie's throat was so dry she could hardly speak, and the effort to do so brought tears to her eyes. She stood gasping, and the man sat there looking at her indifferently as though she were some blue-tailed fish behind glass.

"I have a note," she finally managed to get out, and handed it over.

"Sit down." He pointed her to a chair and opened the note. It read:

> Ernie, lend me ten shillings. I have bronchitis. If you can make it a pound so much the better.—WAINWRIGHT.

"Maurice Wainwright," Ernie said bitterly. "I might have known it. Where is he?"

"At my place."

Ernie gave her another glance. "He would be," he said cryptically. "Where does he think I'd get ten shillings from?"

Bessie shook her head dumbly.

"I suppose," Ernie went on bitterly, "he thinks it just rains money. He always did."

Bessie found her voice. "He said to come out and bring The Book."

"Is he sick?"

Bessie nodded.

The man grunted undecidedly. " You're sure he's really sick ? I've been caught this way before."

" Oh yes."

" Well, you'll have to wait half an hour. I've got some work to finish." He said it defiantly and turned back to the table. " What does he think I am anyway ? " He began a ferocious onslaught on the battered typewriter. " Here. Come and read this out to me. What's your name ? "

" Bessie Drew."

" Right-o, Bessie. Read from here." He indicated the place on the list of figures. Bessie began to read. " Hey, not so fast." He spoke as though the whole world were imposing on him.

Bessie read slowly. She very much wanted to go home. She was thirsty. She was afraid of the dark landing, and she was tired. But she read on steadily.

" Right," Ernie said at last. He put on his collar and tie and reached for his coat. " Lead on, Bessie." He went over to a shabby bookcase and extracted a book covered in brown paper, evidently The Book.

Bessie hung back. " There's somebody on the landing," she objected.

" It's the little mad woman," Ernie explained reasonably. " From downstairs. She's quite harmless. Here," he added, almost kindly, " I'll go first and turn on the lights."

The house was a dreary, faded residential, in the glow of the dim electric light. It was not at all the abode of mystery and horror Bessie had nerved herself to enter. There was no sign of any crouching figure.

" Well ? " Ernie asked laconically. " Satisfied ? "

" Oh yes." Bessie gave a sigh of relief.

He locked the door behind them. " Where do you live ? "

" Archer Street, Redfern."

" How do you get there ? "

" You can take a tram."

" Come on then." He strode off at a pace that even Bessie found a trial.

" How long's he been living with you ? " Ernie asked when they were sitting opposite each other in the tram roaring towards Central Square.

" What did you say ? " Bessie called across the rackety noise of the tram.

" How long's he been living with you ? " Ernie bellowed. People in the next compartment turned to gaze at them.

" Three weeks."

" Never known him stay that long in one place." A thought struck him. " When I say living with you . . . *Is* he living with you ? "

Bessie looked puzzled. " Of course."

Ernie relapsed into a series of displeased grunts. " How old are you ? " he shouted next.

" Seventeen. Nearly eighteen," Bessie replied dejectedly. Now that she had delivered her message and brought back the mysterious Ernie, the excitement of the adventure was dying down, and the thought of the coming row with her parent was not inspiring.

" What's worrying you ? " Ernie asked, as they got off the tram. " I suppose I'm stupid to ask. Anyone who has put up with Maurice gets that worried look."

" Have you known him long ? " Bessie enquired.

" About twenty years."

Bessie's eyes widened. " You must be quite old." She regarded him with the kindliness she reserved for old people.

Ernie chuckled. " You're a character," he said more cheerfully. " Do we keep walking all night."

" No. But I'll have to go in the back way. If Dad hears us, he'll start roaring. It must be past eleven."

Ernie glanced at the large, capable gun-metal watch on his hairy wrist.

" Half-past," he announced. " What of it ? " His disgruntled eyebrow demanded whether the girl had anything up her sleeve.

" Gosh ! It can't be as late as that. Let me go ahead and hold the dog."

Presently she beckoned him from the back door. " In there," she whispered. " And don't make a noise."

Ernie flung the door open with a cheerful slam. " Hello, you old bugger," he said loudly. " What's up with you this time ? "

To Bessie it seemed that the whole house shook with the noise. She waited ; but nothing happened except that the cultured though temporarily wheezy voice of Mr. Wainwright replied :

" Come in, Ernie, and shut the door. Did you bring The Book ? "

Bessie crept upstairs feeling somewhat left out of things. To go to an unknown street and bring home an unknown man, and to do it without being apprehended struck her as something deserving of hearty congratulations. She edged into the little cubicle she shared with her elder sister.

" Where you been ? " Beryl demanded peevishly.

" Sssh ! Did Dad say anything ? "

" He was in bed when I got home."

Truth to tell Bessie's family had taken it for granted that she had retired hours ago. Lying very still, so that she would not disturb Beryl, she could hear the murmur of Ernie's voice in the lodger's room below.

" I'd like to know," she thought, " what The Book is about. Perhaps I can ask Mr. Wainwright to-morrow."

She had a whole week-end to, nurse her friend, and the prospect pleased her. But suppose he died ? Uncle Jeff had died and he had coughed like that. But this man wouldn't die. She would look after him. They were friends even if they were so different. I am a bit stupid and ordinary, Bessie argued. Unless I join with someone who has strange things happen to him, I will never have adventures or excitement. I'll just stay working and plodding and coming home to Archer Street.

She fell asleep and dreamt very pleasantly that, armed to the teeth, she was a pirate boarding a ship from whose side peered down at her the frightened face of Maurice Wainwright.

" But aren't we friends ? " he was saying, almost pleadingly.

" Of course we are," she replied in her dream. " Of course."

Ernie, having run through a list of reproaches, gave Wainwright another dose of medicine " for luck ".

" Where did you pick that kid up, Maurice ? " he asked, as he stood holding the spoon.

" Who ? "

" Bessie." Ernie's tone was as casual and disinterested as if he were discussing the weather.

Wainwright fixed on his friend those piercing, dark, protuberant eyes.

" What are you getting at, Ernie ? "

" It isn't any of my business."

" What isn't ? "

" It's your own affair entirely."

" Ernie Johnson," the invalid croaked bitterly, " I have a temperature."

" I heard about it."

" Do you want to make it worse ? All this . . ." He raised his hand in that all-embracing gesture.

" She said she was living with you. She told me so herself."

" Oh, go away," Mr. Wainwright said acidly. " Do I look like it ? If you've just come out here to be funny . . ." He pondered. " I wonder what her idea was ? "

" It's none of my business." Ernie's eyebrow remained sceptical. " Nice girl, that's all. You send the poor little brute trapesing round Sydney looking for someone she's never seen. She must be gone on you to put up with it."

" When a man is ill," Wainwright protested, with a pontifical air somewhat marred by the stubble of beard, " when a man is ill, the least he can expect is some degree of courtesy and attention. I see you brought The Book. Where were we last time ? "

" Weaning." Ernie turned interestedly to the well-thumbed copy of *Care and Nurture of the Young Child*. Years before, Wainwright and Ernie had formed a pact that, if either were ill, the other would come and read aloud from that excellent and sleep-producing work of Sir Truby King. In an optimistic moment Ernie had bought the works of Truby King, but in vain. They had gathered dust on a shelf for years after his divorce, until Wainwright discovered them and insisted that they were enthralling.

" Knowledge," he had announced to Ernie, " is never a burden. Besides, I'm tired of being told what not to do to babies. I'd like to put women in their place for a change. You and I, Ernie, are going to be Experts."

They had never progressed farther than weaning because, knowing nothing about babies, there were so many knotty points to ponder over.

At a quarter to two when Ernie rose to go, he thought Maurice was asleep. As he reached the door, the figure on the bed stirred.

" And you keep your paws off," it mumbled offensively.

" What do you mean : Keep my paws off ? "

" Her." The mumble was stern. " Nice kid. Protect her. Be out to-morrow, Ernie ? "

" Sure."

" Remember. No funny business."

Ernie was grinning as he let himself out.

CHAPTER II

SATURDAY, with a wet blanket of grey cloud dripping above Archer Street, was so sooty, so dreary, that it might have been chosen to blend with the grey paling fences, old sheds with broken windows, grass-grown heaps of rusty machinery, black chimneys and brick-pits with which the area was encompassed.

The jarring patch of colour was supplied by a beautiful purple-and-gold taxi which drew up before 71 Archer Street a little after ten o'clock. The children who flocked up, hopeful of entertainment, were not disappointed, for the lady in the taxi appeared to be having quite an argument with the driver. Finally she beckoned to one of the neighbours who was leaning casually in his front doorway.

" Would you mind helping to carry these in for me ? " she demanded.

While the neighbour reluctantly joined the driver in an effort to drag out two heavy objects, the lady rang the doorbell of the Drew residence, glancing with a certain distaste at the cardboard slip printed with the word " Vacancies " which Mrs. Drew still displayed in the front window from force of habit.

The visitor was as little in harmony with Archer Street as the purple-and-gold taxi-cab. From her small black hat depended a cute net veil that just touched the tip of her nose. On her glossy dark furs she had pinned a gardenia, while long, black, kid gloves met the fashionable puffed sleeves of a black, figured marocain street frock. Her complexion was superb, her fair hair beautifully coiffeured. She gave the impression of careful corsetry restraining a much-curved amplitude. Her voice was deep and rather throaty.

"Which is Mr. Wainwright's room?" the visitor asked, as Mrs. Drew suspiciously opened the door. That lady laconically pointed down the hall. "Come on, men," the visitor commanded. "This way."

She sailed ahead majestically as the driver and Mrs. Drew's next-door neighbour staggered into the doorway. They were bearing what looked like a metal desk, which had on its front two little disks, one red, the other green, together with a number of interesting slots and handles. Dumping this in the corner of the invalid's room, they tramped out somewhat sulkily and returned with another contraption shaped like a barrel of white enamel with a short funnel projecting from its top. The funnel had a little white enamel lid to which was attached a long brass rod ending in what looked like a piano pedal.

"I've brought them back, Maurice," the lady explained. "As soon as Ernie rang and told me where you were, I hurried straight out." She turned to the taxi-driver. "You'd better wait. I won't be long." And on the helpful neighbour she lavished a sweet smile. "Thank you so much." She turned to Wainwright again as the door shut on her unwilling helpers. "So perverse of you to catch a cold. So characteristic." Her voice took on a tone almost pleading. "Believe me, Maurice, I'm so dreadfully sorry that I couldn't do anything about those machines." She indicated the two objects behind the door. "If you only knew what it's been like to live for all these weeks with the Wainwright Absence Register and the Wainwright Patent Garbage Sterilizer! Don't scold me for bringing them back."

"But, Jenny, you have the *contacts*," Wainwright said decisively. "You could interest capital. You could show the models to people you meet socially. I'm disappointed in you, Jenny."

"But, Maurice, I can't possibly. I've tried — hard." She sat down rather timidly. "Perhaps I'm not good at explaining how they work. Have a cigarette?" She lit one of her own from a gold-monogrammed case. "I can't possibly keep them, Maurice, not even for you."

"It doesn't matter." Wainwright tried to conceal his disappointment. "If I could only get one of these inventions taken up in America, I tell you there's millions in the Absence Register alone." He awkwardly turned up the collar of his pyjamas. "I'm sorry you had to see me like this. You're looking splendid as usual." He tried to smile. "Glorious Jenny Evison. I heard your broadcast. Very good."

"Did you really think so, Maurice?" She was as embarrassed as he was. I would never have guessed, she was thinking, that Maurice was so dreadfully hard up. He might have let me know. She was hurt at his lack of confidence in her. She wanted to offer to help him out of this dreadful place, but he would be offended if she tried. All she could do was disappoint him about his silly old inventions. If only he knew how everyone had teased her about them! She had tried so hard to "interest capital", and had made herself ridiculous for his sake.

"I didn't know," she said with an effort, "that you were so sick."

"You are one of the people with whom everyone tries to be at their best, Jenny." He rubbed his unshaven chin ruefully. "I would have given — yes, even the patents to keep you from finding me in a place like this. I think you might have told me . . ."

Wainwright was saved the trouble of further excuses. There was a knock on the door and Bessie called: "I have your inhalant, Mr. Wainwright."

Maurice was obviously relieved at the interruption. "Come in," he called. "Bessie, this is Miss Jenny Evison." Bessie inspected the visitor from her expensive small hat to her even more expensive shoes. "Jenny, this is Bessie Drew. Bessie's been very good to me while I've been sick."

Miss Evison's little, gracious nod relegated Bessie to the servants' hall ; just another of Maurice's interests, one of a series of little girls who had attracted him and been dismissed in due course.

" The taxi-driver wants to know if he's to wait any longer," Bessie said, addressing Wainwright.

" I'd forgotten all about him." Miss Evison rose. " I really must go. Now, don't forget to give me a ring, Maurice. And get well soon." She imprinted a kiss on Wainwright's rather bald, domed brow. She did not look at Bessie, as she said : " Good-bye, Miss Drew, so pleased to have met you."

" Why ? " Bessie asked in rather a hostile tone as the door shut.

" Just one of the things people say." Wainwright's voice was hard. " She just brought back a couple of inventions she was minding for me," he explained. " You've heard of Jenny Evison ? " Bessie shook her head. " Good Lord, why she's one of the most famous contraltos in the world ! "

It touched his vanity that this child should not realize how famous Jenny was, what an honour it was to know her.

But Bessie remained unimpressed. The secret conviction abode with her that the visitor was too fat. With the cruel intuition of the young and feminine she had decided that Miss Evison would like to marry Maurice Wainwright even if he hadn't a penny. However famous Jenny might be, she had paid Bessie the compliment of disliking her, of trying to put her in her place.

" Swank," Bessie declared under her breath. She turned and inspected Wainwright's inventions gravely. " Did you make these all by yourself ? "

" Of course."

"I s'pose it took a tremendous time?"

The inventor looked pleased. "Not a bit. You get the idea in an instant. The real work lies in studying out the details. Take the Absence Register for instance . . ."

"Bessie!"

"That's Mum. I'll have to go."

"Pretend you didn't hear. Now I had the idea of the Absence Register simply handed to me — you might say. I was waiting on the street corner for a — a business acquaintance one night and he didn't turn up. And as I waited, I thought 'Why isn't there some gadget like a weighing machine or a chocolate machine so that you could drop a penny in it and leave a message?' Then, when your friend arrived, she would see her name, put in the penny and get out the message. You know yourself what a nuisance it is waiting? A man gives it up as a bad job and goes off, then the other person arrives and gets indignant. It causes unpleasantness all round."

Bessie nodded vigorous agreement, as though she were quite accustomed to keeping people waiting.

"Now, when the Absence Register is put in at all the street corners and tram stops and railway stations, people will just go up and glance down the row of names. If there's a message for them, they put their penny in the slot and get it out. If the red light is showing against a name, that person knows that whoever was waiting for him went without leaving a message. If the green light is showing, it means: Keep on waiting, I will be back."

Wainwright looked a different man when he talked about the Absence Register: a young, eager man; not a sick, dispirited one. The heavy lines on his face smoothed out; his eyes lit up.

"I think it's marvellous," Bessie said decidedly.

"You do, eh? I have the world patents for it."

"Bessie! Haven't you finished sweeping that verandah yet?"

" I'll have to go. But will you tell me about the other one after lunch ? "

" Certainly. I don't suppose you have a cigarette about you ? "

" I haven't. I don't smoke."

" Well, just duck down to the corner and get me a packet, will you ? "

" No." Bessie was firm. "You can't have any." She shook her head reprovingly. " You know you shouldn't smoke with that cough."

" But I like to think that if I wanted to smoke, they're there. Be a good kid."

Bessie took sixpence from the dressing-table and went towards the door.

" And I want you to ring a man for me. This is the number. Ask to speak to Mr. Hodges. He is the man who is going to put up the money for my new studio. I was to see him to-day. Tell him I can't get in to town until Monday."

" You won't see him on Monday."

" Oh yes, I will."

" And breathe bronchitis all over him ? "

" It's a matter of striking while the iron is hot. You wouldn't understand." He spoke impatiently. " When you have interested capital, it is very necessary to keep it interested."

" The only thing you'll be interested in is a funeral, if you go into town like that."

" Bess . . . ssie ! "

" I'll go and 'phone in a minute. And I'll make you an egg flip. You'll drink it or I won't 'phone for you." The door shut behind her.

In the kitchen Mrs. Drew was angrily banging plates on to the table.

" If you think you're practically going to live in that man's room, you're mistaken," she began. " As soon as

25

your father comes in, I'm going to tell 'im."

" Oh no, you don't." Bessie calmly commandeered an egg and the egg-beater. " If you do, I'll tell him about that last cash order you're still paying off. And he'd raise much more of a row about that cash order than he would about me. You say one word and see."

Mrs. Drew changed her tactics. " What you see in that man to fuss over I don't know. It isn't as though you could be struck on him like you could on a boy friend your own age. Why, 'e's old enough to be your father . . . and 'e ought to be drawin' the dole from what I can make out."

" You just wait. He may be down-and-out now, but he's too brainy to stay that way. He's going to make millions with an invention." Bessie's confident tone impressed her mother.

" Well, I don't know," Mrs. Drew said sulkily. " But I never seen a man that looked less like it. Even if he does, I doubt if I'll get my rent."

Bessie disdained to answer. She bore off the egg flip to the invalid.

" I'll go out and ring up your Mr. Hodges now," she announced, as she pushed open the door with her foot. " I think all the same . . ."

Bessie stopped embarrassed. Her friend was crying. He lay with his face buried in the pillow, his shoulders heaving under his yellow and green striped pyjamas. He was sobbing aloud without the least attempt at concealment. Bessie awkwardly put out her hand and patted him on the shoulder. It did not have the slightest effect. So she put her arm around him and hugged him.

" Stop it," she said gently.

" I can't," Maurice gulped. " I had the chance to set up a business again. Hodges said he would advance the capital. And then I get this bronchitis. The idea that Jenny Evison might be doing something about those patents was sustaining me. Now that's finished." He sat up and wiped his eyes on a corner of the sheet. "You couldn't understand. One may feel there is nothing left in life and at the same time hope . . ." He gulped again. "If I were younger, it might be different."

Bessie hugged him again ; and this time he did not push her away. He leant on her shoulder. It was such a strong young shoulder.

"You'll see this chap Hodges on Monday," she suggested, "and fix up about starting a new business. And then you can work like blazes and be rolling in money in no time. You can get those patents fixed and all."

The invalid shook his head so that it moved against her shoulder like a warm stone.

"I hate taking photographs," he said, the tears still running down the deep creases in his face. "Pot-boiling, miserable work. Not what I wanted. All my life I have been frustrated. I wanted to be a musician and I broke the sinews of my thumb. I wanted to be an actor and I can't remember two lines. I know all about painting and design and weaving and writing — in theory. I am a failure, you see, Bessie."

"Not on your life," Bessie said, holding him tighter. "Don't you believe it. No one's luck goes on being bad all the time. If you haven't had a good break, now's the time to say : I'm going to make up for all the good breaks I haven't had."

"That's true." He sat up straighter.

"Anyway, I don't believe in luck," Bessie said stoutly. "It's like church. Just a put-up job."

Maurice looked at her doubtfully, his eyes full of tears. "Queer little person ! But there's something in what you say. Henley, it was, wrote that poem. You know it ? "

"I don't know any poetry."

"'I am the master of my fate, I am the captain of my soul.' It runs like that :

27

Beyond this place of wrath and tears
  Looms but the Horror of the shade,
And yet the menace of the years
  Finds and shall find me unafraid."

" Thought you said you couldn't remember two lines,"
Bessie encouraged him.

Wainwright was beginning to see himself in the part.
As he recited in a voice weak but dramatic, he disengaged
himself from Bessie's encircling arm and threw out his
chest. Bessie, regarding him with a fond cynicism, decided that it would be hard to find another man who
would recite poetry in striped yellow and green pyjamas
and an old woollen muffler.

Maurice went on earnestly :

" It matters not how strait the gate,
  How charged with punishments the scroll,
I am the master of my fate :
I am the captain of my soul.

" The captain of my soul," he repeated, drying his
eyes on the corner of the sheet once more. " I have
always been the captain of my soul, Bessie. No one has
ever been able to dictate to me. *That* is the reason I am
lying here . . . now. I have always managed to pre-
serve my independence, thank God. I am — the captain
of my soul." He sank back on his pillow very grandly,
completely restored to self-esteem.

" I guess you need a mate," Bessie suggested abstractedly.

" Eh ? "

" Even if you're going to be captain of your soul, you
need a mate."

Maurice turned over towards Bessie and smiled with
so mischievous a sparkle that she was startled. He hardly
seemed the same man who, a moment before, had such
a grandiose delivery of poetry.

" Applying for the position ? " he asked.

Bessie looked him full in the eyes. For the first time Wainwright noticed that Bessie had green eyes. Or were they grey ? They looked at him so steadily that he began to feel uncomfortable.

" I might."

He tried to turn it off as a joke. " You're a queer person. You do take me so very seriously." He began to laugh weakly and then coughed until he was exhausted.

" Drink your egg flip." She went out without another word.

" Queer little person," Maurice repeated.

As he sipped the egg flip, he began to feel stronger and more resentful. He did not want this girl to get out of hand, he told himself. Strange friendships budded unnaturally in the hothouse atmosphere of a sick-room. He had been forced into a position where he had to accept her casual help and, of course, accepting her help, he had been polite to her. But he could not, no, really he could not become entangled with a little factory girl. He sent her on errands and naturally spoke to her affably ; but it was absurd of Ernie to give him irritating hints. Still Ernie at least had put him on his guard. The trouble with women was that they took too much for granted.

Bessie was an interesting little girl ; but it would not do at all to raise expectations in her mind. It would be cruel — unjust. Good Lord ! he hadn't spent years staving Jenny off for nothing. He ought to be able to keep Bessie from becoming a nuisance. It was distinctly annoying of her, just when he was sick and worried, to force herself on him in this way. She had put her arm around his shoulders. She had deliberately hugged him. The girl was taking advantage of him ; that was it. And telling Ernie — what was it she had told Ernie ? Oh yes.

By the time Bessie appeared with his luncheon, Maurice

C

had worked himself almost into a state of fury.

" I've had mine," she said, perching cheerfully on the foot of the bed. " So if you like, I can stay and take the tray back."

" Perhaps it would be better," he said coldly, " if you were to assist your good mother. I'm sure I don't wish to take you away from your duties."

" What's wrong with you ? " Bessie looked at him surprised. " I suppose you're mad because I saw you crying. Don't worry. Uncle Jeff used to cry every time he got drunk." She added reflectively : " He was drunk most of the time. I'm used to it."

" I've no doubt you are." Wainwright's manner was even more chilly and polite. " I thought perhaps your family might object to your spending so much time with me."

" Not a bit," Bessie said cheerfully. " They like it."

" Surprising ! "

" I have them almost convinced that you're a millionaire in disguise. Naturally they're feeling better." She jumped up suddenly. " You haven't had your medicine. Don't touch a bite till you've had your medicine."

" You can't give it to me now, kid." He quite forgot to be chilly. " It says before meals, and I'm half-way through."

" Well, I suppose I'll have to let you off." She shook her head disapprovingly. " Don't gulp like that."

He glared at her. " I am not gulping, and I wish you wouldn't be so rude."

" Your food doesn't do you any good if you gulp."

" Well, it's my food and I'm eating it." He collected himself. It was ridiculous to argue with this wretched girl. " You need not wait, Bessie," he said coldly.

" I forgot to tell you what Mr. Hodges said." Bessie coiled her foot more comfortably round the iron bed-rail. " Monday will suit him. He was sorry to hear you were sick. He said to take your time getting better."

" Now just what did he mean by that ? " Wainwright brooded. " He's as slippery as a basket of snakes. If he thinks he can slither out now, he can explain how in a court of law. Oh, well . . ." He dismissed the matter.

" Is Ernie coming this afternoon ? " Bessie asked. It seemed outrageous to Wainwright to hear his friend called " Ernie " by this brat of a girl. She added, as though she had read his thoughts : " I don't know his other name."

" It's Johnson."

" He's nice."

" He is not nice. He's the hard, unpleasant type with no respect for anyone. He's a woman-hunter into the bargain."

Bessie looked at Wainwright astonished. " But he's so old ! "

This gave Maurice the same outraged feeling that he had when she called Ernie by his Christian name. Maurice was forty and Ernie was forty-three. He felt as though both of them had been dismissed to the rubbish-heap.

" Of course, to you, my dear child, *thirty* must seem a very reverend age," he observed, with a twist of his lips that was meant for a condescending smile.

Bessie was beginning to suspect that when her friend adopted that tone and used long words, he was trying to crush her. She remained sturdily uncrushed.

" Miss Evison, for instance," Wainwright was calm and lofty, " has, you may have noticed, a certain poise, an aplomb, that a younger woman would lack. She is not a girl any longer, but there is an added charm, a maturity, as I said before — poise. And poise, Bessie, is one of the most beautiful attributes that a woman can acquire. Try to cultivate poise."

" What's poise ? "

"It is — well," he waved his hand, "a matter of never being ungraceful — of a calm and unhurried demeanour."

"You can't move so fast when you're getting fat."

Her crudity, her vulgarity, her stubborn independence, infuriated him. For a long time Maurice had in his secret heart considered Jenny slightly too plump. He lay back on his pillow and shut his eyes.

"Have it your own way," he replied coldly. "If you insist on associating with elderly persons, you must endure their efforts to improve your manners. I suppose I . . . I seem quite old to you ? "

"Oh, I never think about it really," Bessie said earnestly. "You remind me a lot of Uncle Jeff. Ever since he died I've missed him — sort of . . ." She tried to explain. "You see, I don't feel as if my mob are really related to me."

"Your family ? "

"That's it. Uncle Jeff was related to me. He'd take me out when I was a kid, and he taught me to whistle. You might say he brought me up."

"And he died ? " Wainwright's voice was low and sympathetic.

"He got D.T.'s and they took him to the Home. He used to scream the house down. I'd come and sit with him at night sometimes, but he didn't know me in the end. He'd fight me." She looked round reflectively. "This was his room. And seeing you in bed reminds me of Uncle Jeff."

Wainwright's feelings moved sharply from sympathy to annoyance. What a fool he had been to think the girl was trying to entrap him ! The little idiot regarded him only as an elderly relation. Somehow the thought depressed him.

"I can talk to you," Bessie went on in her slow, even voice, "like I could to Uncle Jeff. Like an equal."

" As an equal," he corrected grumpily.

" All right. I can tell you things. For instance, when I said this morning that I might apply for the job of mate, I meant it." Wainwright moved uneasily. " What-I-mean-to-say, you're going to start in business again. Now I learnt to type at school, not very well, and I could answer the 'phone or go messages. I want a job. I don't care what the pay's like. I'm sick of the factory. See? I want to work with you."

Wainwright began to hedge. " My dear child, I was only joking. Good heavens! it's impossible. I may never have the business you talk about."

" You'll be sick for a long time yet," Bessie said gravely. " And you'll need someone to look after you, as well as look after things at your office. I mean — a sort of all-round mate."

Wainwright laughed. " It's very good of you, kid. But the idea's fantastic. You see, I'd need to employ someone with a knowledge of the business, a receptionist, to meet customers and take their addresses and make them at home, and do all sorts of delicate jobs."

" I could learn."

" Listen, Bessie," he said kindly, " I don't want to hurt your feelings ; but it's not only intelligence — you have plenty of that. It's a matter of clothes, and the way you speak, and your manner." He added cruelly : " You need poise, culture."

Bessie did not flinch. " You wait till you've seen me dressed up," she said.

" I'll think it over."

So that was why she had been so assiduous. She wanted a job. And he had thought she really liked him. Something deep down, an innermost vanity, was pierced. It was because he was sick, he told himself, that this child had the power to hurt him. He was physically weak ; and so she could impose her personality upon him. When he was better, when he was in a different environment, he would laugh at the distorted, preposterous set of circumstances that could allow her almost to dictate to him. He would shake her off like a symptom of this accursed bronchitis.

Then another side of the proposal struck him. Why should he not employ her? He felt magnanimous at the thought of giving this girl a chance to better herself. He would not have to pay much for her services, all the less as he would be benefiting her by the educational uplift of his company.

"I'll think it over," he repeated deliberately. His self-esteem was beginning to rise like a barometer.

"It's time for your inhalant." Bessie slipped off the edge of the bed.

"What, again?" In a flash he was reduced from the imposing business magnate to a sick and fretful man.

"If Ernie's coming, it wouldn't do you any harm to shave. It would make you feel better."

"It would not," Wainwright protested. "I hate shaving."

"Then I'll bring the inhalant."

Lying with his eyes on a large, green damp-stain, his favourite among all the stains and cracks with which he was becoming so familiar, Wainwright thought restlessly of how small things were eating up his life. He was forty, a troubling age, neither one thing nor the other, neither a young man nor an old one. All the eager busyness, and most of the enthusiasm of his manhood, had gone, leaving him the haggard necessity of maintaining desperately, and with a failing interest, a life stripped of possibilities.

He was not old enough yet, he told himself ironically, to live on the capital of his past, his memories; though there were plenty of them when the time came. Perhaps he might degenerate into one of those bundles of rags and trembling bones who totter to a Salvation Army shelter, sunk away from the gaze of the respectable ; but who, nevertheless, when addressed, answer in a cultured voice.

Memories trickled through the burning torment of his head : little flashes of streets in many cities ; faces of friends ; his mother's face, vivacious, indiscreet, with all its emotions flashing on it, the face of a woman, wilful, delightful, always in debt, moving in a gaiety of social trifles ; his father's face, dark, saturnine—his own face but repellent with a high, domed brow.

The memory of his mother brought him both warmth and wistfulness. He caught at his foolish thoughts as though they were the hem of one of her insubstantial gauze dresses. She had always spoilt him, loved him, provoked his father nearly to madness indulging him.

All his life, Wainwright thought, some female had been meddling her little fingers in his affairs, spoiling him and everything he did. First, it was his mother ; and then Rose, and after Rose . . . He felt tired when he thought of all those girls. There was the little masseuse in Los Angeles ; and the Canadian girl who wanted him to settle down in her father's store ; and the little Greek in Hawaii — any number of meddling women, managing, arguing, bullying, deceiving, loving him and wanting him to do things for his own good, to be thankful for small mercies, to stay in one place, and above all to settle down. Damn women anyway ! They had set convictions and a narrow concentration ; and both these things, in the long run, bore a man to tears.

He might have been infinitely kinder to Jenny, had she not seemed so inevitable. With a placidity, a bovine placidity, she maintained this pretence of friendship, this long-continued kindness ; certain that, like some good-natured Juggernaut, she would end by crushing him into compliance. It was no use being irritable with her, because she laughed it off with a deep, hearty laugh that jarred his nerves. She was out to get her own way. Women were like that. They simply took an axe and chopped their way through all the polite, small subterfuges that civilized people opposed. Take this brat, this kid Bessie ; she might look easy ; but when it came to getting his own way, a man had to play his weakness, his sickness, for all it was worth or he just wouldn't stand a chance.

Wainwright's resentment against the masterfulness of women increased, as Bessie solemnly bore in a thick china bowl that announced its contents by a choking odour.

" Here you are," she said severely. " And see you breathe it in."

As Maurice bent over the bowl, gasping and coughing, his swollen eyes starting tears, his mouth hanging open with the effort to breathe — a towel draping the pink dome of his head — he might have been some minor prophet dazed by the oracular vapours of an unfortunate future. But the only prophecy he spluttered out was : " If you don't take this stuff away, I'll choke."

Then he bent meekly to the insufferable bowl once more. Bessie regarded him critically. Her look, it seemed to Maurice, was that of one who watched an improvement to her property.

CHAPTER III

ON Monday Wainwright was still very ill indeed. Bessie looked in on her way to work and noticed that he was breathing with difficulty between fits of coughing.

" You can't go and see anyone like that," she said firmly.

"I can't put Hodges off again. That's the position."

Bessie hesitated. She had already almost decided on her course of action ; in fact she had planned hopefully for this very contingency.

"If you like," she offered, "I could go with you."

Maurice turned over with his face to the wall. "I'll manage," he answered peevishly. "You go off to work and leave me in peace."

Bessie whistled softly, absent-mindedly, as she stood in the doorway making up her mind. It seemed to her that this position, half leaning against the doorway of Wainwright's room, was somehow symbolic of her own mental attitude. Wainwright made her feel like an intruder, when all the time he was only a sick man too proud to realize that he must have help. She could go away and leave him, or she could take matters into her hands for good or ill.

"I'm coming with you," she said suddenly. "You're too weak to go alone and I'm coming and that's flat ! "

"Good Lord, no ! "

Bessie, for Wainwright, was part of Archer Street, part of the private grim misery he hurriedly pushed behind him when he emerged into the world of business and his own associates. He did not want Archer Street seeping into other compartments of his life.

Bessie looked down at the little packet of lunch she carried, at the brown paper parcel which contained her starched white overall. It would be strange not to go to the factory, not to have a regular job. But, in any case, she would be discharged when she turned eighteen. The family knew she would be put off ; and they would nag only on principle, if she left before the firm told her to go. Even so it required a good deal of courage to take the decisive step.

In a quiver of nervous tension she walked to the factory, told the forewoman there was sickness in the family, collected her small belongings and said good-bye ; but a new sense of freedom uplifted her out in the sunlight with the streets busy around her, instead of the monotonous humming and stamping and clatter of the packing-room.

" Well I never ! " Mrs. Drew exclaimed, as Bessie strolled in and hung up her faded beret.

" I got the forewoman's back up," Bessie explained untruthfully.

" What will your father say ? " Mrs. Drew began. " He'll thrash you within an inch of your life and serve you right."

" He'd better try."

Bessie had acquired the indifference of those who live on the edge of a volcano. She unwrapped her lunch and took a large bite out of a cheese sandwich.

" You let me break it to him, Mum. I don't think I'll say anything until Friday. Then I'll just tell him I was put off."

The other members of the family were always ready to join such small conspiracies by which their father's temper might be lulled into temporary quiet.

Wainwright had an appointment with Hodges at eleven o'clock. By ten-thirty Bessie had helped Maurice into his clothes ; brought him shaving water ; stitched on two of his buttons ; purloined a clean collar of her father's which was much too big ; brushed his boots and sponged his waistcoat. She left him sitting dejectedly on the side of his bed while she rushed upstairs ; flung herself with a ripping sound into her sister Beryl's second-best black frock ; hurriedly pinned it together ; snatched Beryl's best hat from a cupboard ; and, perspiring with excitement, went off to telephone a taxi.

A week ago the idea of riding in a taxi would never have entered Bessie's head. It had been put there by Jenny Evison. Bessie had not the faintest idea how much taxi-cabs cost, and she was so sure Wainwright would laugh at her for asking that she did not confide her fears.

" If it's more than fifteen bob," she thought, laboriously scraping her savings together, " we'll have to get out and walk." She knew she was mad and reckless but she liked the exhilaration of it. Every minute of her taxi ride she lived as intensely as if it were taking her to the guillotine.

Wainwright accepted the taxi as a matter of course. He reached into his pocket feebly for the fare, but Bessie had paid the man off with a proud and satisfied air.

" Here on the tick ! " she declared triumphantly, looking about her at the black-and-white marble vestibule of the lawyers' warren in which Wainwright was to meet Hodges. " Right on the tick," she repeated. " What floor is it ? "

" I think I'd better go up alone," Wainwright replied evasively. " It's a business appointment, Bessie. Naturally he'll expect to see me by myself."

Bessie did not flinch. He might just as well have told her that her clothes were the clothes of a little shop assistant ; that her shabby shoes and stockings, even the independent way she stood with her feet planted apart, marked her off from the inhabitants of places with marble vestibules.

" Right-o," Bessie said steadily. " I'll wait on the corner."

There was a hot, dusty wind blowing. Trams roared past, contemptuous, impersonal ; people dressed for shopping and business streamed along the asphalt, brushing against Bessie without seeing her. The roar of the trams, the people, the wind, all seemed to be voicing the one criticism of her existence. She breathed dust, tasted it. It stung her face and got into her eyes, making them water and making her ridiculous, abject, sad. The tears might be caused by dust but her feelings matched them.

"A fine blooming goat I am," Bessie remarked to herself, gulping.

Behind wooden palings on the opposite side of the street workmen were drilling out the excavations for yet another imitation marble monstrosity of thirteen floors. Enormous lorries, splashing clay and muck, backed out with roaring engines, in front of the trams and motor cars, holding up the flow of traffic in a leisurely, large way. The racket of the drills came up out of the great yellow hollow as though a machine-gun and a knife-sharpener had gone into partnership.

The trucks reminded Bessie of her father. It wasn't an easy job driving a truck through that demoniac traffic all day. It made Dad a bit cranky. He roared about nothing, like a big lorry coming up a steep grade. But he didn't get drunk except on Saturdays, and he worked hard. Not what you'd call clever. Towards the workmen in their sweaty woollen undershirts and clay-splashed boots Bessie suddenly felt a warm friendliness and sympathy. They were her kind of people. They didn't care about their clothes.

She huddled against the window of a book-shop, seeking some shelter from the grit and wind, watching with critical eyes the girls who passed her. When she had earned some money, she decided, she would buy herself a dress of green stuff with little flowers on it and a white collar. She would wear flat brown shoes and a brown hat. "I look like nothing on earth in black," she reflected.

Clothes did matter, she admitted to herself, shame-faced. If her clothes had been better Mr. Wainwright might have wanted her to go with him to see this business man. Her working overalls, Bessie reminded herself, were starched and fit for a surgeon. Perhaps she could wear them in Mr. Wainwright's office, if he ever had an office, or if he let her come and work in it. Why, she wondered, was she so keen on working for Mr. Wainwright? What did he represent that she wanted? And the answer flashed immediately to her mind : Escape from Archer Street.

Whatever Maurice Wainwright was, and as yet she knew little about him, he measured to none of the standards of Archer Street. He wore his clothes differently ; even his hat had an elegance almost womanish. The men in Archer Street went to work in shabby suits that cost at most a few pounds on the time payment system ; but if you wanted to dress Mr. Wainwright the way he ought to be dressed, it would take twenty pounds at least. Even his dreadful hat seemed, on him, a distinction. He was so different from everything she had known that he was worth watching and studying.

Wainwright was an open door into a different life ; while Archer Street, with its walls, its acceptance of factory and family; its S.P. betting on Wednesdays and Saturdays ; its children screaming at hide-and-seek round the back lanes ; its Saturday afternoon drunks ; its rigid attempts at decency ; its constant fear of being out of work, of owing the grocer and the rent man, of being put out of the house and losing the furniture ; all these things that made up Archer Street, sought to enclose her ; to grind her into their substance and absorb her.

She would go working in some factory until she married or had a baby, or both, and then she would live in rooms or one of those tiny dark flats that smelt of linoleum polish and dinner cooking and phenol and unwashed napkins. She would grow old and baggy and go shopping in bare feet and slippers ; and, if she had a house, she would go out to wash down the footpath in front of the gate, casting contemptuous eyes on the unwashed bit of pavement in front of the house next door.

Bessie had seen all her mother's talent for efficient management and methodical neatness crumble into a haggard worry and nagging. She had seen her father's dogged, rough good spirits become sullen and angry, chafed raw by Archer Street and children and want of money. She was not going to be like that, ugly and mean. For her, life surely held something wide and open and clean. Orderly it must be and well arranged, sure of a future good and work welcome and abounding. But a life without quarrels and rages.

Her mind flashed up a little picture of Wainwright conducting her into a big, shiny office full of mahogany furniture and typists and big filing cabinets, and saying to some distinguished strangers : " I brought my secretary. She has all the necessary papers." And they would say : " Take this chair, Miss Drew." And Miss Drew would take out a note-book and cross her legs in sheer silk stockings and look cool and efficient, a secretary such as Bessie had so often seen in the films. One of those secretaries who managed her manager, who directed things and saved the situation when all looked black. At this very minute Mr. Wainwright was probably pulling off a deal that would give him a new start. And she, Bessie, had managed things so that he was in time for his appointment. She had brought him there. Already she had made a beginning as the perfect secretary.

Wainwright, had she known it, was bitterly regretting that he had come at all. His lawyer friend, Sid Wilkes, had put his dingy little office at Wainwright's disposal for this all-important discussion with Alfred Wedgworth Hodges, and had conveniently gone out himself, leaving the coast clear. Wainwright could hardly speak above a whisper and, if Bessie was feeling abject, Maurice was feeling infinitely worse. He liked to dominate a discussion, and here he was, not only listening to Mr. Hodges, but nodding his head feebly when he should have been urging objections. The noise of the trams bothered him and the dreadful shrilling of the electric drills gave him the feeling that he was deaf as well as dumb.

Mr. Hodges had a grey moustache that acted as an ambush around his mouth, any incautious word being mangled as it emerged. "Hodges' Home Preserves" had a reputation. The respectability of the firm was unquestioned. Mr. Hodges himself looked like the embodiment of "Fifty Years of Honest Trading". He was a sparse, elderly man with a narrow, wrinkled forehead, gold-rimmed pince-nez, and a high white collar cutting into his chin. He sat primly, his hands folded on a walking-stick. Beside him lay a straw hat with a black band, the kind of straw hat that men wore in the year nineteen-twelve. Wainwright wondered wearily where he managed to buy such a hat.

"I'll have to think it over," Mr. Hodges was mumbling. "Think it over. Can't do anything without Advice. I can't go rushin' inter a thing like this, Mr. Wainwright — you can see that for yourself. If we could go inter the details of it, when I'm not in sich a 'urry. I can't exactly see where the returns you talked about come in. Seems to me if I cleared what I put inter it, I'd be lucky."

"I need the capital to fit out the studio. And I need an advance until commissions begin to come in." Wainwright tried to be decisive, business-like. It seemed to him that Hodges had been there mumbling for an eternity. They were like two dummy figures in a nightmare, making meaningless gestures, staring at each other through a haze. "You can adopt the proposition or leave it, but you'll have to advance me fifty besides the capital."

"I'll advance fifty. I'm ready to go as far as that, but I can't let you have the two-fifty."

"I can't fit a studio up without it."

To Alfred Hodges, Wainwright looked like an excellent investment. He knew he had the photographer at his mercy. No bank would advance money on Maurice's security. Wainwright had insisted that he needed three hundred pounds if he was to set up a studio, equip a dark-room, and really start on a square footing. So far Hodges could be brought only to consider advancing a hundred pounds for the studio and fifty for expenses in return for a third share of the profits over a period of three years.

" It's impossible," Wainwright declared. "No business could carry on on your terms."

" Well, I'll tell you what I'll do," Hodges mumbled expansively. " I'm a fair man. I don't like to down a man just because he has to take my terms and can't get others. I like to help a man I know'll succeed. I tell you what, and this is my last offer. If you can find a suitable premises, and the cost ain't above a hundred and fifty for fittin' 'em, I'll go to advancing the hundred and fifty. Only mind, I pay the bills as they come in, and then there's the fifty for coverin' the runnin' expenses until you get started. But the papers will have to be drawn up. An' I get a half share, see ? " He leant back and patted the end of his grey moustache, as though congratulating it on its owner's benevolence. " How's that suit you ? "

" All right," Wainwright muttered. " We'll leave it at that. Will you get Sid to see to the agreement ? " He had a feeling that he was being cheated somewhere, but never before had he so desperately wanted to get anything over.

Mr. Hodges rose. " I've got an appointment," he mumbled. " Very important. Suppose I meet you — day after to-morrow — finalize matters ? "

Wainwright gave him a good start. He left a note for his legal friend explaining the position, then he limped out to the waiting Bessie.

She was standing against the book-shop window, but

when she saw him coming she hurried forward and put one hand under his elbow.

"How's things?" she asked eagerly. "Did you fix it?"

Wainwright straightened his shoulders. He flicked a speck of dust from the lapel of his coat ; then, somewhat in the manner of a tortoise, he moved his head from left to right, stretching his neck as though the too large collar hurt him.

"Finance is adjusting itself," he said, with a vague wave of the hand. "Yes, I think with a little patience I can see my way clear to a satisfactory issue."

"Where to now?" Bessie asked. "Coming home?"

"Lunch," Wainwright declared. "There used to be a place round here . . ." He shivered. "Let's get out of the wind. And then I want to look over some rooms. I think they'll suit." He looked at her questioningly. "I don't want to keep you, Bessie, but I'd be glad of your company. I'm still," he swayed a little, "I'm still feeling slightly . . ." He waved his hand again vaguely. "That is, if you don't mind," he added almost humbly.

"Oh, I don't mind," Bessie assured him warmly, trotting alongside, her hand still protectingly under his arm. "I don't mind. Not a bit."

CHAPTER IV

I

THE following weeks were feverish with hurry and makeshift ; arrangements cancelled as quickly as they were made or changed for others. Soon Wainwright realized that without Bessie he could never have carried on. Day after day he would call up the last dregs of his vitality and hurl himself in to the city ; beseeching small loans to tide him over ; seeing friends ; using influence ; wearing himself to a gaunt shadow that still hoarsely croaked out orders to a tired, stocky girl, orders about electric light, furniture, showcases, appointments, deposits, letters that must be sent, business men who must be interviewed about necessary equipment for which Hodges was reluctant to pay.

Then, at nightfall, Wainwright would collapse into a coughing, exhausted wreck ; and Bessie would take him carefully home and put him to bed with lemon drinks, aspirin and nerve tonic. He worked like a dynamo ; he cursed like a navvy ; and he showed a brilliant flair for getting his own way. Together he and Bessie knocked the studio into shape almost by will-power and their unaided muscles.

As emergencies arose, Wainwright met them with the energy of a desperate man. The company with which he had stored his furniture delivered it to the studio with a bill which Maurice had neither the means nor the intention to pay. By the time he had argued the carriers into leaving the furniture and taking a couple of valuable rugs in exchange for storage and cartage, he had expended enough energy to cut through a battleship with a blow-lamp.

At night he was too tired to eat, too tired to do anything but sink wearily into a sleep that more resembled coma. Bessie, trotting to and fro with hot-water bottles, anxious as a young mother, wondered what would happen if Wainwright collapsed just when he had overcome so many obstacles. Even her family began to share her concern. Now that their lodger showed signs of paying rent, the Drews were tolerant, and, at times, almost affable, listening with an unusual credulity to the glowing tales Bessie brought back from the " Wainwright Studios ".

If, when the studio was still little more than a promise, it shone with a lustre of Bessie's own imaginings, who could blame her for her small exaggerations ?

Just before the studio really began to function Wainwright had one of his brain-waves. Why should he lodge any longer with the Drews ? Why, he demanded, should he not sleep in the studio where there was a couch much more comfortable than the Drews' third-best bedstead ? In the studio he felt at home ; there he could relax and rest instead of tossing miserably in his lodgings.

" You're mad," Ernie declared. " Got the girl waiting on you hand and foot, and you chuck it in to camp alone. Serves you right if the rats eat you."

" There is a different atmosphere in the studio," Wainwright insisted. " The atmosphere in the Drew home is, with all respect to Bessie, sickening. It saps my strength to live in such a dump — a place for cast-offs, left-overs, the dregs of humanity."

Ernie shot his eyebrows as some men shoot their cuffs. " There's a clause in the insurance to prevent anyone living on the studio premises. The owner'll terminate your lease and the caretaker'll shoot you."

" They need never know," Maurice said simply. " I have had duplicate keys made."

Mrs. Drew's indignation at losing her lodger vented itself on Bessie as the link with the departed. There was a sudden, almost relieved, reaction in the Drew family against the extraordinarily placid conditions that had been prevailing.

" And I s'pose as far as my rent's concerned I can whistle ? " Bessie's mother asked shrilly during the in-evitable tea-time row. " You can just tell 'im from me that 'e's not getting them big tin things of his till I get my money. If 'e thinks 'e can put 'is grand ways over me, 'e's very much mistaken. I always knew 'e was a criminal. 'E may be able to impose on a bit of a girl . . ."

" 'Ipnotized 'er." For once Mr. Drew was in agreement with his marital enemy. " I says to the boss at work to-day, ' Joe,' I says, ' what can you do about a 'ipnotizer that 'ipnotizes your girl ? ' ' Put her in a 'ome,' 'e says. ' That'll fix her. Send her to one of these girls' gaols,' 'e says. ' Uncontrollable, they call it, and the perlice just take them away and there ain't no more trouble.' "

" Will you let me get a word in edgeways ? " shrieked the exasperated Mrs. Drew. " I won't have any daughter of mine associating with the kind of girl that gets in gaols, and that's flat. But I 'ave a right to my money, and you can tell 'im that from me."

" Here's five shillings of it," Bessie said. By walking to and from the studio she could save something. She had to give her mother ten shillings a week for board, and Mrs. Drew had a legitimate grievance that it was so little.

" Expect us to keep you," she flung at Bessie. " Getting high and mighty, aren't you ? And your poor brother and sister and father got to keep you, so that you can go smoogin' to a man old enough to know better. You may think it's all very well while 'e's fawning round your feet and sweetheartin' to you, but you just wait." She glared at Bessie. " What do you think you're grinnin' at ? "

" You." The indignation of her parents, suspecting that they were being deprived of their rent and their daughter's virginity, recalled to Bessie how Wainwright had expressed his resentment of the Drews' lack of courtesy.

" I was hoping that your father could have taken time off to bring in my models for me," Wainwright had sonorously complained. " I'll have to send out a carrier to get them, I suppose. You really belong to a most disobliging family, Bessie. I have never known them

48

show any of the niceties, any of the little acts of consideration one expects as a matter of course from those with
whom one associates."

Maurice felt that he was right in resenting this boorish-
ness now he had fulfilled his half promise to give Bessie
a job. He had officially installed Bessie to perform those
tasks generally carried out by a " capable junior " at a
wage of a pound a week. Over and above such occupa-
tions as attending the telephone, typing letters with three
fingers, receiving the more insignificant sitters, staving off
creditors, telling all official lies, answering enquiries and
running messages, Bessie hammered in nails, bullied Sam,
the caretaker, cleaned the studio, took home Wainwright's
washing, brushed his suits, sewed on buttons, brewed tea,
and attended to all the pressing, cutting, filing, pasting,
mounting and posting of the work, jobs for which
Wainwright was for ever meaning to engage a " capable
woman " and then forgetting about it. All these tasks
Bessie accepted automatically as part of the white woman's
burden ; and it never occurred to her that the reason she
was losing weight was not, as she thought, that she was
still growing, but that she was nearly worn out.

Bessie's tasks were not made any lighter by Mrs. Raine-
Smith who was officially supposed to direct and teach
her, but who treated the studio as a convenience and
Bessie as someone born to save more intelligent people
from exerting themselves.

" Billy " Raine-Smith was on a " commission basis ".
She had social contacts, and moved in the circles of the
fashionable and moneyed, luring her acquaintances to
the Wainwright Studios to have a " study " made. She
also used her influence with the editresses of social
columns to get the portraits published ; and the word
passed round that " Billy Raine-Smith was simply marvellous at getting people into the newspapers ". Socially-
minded females in increasing numbers availed themselves

of her publicity methods, and Wainwright's knack of altering a face not quite out of recognition. People who detested him did not deny that Maurice could photograph an old garbage-tin and make it look beautiful and distinguished.

Even the situation of the " Wainwright Studios " in an enormous, inconvenient attic atop a musty, gloomy building calling itself Fullman Chambers had not discouraged the flow of society. The studio was " quaint " ; it had " atmosphere ". Even the ancient lift moaning up and down was " quite quaint ". The landlord of Fullman Chambers had nearly fainted with joy when he realized that, after five years, someone wished to occupy his uppermost floor and pay him for the privilege. Little did he know that the Wainwright Studios depended on Mr. Alfred Hodges, and that Mr. Hodges was suffering badly from cold feet. He had begun to mumble that to rent a studio did not mean he was agreeing to pay for a desert with a glass roof. How much, he enquired, did Wainwright think it would cost to install plumbing fixtures on the top of a ruin ? Maurice had not considered that small point. Finance and the arrangements for such necessities as plumbing were Hodges' concern. For himself, he was occupied with the creative side of the business.

When Hodges thawed out some money, Wainwright hoped to persuade him to put in a dark-room ; in the meantime there was nothing to do but to struggle on desperately, getting into debt for even such small items as plates and stationery. Without a dark-room, without sinks and screens to do his developing, Wainwright was dependent on the good-will of a fellow photographer who had been dazed into allowing his dark-room to be usurped at a nominal charge. He discovered too late that a couple of men in a dark-room are as bad as two women in a house.

With appointments for sittings daily increasing, Maurice, outwardly pleasant, almost majestic, but inwardly raging, realized that he was barely making a living. Something must go towards the payment of debts that he had incurred despairing of help from Hodges, who now waited like an elderly leech to batten on what Maurice was building, without having given much more than moral support.

"I'll take him to court," Maurice raved. "He can explain there just what he means by a partnership. What am I getting out of this place? Not even bread and water!"

He tore at his hair, pulling it with both fists like an angry girl. Maurice had bushy, black masses of hair; but wilful as the rest of Maurice, it refused to grow on the top of his head. Hair would grow splendidly round his ears, on his face, or on the hills and valleys of his person, almost anywhere except on that pink dome from which it had receded as before an ice age, leaving Maurice's brains to function in lofty and, in winter, chilly heights. However tenderly he cultivated certain long, black wisps, training them across the tonsure for warmth, sooner or later they always rose up from where they lay and, stiff and uncanny as the ass's ears of Midas, refused either to disguise or be disguised.

"The exasperations!" he shouted to Bessie, "the petty exasperations! Good God! Does Hodges think I thrill with joy when some old cow comes in to have her double chin disguised for posterity?" He looked accusingly at Bessie who, as usual, formed the sole audience for these monologues. "Now, if I'd concentrated on the Absence Register, there would be none of these annoyances. I'd be on my way to millions, instead of conducting a hypocritical sink of social iniquity."

Bessie nodded sadly, her heart heavy with foreboding. Usually when Maurice launched into a tirade, she took it much as she did a row at home, letting it blow over and bending before the blast. But when she heard the Absence Register mentioned as a rival for her dear studio, she hated and feared the Register with all her heart. Much as the Absence Register was Maurice's creation, so she felt the studio was hers, the result of her love and labour.

A month or so after the studio began to flourish, with returning health and comparative prosperity, Wainwright began to hanker for his brain-child. On the impulse of the moment he diverted current revenue to the making of a new model of the Absence Register embodying several improvements. Bessie, despite forebodings, uttered no protest. Then towards the end of the summer Maurice had a new flash of hope when an American motor magnate, whom Billy Raine-Smith had snatched off a luxury liner, evinced polite interest.

" If I get this invention under way," Maurice gloated to his secretary-typist-scullerymaid-valet, " I'll be able to scrap this blasted studio. There'll be none of this petti-fogging and cadging."

Elated at the prospect of success, bracing himself ex-citedly to meet objections and conquer arguments when he showed the Absence Register to the interested American, Maurice looked round the studio and snapped his fingers.

" That ! " he said, " to the portrait ramp."

Half an hour later the magnate sent a telephone message that he was sorry he was unable to meet Mr. Wainwright as arranged, but circumstances required his presence at a dinner. After that nothing was heard of the Absence Register for quite some time. It lurked in Maurice's special corner of the studio, its little red and green lights gleaming maliciously, ready to be explained to anyone so incautious as to ask : " What's that ? "

It was a robot egotism at which Bessie cast many an inimical glance. She would not even dust it ; and on one occasion she set a vase of flowers on its inviolate head, later receiving a furious reprimand for sacrilege.

II

" Room to expand ! " Wainwright had cried enthusiastically, when he first saw the wide, open spaces of the studio. But, little by little, like the cosmos taking shape and form in the void, the studio had been divided into little spheres and compartments. Bessie's sphere was the ante-room, where she sat behind a typewriter and a telephone, on guard for those who should not pass, particularly debt-collectors. Over the studio itself presided a camera, a quite inferior camera, which had been fitted on to such a massive, wheeled base, decorated with so many screws and steel knobs, that even people who had been X-rayed quailed before its looming personality.

On the far side of the studio, behind tall green curtains, once the property of a short-lived repertory society, Maurice had a comfortable and untidy burrow, chock-a-block with a big desk, a swivel chair, his couch, bookshelves, and odds and ends of inventor's litter ranging from screws that might come in handy, and a collection of old pipes, to part of a diesel engine. Coils of flex, lamps and files of photographs were bestowed around the floor. Before any important interview Bessie almost had to fight for permission to tidy up the mess. Usually she seized her chance when the owner was out.

The curtains cast a green, underseas gloom over Maurice's lair, making a reading-lamp necessary on dull days. Friends, plunging from the hard clarity of the studio into the curtained recess, where the lamp cast romantic shadows on Maurice's striking features, invariably demanded why he had " rigged up those curtains to shut out all the light ". To which Wainwright invariably responded : " One must have privacy ". It was characteristic of him first to choose the studio for its spaciousness, its flood of light, and then to wrap himself comfortably away from both.

The first thing that struck the visitor to the studio was those tall green curtains on the far side of the room, dominating it, as though they were the embodied will of the owner. On the left, a row of windows had their unsightly view screened in more green silk ; on the right cubicle dressing-rooms stood enigmatic and impassable as the Wall of China, barring from the view of the un-privileged those wide, open spaces where mice, brooms, buckets and refuse of all descriptions had a congenial home. This was the behind scene of the theatrical impressionism of the studio.

Around the walls of the studio proper hung enlarge-ments of Wainwright's work, studies of old cobble-stones or boats ; doorways that had interested him ; shadow patterns or bits of lace or bottles. There were auto-graphed portraits of stage celebrities or former Hollywood stars ; black-and-white sketches by fellow artists ; and two large tapestries, pseudo-eighteenth century. A few exceedingly uncomfortable chairs completed the im-pression that the stage was set and that presently the green curtains would part for an invisible audience. Even the lighting overhead heightened the feeling that spots in the fly gallery were training down on the insig-nificant sitter, the puppet below.

Scattered about, it might seem carelessly to the uninitiated, were rugs of diverse breeds and brands, affording scanty protection to the brilliant surface of a floor that had been painted in red, green and black triangles, to give, as its designer proudly maintained, a " surrealist effect ". Maurice, ever since the inspiration struck him, had lavished love and attention on that tri-coloured floor. He moaned to see its surface marred by a footprint. Unluckily, the floor exposed straying footsteps like a guilty conscience ; and, in vain, Maurice tried varnish and anguish, polish and curses, and more paint. He hired a man to scrub the floor every second day, but the man went on strike, so Bessie usually did the scrubbing.

Days when the floor's face was clouded were likely to be days when Maurice's temper clouded too ; but to see the floor impeccable cheered and inspired him. The little islands of rug were, therefore, planted strategically to trap the unwary or daring foot ; and Wainwright's " gang ", now beginning to " drop in " in increasing numbers as the studio prospered, would leap from one area of carpet to the next, encouraging each other with hoarse cries.

Protecting Maurice from his friends began to be one of Bessie's major problems. They would " drop in " and kill an hour or so in cultured conversation. They would arrange to interview business associates with whom they were " pulling off a deal " at " Maurice's place " because it was so convenient. On one occasion Bessie informed an indigent stamp-collector who was arranging his collection at ease in the best armchair, that " Mr. Wainwright wanted the room. He had a sitting in a few minutes."

" Let him go ahead," the collector said negligently. " I won't interfere."

Bessie bared her teeth. " Clear out," she said briefly.

The surprised philatelist hastily, but with dignity, gathered his litter and departed. He complained later to Maurice that " the girl's manner was insulting. It creates a bad impression to have her about."

" I'm very sorry this should have happened, George," Wainwright apologized weakly. He was too kind-hearted to hurt George's feelings himself. " But she's a good little thing and usually quite civil."

Wainwright could never refuse his friends ; he was

always ready to do small favours, to lend them money. Though it interfered with business, he liked to have people drop in. So popular did the studio become that Ernie declared it resembled one of those caverns where every beast and bird had each his refuge and lurking-place.

Of all those who staked a claim in the Wainwright waste spaces, among the brooms and buckets, Mr. Montgomery was the most thoroughgoing. Having become bankrupt at the same time as Wainwright, he felt it established a bond between them. He gave his approval to the studio by moving in a complete set of office furniture which he stored in two of the cubicles. He would come and consult his files quite as comfortably, as he often said, as if it were his own office.

Bessie had a soft spot for James Everard Montgomery because he treated her, not as a hard-working typist-cum-scullerymaid, but more as a lady who had come to order a portrait of herself in court dress. Had they been fashionable, Montgomery would have worn a top-hat, and looked well in it. He always carried a gold-headed cane, and upon his silver hair he wore a beautifully brushed bowler hat. His conversation was mainly of his debts ; but he mentioned them much as a picnicker might deplore the prevalence of sandflies.

" And now," he said on one occasion, having lectured Bessie on moth and silverfish prevention for the best part of half an hour, " I really must hurry. I have a most important conference with a board of directors. Should they adopt my suggestions, it may mean affluence again. Have you five shillings till Saturday, Maurice ? Thank you . . . thank you. *Au revoir*, Miss Bessie. Wish me luck."

" What's he do for a crust ? " Bessie asked, as the lift bore Mr. Montgomery away.

" He specializes in political and economic problems," Wainwright said, with a note of reverence in his voice.

" He writes articles for the quarterlies and the financial pages of the daily papers. I don't suppose you have ever read his *Analysis of Factors governing Economic Norms in Australia*, but it's a very well-known booklet. He always gives evidence at unemployment commissions and wage enquiries."

" What I want to know," Bessie complained, " is where are *you* going to fit in if any more of your friends camp here ? "

" I don't grudge old Jimmy storage space or the loan of a few bob now and then," Wainwright amiably dismissed the matter. " After all, it's the least I can do."

Bessie gulped and gathered her courage. Maurice was in one of his most expansive moods. He was talking to her as though she too painted or sang or wrote for magazines. " All my friends," she had heard him say once, " *do* something." And it had cut her to the quick that, though he lent her books and had tried to improve her, she could never repay him by any desire to " do " something, turning out clay pots or embroidering peasant motifs on bits of old canvas. Bessie felt that only when he was at his kindliest did Maurice count her as a friend. Other times she was just Bessie, an institution for cleaning and defending studios.

For some time now she had been nerving herself to assert the right, not of a friend, but of an ordinary employee, the right to a living wage. Since Maurice was very far from being an ordinary employer, so must her approach to the subject be far from a bald demand for money due. She gulped again and plunged into the embarrassing problem.

" Maurice," she said, almost in a whisper, " Maurice, could you lend me thirty shillings ? "

Hitherto she had always called him Mr. Wainwright. The use of his Christian name startled Maurice almost more than the unheard-of request. Bessie was stationed in the ante-room to keep persons with designs on his purse from reaching him. He had even come to refer his friends to her with a vague : " Ask Bessie, she looks after the petty cash." Here suddenly was a revolution ; the guardian inexplicably turned menace.

" Why, of course, Bessie," he said hastily. " Of course. I haven't got it now, but towards the end of the week . . ."

Bessie was determined not to be brushed aside. If Maurice could bestow largesse on all and sundry, her dignity demanded that he should hear her just feminine claims.

" There's a dress," she said breathlessly, her eyes large. " I've got to have some clothes. I . . . I can't really manage any longer. . . ." Her voice trailed painfully away.

Wainwright's face lit with interest. " Of course, you must have a dress," he agreed. " One has to dress well." Maurice's boots were never polished unless Bessie polished them. His best suit constantly needed a visit to the cleaners for spots and stains, careless memories of bygone meals.

Bessie's face shone with pleasure because Maurice was really listening to her, paying attention and sympathetically considering her right to a pretty dress.

" It has little flowers," she told him eagerly. " It's green — something of the colour of the curtains — apple green."

Wainwright eyed her narrowly. " You'll need shoes and stockings," he said decidedly. " And a hat, I suppose. It isn't one of those yellow greens ? "

Bessie shook her head. " Oh, no," she assured him. " You'll like it."

He smiled, amused at so childish a display of earnestness.

" Well, anyway, you have to have it." He dug into his vest pocket. " Here's the bank. Let's see. I've got five pounds nine and threepence. Here's three pounds. Your share. Sure you can get all you want on that ? "

Bessie almost blushed as she stuttered out, " I'll have to . . . pay you back . . . Mr. Wainwright."

" It's a bonus in advance," he said gravely, looking down into her green eyes. " Why don't you always call me Maurice ? "

She was so attractive when she relaxed that serious, stiff, business manner, so delightfully young. Surely nothing quite so young and pathetic as Bessie glowing in the realized dream of her new dress had ever brightened the studio. It seemed to glow with her pleasure.

For the first time in months Wainwright heard her whistling as she put on the electric jug for his afternoon tea. It made him feel old and just a little sad to think how she must have suffered before she screwed up courage to ask him for that money. Bessie was, now he saw her out of the enveloping white overall, very much thinner. She was paler too, the little dusting of freckles faded out. He noticed she was taking care of her nails and was wearing a more becoming shade of face-powder.

" Gee," she said, beaming on him, " you're good to let me have that three quid."

Her speech had improved not one iota, had not a trace of his own mellow, measured diction. It was a husky, rather deep growl, resembling her father's as velvet resembles sacking.

Bessie had learnt something about Wainwright that she had not realized before. When she borrowed money, Maurice treated her as a friend ; when he had to pay her wages, she was just an employee. It would be much better, Bessie considered, to borrow her wages in the future and be treated as an equal. None of his friends ever paid Maurice back ; they sometimes lent it to him again. Bessie was sure that, if she " borrowed " her salary on a Friday, it would put her on a different footing, although, of course, Maurice would inevitably attempt to borrow the money back again.

When she brought the tea he looked at her with a rather wistful expression.

" That dress suits you," he said. " You have an eye for colour, Bessie. You should do something in that line."

Bessie's face fell. He was going to urge her to study art or design, to read more books and take an interest in politics.

" I can whistle," she said to divert him, defending her one accomplishment with a half-shamefaced grin.

" Too bad." He threw himself back into his swivel chair. He seemed suddenly to have lost interest in her. " Did you get those prints ? "

" Why, yes," Bessie replied in a stifled tone. All the glow had departed from her. She was just Bessie again, an adjunct of the studio.

CHAPTER V

THE change in Bessie might have begun with Maurice's memorable party, or perhaps earlier, on the day the piano arrived. She did not even know her employer owned a piano until a girl generally referred to as " Bill's Girl " or " Bugs " strolled in and draped herself on Maurice's sofa for a little leisurely gossip, just at a time when the studio should have been at its busiest. Maurice hinted that he was rather rushed, but the hint had no effect.

" I suppose you know the Corner Theatre is closing down ? " she mentioned, surveying her brightly painted toe-nails where they protruded through frayed gilt sandals. She giggled. " That was the funniest thing."

" What was ? " Maurice could have been more impatient. Bugs had a very beautiful frame that made all her clothes appear inadequate. " What was ? " he repeated, surveying her with an indulgent eye.

" The landlord asking them for rent . . . the funniest thing. And the producer, Tim Healy, all covered in boils, which comes of living on meat pies and coffee, and sleeping on the club-room floor ; and Joe Ashley being expelled for pinching George's wife and spending the funds on rum — and then, on top of it all, the landlord asks for rent ! " She went off into a peal of laughter.

" Nothing funny about that."

" Oh ! but they fixed him. They talked him out of it. They gave him the piano as full payment. He didn't want to take it at first."

Maurice rose excitedly. " But they can't do that ! " he cried. " That's my piano, the hounds ! I only lent it to them because I had nowhere to put it."

Bugs yawned. " Was it your piano ? I thought it couldn't belong to the Corner Theatre. Anyway, it's no use crying over spilt milk."

" Spilt milk indeed ! " Maurice was virtuously indignant. " A man does what he can to assist the movement for culture among the masses. Lends them his piano ; and this is what happens ! Anyway, I'm not going to let them get away with it. Bessie ! "

Bessie came hurrying.

" Ring up a carrier and tell him to go to the Corner Theatre and collect my property. And they oan bring it here. I didn't mind the Corner people using that piano, but I'm damned if any landlord is going to detain it. The hide of them doing a thing like that ! "

The next morning two brawny carriers appeared at the door of the studio to enquire if it was " the place where the piano was to come ".

" Right in here," Bessie encouraged.

" That's all very well." One of the movers pushed back his hat and scratched his head. " But how we goin' to get 'er 'ere ? "

" What's the trouble ? " Maurice asked, emerging from his corner.

" They don't know how to get the piano up here."

" Won't it come up in the lift ? "

The carrier in the felt hat looked at his mate in the leather apron. " Here's a bloke," the glance seemed to say, " who was dropped on his head when a child."

" You might haul it up through the window," Bessie suggested ; and there was an exodus to the window.

Two floors below projected a corrugated iron roof shading the footpath and the shop fronts. Below that again a truck might be observed with a battered old piano standing on it, a policeman with a suspicious look keeping watch just behind, and a " No Parking " sign just in front.

" One of you men," the owner of the studio observed hopefully, " could slide down a rope and wait on the roof to guide the piano up."

There was again between the two carters that silent interchange of opinion. Ernie had now joined the committee as consulting expert, having come up behind and taken in the situation at a glance.

" Thing's perfectly simple," he said contemptuously. " What's wrong with you ? Lug it up the stairs."

The piano-movers were inclined to regard Ernie with some degree of deference. His tone was so assured.

" Thasso, Bert," the leather apron chimed in. " What's wrong with that ? "

" Nothing's wrong with that." Again the felt hat shifted for the scratching process that encourages thought. " Looks a bit narrow. Anyway, I guess there's no other way."

" Unless you lower it through the roof," Maurice suggested humorously.

Again that look.

The advisory committee accompanied the executives down to the lorry, and Maurice engaged the policeman in conversation while the piano was lifted off. It was one of those pianos which have obviously had a hard life, serving overtime as a sideboard, a place to stow beer, a dressing-table and shelf combined ; a scarred tom-cat of a piano accustomed to lift its unmelodious voice into the small hours. It had a drunken lurch where a castor was missing and looked as though its only fitting environment was an inebriates' home.

" Ho ! Bert." With a dexterous humping movement the leather-aproned carter received the weight of the piano.

" Ho ! Jeff." The one with the felt hat had the other end. They marched with it as though it were a feather to the end of the staircase, their advisory committee following in single file.

" Hup ! " The piano " hupped " ungracefully, with sundry bangings at the turn of the stair, and settled on the first floor while its urgers took a firmer grip. The committee of three had been augmented by Sam, the caretaker, with a broom and basket which he laid aside gratefully, having spied an excellent chance for a guerrilla exchange with his hated enemy, Wainwright.

" Where you taking that ? " he enquired.

" Where do you think we're taking it ? Upstairs of course. Does it look," Ernie asked, " as though we were stowing it in a cellar ? "

" Got to get the landlord's permission," Sam maintained. " Can't have pianos moved in. It's not in the lease."

No one took any notice. " Hup, Bert." The piano recommenced its majestic ascent.

" I'm telling you, you can't take that upstairs without askin' Mr. Fullman. I'm in charge here, and it says in the lease nothing that will in any way disturb the other tenants. If that there piano ain't goin' to disturb 'em, I'm a bit out."

" If you wish to make a complaint," Maurice responded, chilly as a public servant, " you can make it to Mr. Fullman. I am well within my rights in moving in my furniture."

" Ho, we'll see about that." Sam had abandoned his bucket and broom and was hot-foot down the stairs.

" He has a long way to go to get old Fullman," Maurice observed placidly. " By the time they get here, the thing will be in, and he can't do anything."

Unfortunately this prophecy was uttered too soon. The piano made the grade to the second floor, but there the stairs narrowed considerably and jerked upward in a dog-leg, complicated by a low ceiling which jutted over the landing.

Bert and his mate stood back contemplatively and shook their heads.

" But try," Maurice urged. " I don't want a row with the landlord and that man is determined to be unpleasant. I don't mind if the piano is scratched a little. Tug at it this way." He moved in to show them. " You take that end, Ernie, and tilt it like this." Bert and Jeff, jealous of their professional dignity, seized the other side. " Now, all together."

The piano, nearly flattening Bert in the process, went at a lumbering run as far as the dog-leg bend where it jammed.

" She can't go no further," Bert said, slowly scratching his head.

" Well, bring it back and we'll try again," Maurice commanded.

The piano, however, was caught between two floors.

It refused to budge. They tried pushing and pulling and levering but to no purpose.

" Might get a jack and jack it up." Ernie had once owned a car.

" Don't be a mug. The thing's caught on the wooden bit sticking out from the top floor. And it won't come round those banisters."

They were still arguing when Mr. Fullman arrived in tow of the excited Sam.

" I told them, Mr. Fullman, didn't I tell yer there was a clause in the lease about not disturbin' the tenants ? "

By this time the advisory committee was composed of the original members plus three typists, an office-boy, a stout, elderly paint merchant, a traveller for a hosiery firm and two customers of the paint merchant. They were all helpful and they all had theories. Someone had left the door of the lift open on the top floor, and the bell was ringing and ringing unregarded.

" Hey, you ! " the owner of the building shouted to the felt-hatted mover. " Go and shut that lift door."

There was a tramp of heavy boots and presently the lift slid past on its downward passage.

" Well, I don't care what you do," Mr. Fullman cut in on Maurice's indignant discussion of the terms of the lease. " Get the piano up or take it out of here, but don't leave it blocking the stair like that. People want to pass."

Sure enough, on the principle that someone always treads on a sore toe, three people had already sought to use the stairs in preference to the lift.

" But it's stuck ! "

" Well, get it out of there."

The little eddies of interest that the piano had set up began to die down. The paint merchant drifted back to his office, and this reminded Maurice that the studio had been left deserted.

" Good Lord ! " he exclaimed. " The place is open and empty. Bessie ! No, I'd better go myself. You stay here, Bessie, and Ernie, you'd better come with me. We can see from above what's best to do." Wainwright felt conspicuous, being pointed out as the owner of a piano which had jammed in the stairs. " This is a lesson to me," he declared, as he sought the refuge of the lift. " Never again will these theatrical ventures get more than my moral support. I'm tired of being the mainstay of a crowd of hangers-on."

Left to themselves the movers regarded each other thoughtfully.

" Twelve o'clock, Bert."

" Near enough."

They prepared to sit down on the bottom step for lunch.

" But aren't you going to get the piano up first ? " Bessie asked anxiously.

" She won't go up, miss."

" Nothing we can do."

" But it can't stay there for ever," Bessie pleaded.

They shook their heads, and having produced each a packet of sandwiches, enquired if there was anywhere they could get hot water. Bessie trotted off to heat them some and report to Maurice.

There was an armistice on the piano front while the movers had their lunch, while Bessie, Ernie and Maurice had their lunch and drank their tea. It was only a seeming lull, for the inventor's brain of Maurice was busy.

" If we rigged a pulley and took the rope under the piano lid," he explained scientifically, " so that the pull was upwards, we could shift it in next to no time." He went off to inspect the battle-field. " By George, that's what I'll do. There's a beam within easy reach, if you climb up on the banister, and we can put in a rope and pulley on the beam."

" Don't be a bloody goat."

" Mrs. Raine-Smith is bringing in Mrs. Jethro for a sitting at a quarter to two."

" We'll have everything settled by then. Run out like a good girl, Bessie, and buy me a rope and pulley."

" What sort of a pulley ? "

Maurice sighed wearily. " I'd better go myself." It took him some time to finish his conversation with Ernie, a little longer to find his hat, but finally he departed in search of the necessary pulley.

" Maurice is a bloody goat," Ernie said reflectively. " He mucks about."

Bessie made no reply. She was feeling disloyal but did not wish to sound it. The two movers were still having a quiet smoke when Maurice returned and began a search for a hammer and sufficiently strong screws.

At a quarter to two, when Mrs. Raine-Smith and the sitter arrived, Mr. Wainwright, instead of being urbane, smiling, ready to get the best out of a face not originally blessed, was clutching a rope in one hand and howling over the banisters to someone unseen :

" That comes of leaving it to a stupid fool who can't lift his feet out of the way ! "

" A slight *contretemps*," he explained. " My men are attempting to move in a piano too large for the staircase. Excuse me just for a moment, won't you ? This sort of thing needs personal supervision." He dropped the rope, however, and with a divided mind accompanied the interested ladies into his studio. He was out again in a minute. " Bessie ! " he hissed over the banisters.

" Yes."

" Come up here at once. Why the devil aren't you ready to receive them ? "

Bessie had wriggled across the inert bulk of the piano. " Because I can't be in two places at once," was what she would have liked to say ; but instead she responded : " Sorry," endeavouring at the same time to tidy her hair.

Ernie, left in charge of the moving, seized Maurice's discarded rope energetically. Bert and Jeff also seized it.

" Now, when I say three," Ernie commanded. " One, two, three ! "

At the word the lid of the piano detached itself from the remains and sailed into the air, to descend with a splintering crash as they let go.

" Can't be helped. Knew the idea was lousy," Ernie consoled his troops. " What's the next move, boys ? "

Sam, who had hovered and hovered like some bird of evil omen, had at that minute departed.

" What this thing needs," Ernie decided, with a gleam in his eye, " is direct action." He knocked on the paint merchant's door. " Have you by any chance," he enquired politely, " an axe ? "

Unfortunately the paint merchant had an axe. What he used it for was a mystery ; but there was Ernie with a nice, shiny new axe.

" Hey," the movers demanded in chorus, " what're you goin' to do ? "

" Chop it out."

Ernie went superbly to work. He was enjoying this. Chips flew from the piano, the stairs, the wall indiscriminately. He had cut away a section of the banisters and was beginning to break away the jutting beam of the upper floor when the piano, without warning, fell forward on to the floor below, breaking the rest of the banisters as it fell.

" There, I told you." Ernie dusted his hands. " It needed direct action." He returned the axe to its owner. " Thank you."

Bert and Jeff propped up the ruin. " She still won't go *hup*," Bert pointed out.

Ernie waved the objection aside. " It's no longer important," he said, regarding the fragments.

" There's an empty room along the end of the passage,"

the paint merchant suggested. " The caretaker keeps his buckets there."

" The very thing ! Shove, boys ! "

By the time Sam returned, there were only the splintered ruins of the banisters and the bulk of the piano protruding indecently from his storage cupboard. " Hoy," he complained. " Who the hell . . ." But Ernie had departed.

" It all comes," Maurice explained to Mrs. Raine-Smith and her friend, as the sitting concluded, " it all comes of allowing one's self to be used as a convenient source of funds by individuals and organizations with no sense of responsibility. One comes in contact with them, of course. Artists, writers, journalists . . . no method. No real sanity of outlook." He heaved a sigh. " I sometimes feel that those men who go home and tend their gardens are in a happy position. I miss — the quiet dignity, the ordered elegance of other days. I sometimes feel that the period when women wore bustles and kept their pretty heads free of every idea except how to be charming were the times really worth living in."

" How extraordinary of you, Mr. Wainwright ! "

Bessie, listening in the ante-room, knew just what an arch smile her employer would be wearing.

" But even in the days when women wore bustles they didn't only think of their looks."

" Ladies with wide interests and talents, ladies such as yourselves, there have been in every age."

This polished exchange of small nothings would have continued indefinitely had not Billy Raine-Smith broken in : " I wonder you don't give a party, Maurice, now you have the piano. This would be a splendid place for a party."

" That's an idea ! " Maurice was struck by it. Bessie's heart sank. Here he was, up to his eyes in debt, and parties cost money. " After all, what is the use of opening a new studio without you have some ceremonial ? I'll act upon your suggestion, Billy. It shall be done."

He saw the party in his mind's eye as he escorted the ladies to the lift. It would be a party of old friends. Just the people he really liked, distinguished, gracious people, who talked his language, and were still capable of regarding modern vulgarisms as offensive.

" Bessie," he said, returning in good spirits, " I have a great idea."

The red, inflamed eye of Sam glared up at him from the well of the ruined stairs. " I wanna see you, Mr. Wainwright," he breathed fiercely, " about that there piano . . . what's left of it."

" Leave it there," Wainwright said grandly. " I'll have it removed to-morrow if it won't come upstairs. I'll give it away, or sell it, or something." He turned away from the disgraceful incident. " Bessie, I am going to give a party — next, next Thursday."

Bessie said nothing.

" It will serve as an official opening for the studio," Wainwright continued gaily. " Times being what they are, I might have to close it soon anyway. We may as well enjoy life, yes ? "

Bessie still said nothing. Until this time she had regarded Wainwright as a capable man cursed by misfortune. She was beginning to have her doubts.

CHAPTER VI

I

THE morning of the studio party Bessie came in at half-past seven and washed the floor. She had changed into some overalls belonging to her brother and started on the red and green patchwork before Wainwright woke up. He padded out from behind the curtains and regarded her fretfully.

"What the devil are you doing?" he demanded, yawning. "You know I was going to get a man in to scrub the floor. It's no job for a girl." He rubbed his chin with the rueful satisfaction of a man who realizes that he has sprouted overnight. "Gosh! I feel rotten. Couldn't sleep for hours and hours. I'd appreciate it much more, Bessie, if you'd leave the floor alone and make me a cup of tea."

Bessie rose, put on the electric jug, and returned to her scrubbing. Maurice would have liked to ignore her and to return to bed; but you cannot ignore someone who is silently busy about your feet. He regarded Bessie irritably. All that display of competent energy so early in the morning made him feel ill. He had not been able to enter the building until the small hours. Returning after midnight, he had run into an ambush where Sam was lurking on the stairs, and had been forced to retire.

Sam, like the lift he drove, complained bitterly and frequently. He was most in his element slopping dirty water along the passage with a mop. His preoccupations were all in the basement of his body, where he had obscure and repellent troubles that kept him from every joy except a fluent and gifted narration of his symptoms. If the cistern leaked or the lights fused, Sam was nowhere to be found; but at other times he would be lounging in the entrance telling a friend about his inside. He and the cockroaches emerged together after dark.

It was not until two o'clock that, worn out watching for Wainwright, Sam had fallen asleep in the front entrance hall. There were, Maurice felt, certain draw-backs to living at the studio; first the trouble with the caretaker, and now Bessie tramping about in the early hours of the dawn.

" There was no need for you to scrub it," he persisted in an aggrieved tone.

" Pigs' tracks," Bessie replied briefly. " All over it."

Wainwright gathered his flannel dressing-gown about him. " Bad temper first thing in the morning," he reproved, " is an infallible sign. You can always tell a woman by the way she behaves when you wake up." He put his head round the curtain and grinned at her, curiously like a gargoyle in his early morning growth of beard. " You'll get middle-aged spread if you will persist in scrubbing. Just look at the women who scrub. They're dreadful."

Bessie smiled back at him. She felt a warm little glow when he pretended to scold her. She didn't mind cleaning the floor. She welcomed anything that might make her even the least use to him. Perhaps some day he might reach the stage where he could not do without her. But the trouble with Maurice was that he did not depend on anyone, not even on himself. He just took what came.

" Amoeboid," Bessie had heard Ernie fling at him, when they were having one of their usual friendly cursing matches. " You're amoeboid, Maurice. You just react to things. You've got no skin. Drop one sort of chemical on you and you turn blue and green. Drop another and you go yellow. You just roll along quivering and putting out feelers. Now, take young Bessie," he had lowered his voice, " she's got half your intelligence and four times your gripping power. She's a regular little limpet when it comes to sticking, but you haven't got stickers ; you've got suckers."

" And the same to you," Maurice had flung back. " Now let me tell you something about yourself . . ." And he proceeded to tell Ernie his failings with a wealth of language that left Ernie's feeble by comparison.

Bessie, after asking Ernie to spell it for her, had looked

up " amoeboid " in the dictionary, and had discovered that an amoeba was " the simplest of living creatures ". This, she felt, did not fit Maurice at all. There was nothing simple about him.

Despite the looming problem of Maurice's party, she was happier that Thursday morning scrubbing the floor than she had been for weeks. Here she was on terms of intimacy with Maurice again, quite at home watching him pad around looking for his boots. She belonged here. She was making herself a niche. Everyone had to make themselves some sort of place ; carve it out to suit themselves and clean it and improve it.

Maurice did not realize that Bessie regarded this as her property that she was scrubbing. She wanted it to look clean, not for Maurice's sake, but for her own pride's sake. Not because she was fond of him did she scrub. Naturally she was fond of him ; but that was a separate compartment of her mind. She took Maurice with the studio, not the studio with Maurice. She was contented scrubbing her floor ; and she began to whistle with little trills and runs and flourishes. Maurice bounded around the row of cubicles and made frantic signs to her to cease.

Bessie looked up, her mouth still pouted over a note. She eyed him wonderingly. " What's biting you ? " she enquired. It never occurred to her that well-trained typists or charladies do not ask an employer what is biting him. Maurice had often thought he should curb Bessie's freedom of speech, but the hopelessness of the task deterred him.

" I don't want Sam charging in. He'll be getting ideas in his head."

" Oh ! "

She knelt on a little bit of matting, the scrubbing-brush still in one hand. Something about the faded dungarees she was wearing made her look very much

73

more feminine than did the green flowered dress. It was probably only that the dungarees did not fit her. Maurice noticed that her short brown hair was standing out around her head.

" You've been doing something to your hair," he said, almost as though he were accusing her of a crime. He came over and inspected it closely. " You've been shampooing it. It looks delightful."

Bessie almost blushed. " It's for the party," she muttered.

Until that moment it had not occurred to Wainwright that Bessie would be coming to the party. He had not thought to exclude her ; he had not thought to invite her. The idea of Bessie at his party had simply not entered his head.

" Why, of course." He retired to the dressing-room and thought hard. Bessie trotting about the studio, or Bessie perched on the end of his bed, he could visualize ; but scarcely at a party. How would she mix with the people he had invited ? People like Professor Zetkind, a distinguished anthropologist, or Sutcliffe, owner of one of the biggest jewellery stores in Sydney ?

Reviewing Bessie's previous meetings with his friends, he was forced to admit that she had mixed very well. While she did not talk much, she listened splendidly. Bessie might be as difficult to dispossess as a cat ; but she had a cat's trick of sitting unobserved and quite at her ease in the seats of the mighty. There was no noticeable improvement in her speech and manners ; but the manners of society were so bad that Bessie was, comparatively, well-bred. At least she never asked, as one fashionable debutante had done : " And who are you committing adultery with these days, Maurice ? " All in all, he decided, Bessie was much less affected and more intelligent than many society women.

Still he did not like Bessie taking it for granted that

she would be at the party. Bessie seemed to be advancing on him, encroaching a small privilege here and a concession there. This business of cleaning the floor for instance ! Putting him under an obligation to her ! He hated being under an obligation to anyone.

All the time he was dressing and drinking his tea he was aware of Bessie as a problem. It was selfish of her to make herself into a problem when he had so many pressing things on hand. He did not mean to speak sharply to her, but now and then during the day he almost snapped at her :

" Haven't you got that number yet, Bessie ? Why wasn't I told sooner that Hodges had been in ? Where have you put that list of addresses I left on my desk ? "

It was one of those maddening days when everything went wrong. Wainwright was more absorbed in the preparations for his party than in his work. He went through a couple of important sittings almost absent-mindedly. To add to the aggravation, Ernie strolled in late in the afternoon with a nasty look in his eye. Relations had been strained between Maurice and Ernie from the time Maurice viewed the maimed corpse of his piano.

This afternoon Ernie had been definitely having too much to drink, and an odour of coffee berries preceded him by about four feet. Drink always made him more dogmatic and belligerent. He surveyed Maurice's modest collection of bottles, and sneered with his eyebrows.

" Gawstruth ! " he said cuttingly. " Anyone'd know you were a blasted teetotaller." He competently took over the drink problem. " You leave it to me. Needn't think you're going to stave off that mob with three bottles of grocer's claret and one dry sherry. Let me at the 'phone, Bess. Chap I know. Name's Fred. Get the stuff delivered here. Favour to me." He issued rapid orders to Fred. " And Freddie, ole son, put in a dozen of dry ginger ale for luck." He put the telephone down

and waved his eyebrows at Bessie. " You ought to know
better than to let Maurice run things like this. No right
to give a party. One glass of beer puts him under the
table for the night."

Ernie insisted on regarding Bessie as an amorous connection of Wainwright's rather than a business one. He
was constantly deploring to his friend the harm " this
infatuation would do ".

" It won't last, Morrie," he would say in a depressed
tone. " She'll skid off with someone younger and
better-looking."

And Maurice would swear at him impotently. Wainwright felt that same sense of injustice when Ernie devilled
him that Bessie felt when her family took it for granted
that she was her employer's unofficial wife. Just because
a girl washed a couple of his shirts, Maurice protested to
his cynical friend, she didn't own him body and soul,
did she ?

" You look out," Ernie would respond. " No fool like
an old fool." Maurice hated to be reminded that he
was forty.

" *I* am giving this little party, Ernie," he said now,
with the inflection on the " *I* ", " not for a mob of drinkers.
Just a cheery gathering of my personal friends, my more
intimate friends. An evening of quiet, pleasant discussion — a little music perhaps. Miss Evison has
promised to sing."

" Hell ! " Ernie observed vulgarly. " Sounds like an
old maid's funeral. Bess and I 'ull mind the bar, won't
we, sweetheart ? "

He placed his arm round Bessie's waist and she detached it good-humouredly and went on cutting sandwiches.

" Bessie ! " Wainwright said sharply. " I want you
to go over to the dark-room and get those proofs they're
holding up. Insist on having them. Never mind the

76

sandwiches. Tell them I must have the proofs for to-morrow morning."

As soon as she had gone, he swung round on Ernie. "You get home and sleep it off. What the hell do you mean coming in boozed and being offensive to that girl?"

"Jealous," Ernie remarked sadly. "Jealous." He took a large bite out of a sandwich and munched it appreciatively.

"Don't be more drunk than you are. Go on home."

"Staying for the party," Ernie said nastily. "I want to hear this pleasant discussion. Meet your interestin' friends."

Maurice led him to the sofa. "Get a sleep," he said resignedly, knowing from past experience that Ernie would wake with a desire to avoid all society, especially his own.

"Haven't been to bed three nights," Ernie mumbled. "Get the sack to-morrow." Ernie had some mysterious connection with a paper that was always either sacking him or taking him on again. He stretched out comfortably and waved his eyebrows once. "Good ole Maurice," he murmured. "Good ole . . ."

There was presently a sound as though the lift had climbed its four floors and stopped with a grunt. It was Ernie snoring. Left alone in the darkening studio, Maurice decided he needed another shave. If he did not hurry, the barbers would be all shut. Leaving Ernie for watchdog, he seized his hat, slammed it on at his usual erratic angle and rushed out.

The studio grew darker and darker, and Ernie slept more and more noisily. The red, black and green floor had all merged into black ; the curtains were making a gentle, ghostly rustle in the dark when someone stepped out of the lift and called "You there, Maurice?" in a sharp, female voice.

The intruder did not bother to switch on the lights

but padded round the studio softly, inspecting the sleeping Ernest without much interest and settling down in the best armchair, the red end of her cigarette making the only spot of light in that empty place.

When Bessie switched on the lights a quarter of an hour later, she found a tall, stringy female, burnt a light walnut colour and wearing a garment of what looked like brown sacking. Her feet, as they dangled over the side of the chair, were astonishingly large and shod in a pair of disreputable canvas shoes with holes in the toes. The lady's glasses were very thick and they gave her eyes a protuberant look.

" Did you know Ernie is drunk on the sofa ? " the vision asked ; and then without waiting for a reply : " I was relaxing. Nice in the dark. D'you work here ? "

Bessie attempted the last question first. " Yes. I'm Bessie Drew, Mr. Wainwright's assistant."

" Don't look it. You ought to have red finger-nails and stilt heels."

Bessie was saved the trouble of replying.

" For Gawsake don't make such a row ! " Ernie moaned from behind the curtain. " I bet it's Esther Gullick. I know that voice." He stumbled out holding a hand to his head. " Get me a drink, Bess. I've got a mouth like the bottom of a bird-cage." He turned to the visitor. " How's the simple life, Esther ? How's the biology and the mineral elements and the microscope ? How's the hut ? "

Bessie broke in. " There isn't any bottle-opener, Ernie."

" 'Struth, what a place ! " From his waistcoat pocket Ernie fished out one of those penknives that include everything from jam-spoons to implements for removing stones from horses' feet. " If you lose this," he said tenderly, " it will be the last thing you lose." He turned again to Esther. " I was asking about the hut. Delightful

78

place. I suppose the roof still leaks ? "

" It still leaks." Esther rolled herself a cigarette with the dexterity of a kitten patting a dead leaf.

" Bessie," Ernie declared, accepting a glass of beer, " never go near Esther's hut. She lured me up there once — just once. Obvious attempt at seduction. Fed me on health foods and bran to weaken my resistance. Trees breathing down your neck and mountains in the backyard. I had to walk a hundred miles to the train." He finished the beer and rose. " Ooh ! what a head I've got ! Tell Maurice I couldn't stay."

He faltered out, and Bessie and Esther exchanged the tolerant smiles of teetotallers who have had one more proof of the evils of drink.

" You should smile often," Esther said. " It suits you."

" I haven't much to smile about." Bessie ruefully went over to the sandwiches. " I haven't had any tea."

" I haven't had any either," Miss Gullick remarked pensively. " You can't buy anything worth eating in the city. Just stale white bread and bruised fruit. I could do with a cup of tea."

When Maurice arrived with a lift full of guests half an hour later, they were arrested in the doorway by the sight of a weird middle-aged woman with a cup of tea holding forth to a young, rather weary girl also with a cup of tea.

" And what is protoplasm ? " the weird female was asking. " When you examine it, protoplasm, you find, is a set of vibrations, or rather, sets of vibrations. The old theory of solids is . . . Hello, Maurice. Just thought I'd drop in. Heard you were giving a party."

" Why, Esther, this is a surprise," Maurice responded, not very cordially. He had a sinking feeling that if the news of the party had travelled as far as Esther's hut, it must have passed some old and disreputable acquaintances *en route.*

II

Whenever she remembered that party, Bessie was conscious of a bad taste in her mouth. The invited guests arrived in evening dress. The uninvited guests strolled in wearing everything from a sari to beach shorts. The invited guests showed a tendency to cluster in the more presentable half of the establishment ; behind Maurice's green curtains or on the polished spaces of the floor where they admired the pictures in an aloof way. The uninvited made instinctively for the shabby and untidy clutter behind the cubicles, where they sat on old tables, bits of wrecked benches, and other people's knees. They were in a strategic position because the food and drink had been stored in one of the cubicles opening on to the unfurnished parts.

From the first there was nothing of the " old maid's funeral " about the party. The lift roared up and down with groups who " had just dropped in " or " had heard Maurice was giving a party ". Nothing so unimportant as an invitation troubled them.

Billy Raine-Smith arrived with a group of lovely young things, including the niece and nephew of Lady Poindexter, who shrieked that it was " too marvellously quaint " and " so divinely Bohemian ". Jenny Evison, enthroned on a pile of cushions on the sofa, received them like a queen of the Valkyrie. Jenny was looking very lovely in powder-blue velvet, and Bessie felt a little pang of envy as she watched from the lift door, where she stood pacifying Sam.

The invited guests had shown no inclination to greet her as they passed. They delicately turned a deaf ear to Sam's coarse views.

" I've got me orders," Sam was repeating. " I've got me orders, and I want me sleep. I don't want not to do you a favour, Miss Drew, but as for *him*, the only favour I'd do him is to tear him apart and pour out the sawdust.

'Tisn't only a matter of the lights. I'm responsible for this place, and *he* won't rekernize it. *He* don't care if I don't never get no sleep. I'm a mug, Miss Drew, but even the biggest mugs wake up to themselves sometime."

Bessie was not really listening. She was watching Maurice as he playfully attempted to detach a gardenia from Jenny's corsage to put in his button-hole.

" See her ? " Bessie jerked a thumb at the unconscious Jenny. "She's a famous singer, Sam. That's Miss Evison."

" Never heard of 'er," Sam growled sourly. " And if she was as famous as Sheba, I still want my sleep."

" She sings wonderfully," Bessie said wistfully. " If you wait long enough, you'll hear her sing." She heaved a sigh. " I once heard her sing ' Sink, Red Sun, into the West ', and believe me, Sam, when she finished with it — it stayed sunk."

" I got a responsibility in case of fire," Sam whined.

Bessie went self-consciously across the room to where Maurice was leaning towards the fair Valkyrie. Ignoring Jenny, Bessie said curtly : " Sam wants to see you."

Maurice excused himself and beckoned Bessie into one of the cubicles. " What's up ? " he asked in a very different tone from the one he had been using to Jenny.

" He says they've all got to be out of here by eleven or he'll call the police."

" He wants another tip," Wainwright said angrily. " You go and smooth him down, Bessie. He takes more notice of you. Here, give him this."

He turned back and crossed to Jenny's side once more. A lump rose in Bessie's throat, and when she swallowed, it stuck in her chest with a queer pain. She went out to deal with Sam who was waiting, leaning against the lift-well, in the attitude of a marble angel over a tomb. As Bessie appeared, the lift door slammed open ; a gang of foreign, dark-coloured people poured out, and before she could interfere they had swamped Sam in several languages.

They waved their hands and surrounded him ; they all spoke together about the lift ; one faction claiming that Jaska had pressed the wrong button ; another maintaining that the age and debility of the lift were at fault. They were inclined to blame Sam for the accident that had jammed them between two floors until another liftload arrived and formed a counter-faction around Sam, pointing out that Sam had not installed the lift, and that in all fairness he could not take the brunt of what was obviously some contractor's fault.

" Enough of this," one of Sam's supporters declared, seizing him affectionately by the arm. " Lead on. We brought our own gin."

Still protesting, Sam found himself whisked into the stronghold of his enemy, where a dirty cupful of gin was thrust into his hand. By the time he had consumed the liquid, the party had become so interesting that he could not have dragged himself away if urged to do so.

In the more elegant half of the studio a body of the elect had gathered respectfully around Professor Zetkind, while he held forth on the spread of venereal disease among the tribes of the Upper Upopo regions of New Guinea. Another body of the invited were clustered around James Everard Montgomery who was expounding the benefits of an international stabilization fund for falling currencies. But from behind the cubicles came disturbing sounds ; cries of encouragement, shouts of laughter, and the thud of heavy furniture being dragged across a space and bumped into more heavy furniture. Through it all penetrated the champing sound of an accordion about to go into action. There was a splintering crash and cries of " Lap it up before it wastes." Jenny Evison turned an appealing look to Maurice, a mute reminder that she had lent the crockery and glassware.

"I'd better find out what they're doing," Maurice said, rising with the expression of a mother who has left her children innocently playing in the nursery.

Rounding the row of cubicles, he realized with horror that the uninvited had started on the drinks. Two young art students had taken down some curtains to provide themselves with costumes for a Maori war-dance which they were hastily rehearsing in a corner. An elderly lady with her hair dyed purple was, against violent opposition, preparing to give a song recital in Gaelic, while the owner of the accordion, a swarthy little hunchback, stood swaying in the middle of a cleared space, a fixed smile on his ugly features.

"Suppose we all go into the other room?" Maurice suggested in the tone of one who finds the little darlings need a mother's care. "It seems a bit unsociable of you to park out here."

"We like it here," the manager of the Corner Theatre said determinedly. "We'll stay where we're comfortable."

"Try it again, Godfrey, old chap," one Maori war-dancer encouraged the other. "You didn't quite get the intonation of the cry. Waah!"

The Maori howl was almost drowned by the accordion which at last got going in a terrific burst of sound. The phalanx of foreign-looking persons raised their voices as one with the accordion. They began in Yiddish, continued in German, and responded to a vociferous encore in Russian. The invited guests eddied into the ranks of the uninvited; they sat on the knees of the uninvited and accepted drinks from them. Professor Zetkind, beaming from behind his spectacles, assured Maurice that he had seen nothing like it since he left the Upper Upopo.

Everywhere guests were beating saucepan-lids or clapping their hands, shouting inharmoniously or clashing a couple of spoons. The accordion had burst into one of those stirring old sea shanties, so apt to be misinterpreted by people who have learnt only the censored version. There was nothing censored about the version which the uninvited sang, and a few of the *élite* began to glance uneasily at one another.

"Lower away the fore-t'gallant sails, the good ship rides merrily,"

the mob bellowed. There was some dispute over the words, many of them singing "heavily" instead of "merrily".

"Lower away the fore-t'gallant sails, the good ship rides free, Every good ship has a long-boat, every long-boat has rollicks . . ."

"I say," a very cultured-looking person, in a white, stiff shirt-front, asked Bessie, "are you an artist too?"

"No," Bessie said shortly. "I'm not."

The white-shirted one opened his mouth in a vacant way. "Oh!" he murmured, and then brightening, "But he's an artist, isn't he?" He nodded towards a youth in a crimson shirt, green tie, brown trousers and sandals, who was gesticulating so violently that his hair flopped across his eyes.

"No," Bessie replied brutally. "He's just trying to look like one. You don't need to have a dirty neck to be an artist."

The dress shirt gave forth a starchy creak as its owner withdrew in the direction of the niece of Lady Poindexter, who was swearing like a guttersnipe to show how in accord she was with the spirit of the party.

"You know, Bubbles," the shirt-front ventured plaintively, "a girl over there says they're not artists — some of them."

"But, darling, it's too bloody Bohemian for words," the young lady shrieked. "Aren't you enjoying yourself?"

"I don't know," the stiff-shirted gentleman murmured

unhappily. " I would be if I knew they were really artists, but hang it all, if they aren't artists, what are they carrying on like this for ? "

He wandered around disconsolately until he came to rest beside a young lady who worked in a sweet-shop. She had a high, haughty nose and a superior air. Murmurs of their conversation strove through the sea shanties now becoming so rough that they lifted a blush that was more than beer.

" She was my Aunt Josephine," he of the shirt was saying earnestly, when Bessie next passed his way with drinks. " Aunt Josephine was one of the Shropshire Poindexters. She married Sir Charles Blessington, and their children, apart from Cousin Percy who died from a fall at polo, all married Americans. Percy was playing with the Tenterden team on a pony lent him by Sir Renford Tenterden. I was there at the time it happened . . ."

" How marvellous ! " the lady said raptly. " To have been there ! "

A yell went up : " Anyone got a car ? We're running out of booze."

" Ai have," the starched shirt said, rising. They swooped down on him ; and for the next hour or so the relative of the Poindexters was seen only at intervals staggering out of the lift with bottles, and murmuring brokenly about the honour of the family to a young man with beautiful marcelled curls, his fellow carter, who to brighten the laborious task had draped himself in someone's brocade evening wrap. The Poindexter shirt-front was autographed in half a dozen places, and on it was drawn in charcoal a cupid and two intertwining hearts.

" All artis'," the Poindexter explained foggily, " act like this, if they're artis'."

The party was growing brighter. The insatiable

accordion breathing out a barn dance, the guests emigrated into the red, green and black splendour of the studio proper. They whooped and sprang and improvised steps all over the polished floor. They wrote their names on the walls and played hide-and-seek in the passage. Someone left the tap running in the wash-room and the water flowed down into the office of the paint merchant below. Someone else dropped an antique hurricane lantern out the window and went round looking for a rope so that he could rescue it, then burst out crying because there was no rope. Sam, asleep in one of the cubicles, was decorated with red ink and feathers.

In the midst of the tumult Maurice every now and then pleaded for quiet. "It's getting pretty late, you know. We've got to consider others." Two minutes later the row would begin afresh. There was no chance of breaking up the party unless the police broke it up. Whenever Maurice suggested to the accordion-player that he might rest for refreshment, the player nodded and smiled and burst into a fresh tune.

In the end Maurice gave it up and devoted himself to apologizing to Jenny who was thoroughly enjoying herself and could not see what there was to apologize about. He even took a glass of wine to cheer himself up, but it only made him want to cry.

Under cover of the noise Esther Gullick was persuading Bessie to visit her hut in the mountains. "You don't belong here," she declared. "You ought to have seven children, an apron, and a hoe in your hand."

Bessie grinned. "Thanks. I'll stick to the job I have."

"Unhealthy. Maurice is just another of these social column addicts. I suppose he's still a misunderstood genius, one of civilization's finest flowers. Photography! Pah! He used to be good."

Bessie was annoyed. "You've got to make a living,"

she defended. " I mean you've got to work." This one
article of her simple creed she had never questioned.

" It's not just working. It's the kind of work you do
that matters. Cities make me sick. They batten on this
country, sitting round the coast like blood-sucking leeches.
The people who live in cities get that way too. Battening,
mentally and economically, on each other. I know. I
could have been a cloistered research worker battening
on some bequest, doing interesting abstract problems in
biology."

" So what ? "

" So I quit and saved my sanity. I'm really finding
out things now since I ceased being academic." She
stopped abruptly. " A luxury trade, this parlour research. Like most of the trades here." She swept a skinny
arm to embrace the street below. " Advertising, interior
decoration, millinery, jewellery, perfumes, cosmetics, cut
flowers." She broke off. " I hate cut flowers. You
wouldn't cut off a girl's head and stick it in a vase. I
hate the city."

" Hang on," Bessie said confusedly. " There are
people working here. Real hard work."

" And there are people starving here. But they're not
an integral part of the luxury trade that makes the atmosphere Maurice lives in. False values, red finger-nails,
permanent waves. You don't really belong to it, and
he does. He likes the bright lights."

The white shirt containing a Poindexter lurched over
to a mild-looking lad sitting a little apart from Esther
and Bessie. The mild-looking lad had been crouching
there drinking moodily ever since he came in.

" Have another drink, old boy ? " the Poindexter
offered, jovially holding out a brimming glass. " All
artis' together."

The mild-looking lad bounded to his feet with a snarl.
" What the hell do you mean talking to me like that,

87

you greasy son of a bitch ? " he said rapidly, and put himself in an attitude of defence. " Come out and I'll teach you."

The Poindexter was wounded in his best feelings. He had fraternized with artists, and one of them had, so to speak, bitten him through the bars.

" Come, Alison," he murmured. " I think we'd better go."

" Hoy, Stace," his relative agreed, staggering over with dignity. " It bloody well looks like it."

A volunteer corps of the mild lad's fellow guests was uncertainly holding him back and soothing him by bellowing in his ear. This he interpreted only as pro-vocation, and he swore at the departing Poindexters ; he kicked his well-wishers in the shins ; he bit the kind hands that held him and went berserk on the floor.

" For God's sake, somebody go and find Emily ! " a shout went round. " Emily, where are you ? "

Emily pushed forward. " Johnny," she commanded, " stop acting the goat and come here." She seized the mild lad by the hair and lugged him towards the door where Maurice was waiting to say good-bye with a thankful heart. " Sorry, Maurice, he just gets to this stage and there's no doing anything with him."

From the interior came a renewed outburst of shrieks and oaths. Rustling back to his party, Maurice said breathlessly : " Now, what's up ? "

" Hilary said she was going to do a fan dance, and her husband said if she did he'd beat her up, and then she called him various things, and now they're trying to hold him down so he won't beat her up."

A group of interlaced arms and legs and bodies wove unsteadily out of the studio. From the midst of the group an elderly man in a disordered dress suit was endeavouring to break free. He was purple in the face with fury and exertion.

" Let me get at her," he howled. " I'll teach her to disgrace me."

" There, there, old man," his body-guard soothed, wrenching his hands away from the door where he was clinging tenaciously. " Leave him to me, Bert. You go back and see to Hilary. Take her home or something. I'll see to George here."

Maurice mopped his brow. " Bessie," he said, beckoning energetically. " Bessie, come here, quick." He seized her by the wrist and drew her into one of the cubicles. " You little devil, what did you do to those drinks ? "

" Let me go." She was really angry. " I didn't do anything. Professor Zetkind was mixing them. He put in gin and whisky because he said that's the way they used to drink it on the Upopo."

Maurice groaned. " I'm sorry. They've all gone mad. What am I going to do ? "

Bessie eyed the gathering coldly. " Clear them all out."

He hesitated. " I can't do that."

" Why not ? "

" They're friends of mine."

Bessie snorted. " Look at that," she said, real disgust in her voice. " *Some* friends you've got."

A big, heavy girl, barefooted and dressed in a peasant skirt, with a red handkerchief tied under her chin, had suddenly started across the room in the direction of another girl, an artist's model known as Lily.

" I'll teach you," the lady in the peasant costume screamed. " I'll teach you, you white-faced little fraud."

She was restrained from teaching the terrified model by another group of volunteers who flung themselves upon her and pinioned her, one to each ankle and wrist. She was soothed and patted and encouraged by a muzzy collection of guests, all nearly as drunk as she was, while she struggled and shrieked to get free.

" Good Lord ! " Maurice was appalled. " She'll scream the place down. What the devil am I to do ? Stop that row." The accordion still bellowed happily from behind the cubicles. " She's hysterical," Maurice shouted. " Give her water or something."

Bessie woke up. Hysterical ? She knew how to deal with hysterics. She rushed across the room.

" Be quiet, you idiot," she admonished, and competently catching the girl by the hair, she dealt her a sound slap on either cheek. The girl's mouth fell open, her eyes blazed.

" You ! " she gasped. " You called me an idiot ! " She redoubled her efforts to free herself. " I'll show her," she kept repeating. " She called me an idiot ! She slapped me ! "

It suddenly struck Bessie with a sick apprehension that the girl was not hysterical. She stood dismayed, uncertain whether to run from the virago or to apologize. A friend patted her on the shoulder.

" Good on you, Bess," he said heavily. " Madge always puts on this act every party she goes to. If you hadn't slapped the woman, I'd have turned her up and spanked her. For once someone took her seriously and serve her right. She's getting to be a bore."

The poor, trembling model was being hastily taken home, dissolved in tears, with a gentleman to hold each hand.

" I thought it was hysterics," Bessie muttered. She sank down on the sofa appalled.

Two gentlemen friends of the insulted lady lurched towards Bessie and stood glaring at her.

" This bitch of a woman," one of the gentlemen observed with righteous indignation, " called Madge an idiot. No bitch of a woman is allowed to call Madge an idiot. Madge was just brightening up the party and this bitch cut in and spoiled it."

They were towed away from their victim by a hearty group of life-savers. Bessie was so upset that the tears sprang to her eyes.

"I never," she said, biting her lip, "I never saw a turn-out like this before."

"Come on." Esther put out her cigarette. "We'd better be going before they turn Madge loose."

Bessie hesitated. "What about Maurice?"

"Well, what about Maurice? He'll still be here to-morrow, if they don't burn the place about his ears."

Bessie was scarcely listening. "I hit her," she muttered brokenly. "I hit her and she wasn't having hysterics at all. Gee, I feel rotten!" The tears were standing in her eyes again. "I've seen fights down our way but 'tisn't often you see women fighting."

"Cheer up," Esther said. "Don't let it worry you."

The tears had brimmed over. "I hit her," Bessie repeated. "Oh dear!"

Esther led her to the lift door where they met a gentleman naked to the waist. He raised his hat politely and said in a fretful tone : "If someone would give me my shirt and coat, I could go home."

Maurice was far too busy to say good-night to them. He was in one of the cubicles endeavouring to convince a group of models through the partition that no good purpose would be served by holding a séance in the nude and would they be so good as to put their clothes on again.

"Bessie!" he shouted. "Bessie, will you please come here."

But Bessie had gone.

She walked home by herself whistling hoarsely under her breath. The middle of her chest still hurt her. It ached dully as though she had indigestion. The pain seemed to be spreading over the rest of her body. It was tragic to her that Wainwright should be wasting time and money on a party when the studio was so precariously situated. He didn't care. He knew that he could always, in a happy-go-lucky style, find someone to give him credit. He had such charming ways, when he liked to use them. He was much more fascinating than many a handsome man. Women liked him. Men either hated him or lent him their last half-crown. But he didn't care ; that was the trouble. He was irresponsible, undependable.

Bessie licked off a tear that had trickled down the side of her nose. The best thing would be to break away altogether and get a real job, the kind of job she had been meant for all along, scrubbing, or carrying trays or making biscuits in a factory. It was silly to be something different from your own people. They were right to resent it. She hadn't really done herself any good working herself to a shadow for a man who didn't care twopence. She would have to cut it out and get back to earth again.

At the very thought of leaving the studio, the hard, painful lump ached again in her chest. " I'll do it," she told herself. " If I can't have a show-down about the way he's mucking up the studio, I'll quit. I've got to do something."

Not once did she think altruistically of Maurice deprived of his prop and support. She was clearly and logically selfish. She was fond of Maurice. Who would not be fond of him ? But if he wouldn't do as she thought he should, she would discard him. " I'm not going to kid myself," Bessie told herself firmly. " There's too many people going about kidding themselves." But she was still sniffing as she turned down Archer Street and opened the sagging gate of Number 71.

CHAPTER VII

BESSIE was very quiet when she came in next morning to clean up the mess. Maurice did not notice that she was depressed, because he was so depressed himself that anyone else looked cheerful by comparison. He had just glanced at the calendar and discovered that his patent rights for the Absence Register expired the previous week. At any moment greedy manufacturers might turn out thousands of Absence Registers and there would be no power to stop them. He, the inventor, could not collect a penny on one of those machines. What was the use of having world rights if you let them expire?

" Fiddling while Rome burns," he said excitedly. " Giving an incredibly stupid party when the Absence Register is in jeopardy. I've got to save it."

He was away from the studio the best part of the day, while Bessie struggled with any emergencies, including Sam and the paint merchant whose office had been flooded. When Maurice returned late in the afternoon, he was worried but more hopeful.

" I think I can see my way clear to borrow the money," he announced with a Napoleonic air. " I don't know for sure, but I think George Soames will back my note. He still doesn't seem to realize the urgency of this — that we must act fast."

Bessie said nothing. She had tidied all the files. She had cleaned up the odds and ends that accumulate on Friday afternoon. She checked the stamps and letter-book. She removed her lipstick and a worn powder-puff from the drawer of her table in the ante-room. Then she walked in deliberately to confront her employer.

He was lying full length on his dearly beloved sofa with his hands folded across his stomach. His hat was still tilted over one eye. He did not look like a business man ; he looked like a brigand. No business man has any right to have long black eyelashes. He couldn't even wear boots like anyone else, Bessie reflected bitterly. Wainwright's boots were of a particular design that he had worked out for himself. They made him look, not exactly club-footed, but as though he concealed a cloven hoof.

" I want to give a week's notice, Mr. Wainwright." Bessie's voice was level. She might have been reminding him of an appointment.

He opened one eye. " Don't be silly," he said lazily. " Come and sit on the nice sofa and tell your uncle all about it."

It would have been so much easier not to persist. He was in his most friendly mood now that the worry over the Absence Register was smoothed from his mind. Bessie stood grimly beside the desk.

" I mean it," she said.

It dawned on Maurice that she was in earnest. He sat up on the sofa and pushed his hat back on his head.

" What is this ? " he asked grimly. " Don't I give satisfaction ? "

Bessie nodded. " When I came here, you told me the job was only temporary — that you would have to get someone with social connections to manage the receptions." She swallowed a lump in her throat. " You gave it to me straight that I was getting the job as a favour. Well, I don't want any more favours. That's all."

Maurice became dangerously polite. " And what do you propose to do when you leave here, if you will pardon my natural interest ? "

" I can get work as a waitress. A girl I know says she'll get me in at the Colonial Café. 'Tisn't bad."

As she stood there, her feet apart, her head a little on one side, her hands clasped behind her very much in the attitude of an elderly gentleman on his hearthrug, she looked so very young and solemn that Wainwright was irresistibly reminded of a lion cub he had seen at the zoo. It had planted its paws in just that deliberate way ; it had Bessie's wide-set eyes, though Bessie's eyes were green and the cub's were yellow.

" I could do a study of you," he said, much taken with the idea. " You and the lion cub. I couldn't quite make out what it was at first, but there is a certain muscular strength you have — the way that little band of green stuff fits tightly round your arms and makes them firm and heavy. And that dress. You almost expect the muscles to ripple under it. You and a lion cub with, I think, a pattern of shadows from a tree to give the cub the same dappled effect as the frock gives. . . ."

Bessie flared at him. " Cut it out," she ordered, her eyes blazing. " Don't think you can put that soft-soap over me. I'm not sitting for any photograph. I know your line. I've watched you on the job."

Maurice was taken aback. " I assure you . . ." he began stiffly.

" Oh no, you don't," Bessie broke in rudely. " You don't get the chance. I'm through with your acting. Acting all the time." She was gasping, she was so angry. " Acting you're a business man — acting you're a genius — acting you're so intelligent an' cultured an' refined. Too blasted soft for the wind to blow on you. . . . Oh ! " She stopped to catch her breath. " You find someone else to act for. Someone who'll let you go on acting like a silly kid and get away with it."

She realized that by being angry she was putting herself at a disadvantage ; but the realization only made her more exasperated. She could see that Maurice was feeling superior and kindly and that made her furious.

" I still don't quite know what this is all about," he

declared amiably. " I gather I have offended you — hurt your feelings in some way, but I can't quite understand why you should fly into a temper and abuse me."

Bessie swallowed. She clenched her hands, tensing her muscles in an effort to control herself, almost as though she were reining in a team of horses. " That's so," she answered in a strained voice. " I shouldn't have gone off at you. But it's like this. When I come here . . ."

" Came here," he corrected equably, watching her as though she were the little lion cub raging at him through the bars.

" When I came here I was keen to get this job with you. See ? " Bessie's control of her emotions did not extend to her speech. " I says to myself : Here's a chap who'll let me work with him, let me go shares, see ? Take an interest in things."

" Well, that's right," Maurice said calmly. " Haven't I let you take an interest in things ? "

" That part of it's jake. But I can't work with a chap who just mucks about, not caring two hoots whether he makes a go of a thing or not. You got to work like a slave if you want to make anything good, not dabble in a thing and then chuck it when it suits you. You don't work, you potter about."

" Any other complaints ? " His voice was hard. She had touched his vanity on the raw. " Go on. Let's hear the rest of it."

Despite Bessie's efforts to remain calm, the angry tears sprang to her eyes. " That's about all," she said. " You can't kid me into thinking you're the goods, if you're not. It's what you do that matters, not what you are. You can be the hell of a genius, but if you never do anything, I'm not going to stick around and kid myself you'll maybe reform."

" Well, now let me tell you something," Maurice opened up dangerously.

"I'm not going to listen. I've made up my mind and I'll stick to it. I'm through."

"You are going to listen." He caught her by the arm, and when she attempted to wrench herself free, she discovered that Maurice, for all his fat, had very strong wrists.

"You let me go," she demanded furiously.

"Not till you hear what *I* have to say." He sat down coolly on the edge of the desk, still holding her as though she were a kitten. "I'll tell you why you're leaving. I've had girls leave for the same reason before. You're sulking because I haven't taken enough notice of you. You think your little ego should have been expanded, that you should have been encouraged to make a nuisance of yourself about the place. Well, get this. I've staved off older and more cunning females before now. You thought you were clever, didn't you? Foisting yourself on to me, letting my friends think you were my mistress, trying to give that impression. Working in subtle, under-hand ways to get me into a compromising position . . ."

He stopped, taken aback. Bessie was laughing. There was nothing theatrical about her mirth; it was just amused and happy.

"Seduced him," she gurgled. "That's what Ernie said, seduced him. Gee! if you only had on little frilled pants and a big hooped skirt, you'd make a picture."

He flung away from her. "I'm pleased to see you're developing a sense of humour," he said cuttingly. "I often wondered if you would."

Bessie no longer felt that she must run, go quickly down in the lift and never come again. She was herself once more, controlled, good-humoured. In this queer quarrel of wills between them she had swung on top again. She sat down on the sofa and smiled at him provocatively.

"Go on," she mocked. "Tell me some more about the girls who tried to put the hard word on you."

" You think it's funny," he replied angrily. " It's a blasted biological truth. A woman decides on a man and he's got two courses open. He either has to run or get eaten. Once she gets him, he can't call his soul his own. Doesn't matter if he isn't married to her. He's her property. A woman is always out to find a good square meal-ticket. Someone who will build her a safe place for her young, who will do as he's told, and change his best suit when he comes home and not drop cigarette ash on the carpet. I've seen it happen too often, I tell you. You can laugh."

" I'm not laughing," Bessie said soberly. " There's a lot in it."

" I'm glad you admit that. Very glad. And let me tell you this." He shook a nicotine-stained forefinger at her. " I'm not going to have any woman running me." He started pacing up and down his green and red triangles, sadly dirty from the dancing of the night before. " Do you think if I wasn't fond of you I'd bother to talk to you at all ? I'd just dismiss the matter and you from my mind. But I *am* fond of you. Did it ever occur to you that one of the reasons for my trying to keep a distance between us, for my being a bit sharp sometimes, might have been due to a feeling for you that I have done my best to crush . . . out of regard for you ? A man may see a girl and realize that she is physically attractive, but because he has never thought of her as a prospective sweetheart, he doesn't let it affect him. It's a kind of insulation that he wraps round himself. That's the way normal society works. And you have deliberately tried to break down that insulation, to make the relationship between us an impossibility."

Bessie was to discover that Wainwright loved a scene. He was never adverse to provoking a dramatic situation ; and he approved particularly of himself in the part of the world-weary instructor telling the little child what it ought to know. Bessie sensed this in him, but even sensing it, she could not but admire him a little.

"When you came here, I didn't put you on a business basis," he went on, still walking the triangles and unconsciously avoiding the lines of intersection. "You said something about being mates ; and I was weak enough, or damn stupid enough, to think you might mean it."

"I did," Bessie said quietly. "I haven't forgotten."

He changed his attack. "All these months you've been judging me, weighing me, condemning me when I've been a nervous wreck, worn to a shadow by petty little money worries. I haven't been *me* at all. Why do you think I'm trying to launch the poor old Absence Register ? Not for the money." He waved the money aside. "For the chance to be *myself*. How can I be myself without financial security ? How can I produce beautiful things when I'm worried and strained and have no leisure, no capital ? It's the law of the jungle in this city — anywhere. You have to have money to escape the everyday struggle. You have to escape it before you can really be yourself."

"That's all bosh," Bessie said stubbornly. "A chap's at his best when he's battling. Or he ought to be. I'd still be mate if the place sunk under you, but I'm damned if I'll hang round and listen to you wail about not being able to be yourself because you're in mid-ocean and there's sharks about." She was discovering an eloquence that astonished her. "A bloke ought to work. Take Dad for instance. He never expects to get anything out of life except to get drunk Saturday, but he just plugs on."

"I'm sure he does," Wainwright agreed smoothly. "So does an elephant, and it has just as little brain. A woman's idea is always to find a man a secure rut and stick him in it and let him provide. I suppose your idea is that I stay in this damn rut of a studio and give up all idea of ever getting out of it ? "

99

" Well," Bessie sighed, as she rose from the sofa, " I guess we just look at things different."

His whole face and manner altered in an instant. Bessie thought : " He's going to be noble. I know he is ; but what is the use of knowing what he's going to do, if you let him get away with it ? "

" Rather like cutting off my right hand, isn't it, kid ? " There was gentle, winning reproach in Wainwright's eyes. " I hoped you could have stayed a few months more at least. Don't think I haven't appreciated all you've done. It's just that I've been living under these appalling conditions, subjected to a continual nervous strain. I can understand that a place like this — the wages I can afford — are naturally less than I led you to expect." He laughed genially. " I call you my mate and give you the wage of a cabin-boy. But," he threw out his hand, " this poor old dump of a studio — I thought it *meant* something to you as it does to me. There are loyalties, Bessie," he waved his hand vaguely, " loyalties."

" I guess so," Bessie replied heavily. She was tired ; she felt as though he had beaten down her resistance. She would have to go away or give in. If she let him talk long enough, he would win. " I guess I must have been planning to grab you and marry you like you said. I hadn't though of it that way, but I can see now it 'ud be a better idea if I left you be."

" No, no," Maurice insisted quickly. That was not at all what he wanted. " You misunderstand me, Bessie. You misunderstand me completely. When I said that no woman would ever get her clutches on me, I never excluded the possibility that I should have friends, women friends. I have many women friends, cultured women, pleasant women, women of understanding, charm and poise."

" Not like me," Bessie said drearily. What a fool, she

was thinking, what a silly little fool she looked, a design-
ing, stupid idiot, making sheep's eyes at a man who knew
all the time what she was after.

Maurice sat down beside her on the sofa and took
her hand. Bessie's hand was cold and firm. It had
well-shaped nails badly cared for and little hard calluses
on the palm. Wainwright's hand was soft and warm ;
a big, square hand with a skin like dry tissue paper.
This was the first time he had ever touched her hand
except to take a photographic plate or glass of medicine.
She tried to draw it away and then passively left it
limp in his.

" Listen, kid," he said gently. " I got my idea of
what women were like when the girl I was engaged to
jilted me. She was and has been the only woman in my
life. I was twenty then and ready to go out and lick
the world. Whenever I feel like falling in love with a
woman again, I remember Rose."

" She threw you over ? " Bessie asked dispiritedly.

" I had gone to America. She promised to wait for
me and I thought I could do better at this game in
America. She promised to wait. . . ."

" Pretty ? "

" Eh ? Oh yes. Little and dark and gentle."

" With poise ? " Bessie added.

Wainwright refused to be provoked. " She was too
young to have poise."

" Too bad." Bessie was almost recovering her usual
spirits, with his hand so comfortably clasping hers." Go
on, Maurice," she added hastily. " I'm listening."

" She wrote to me, long, long letters. And I replied.
Perhaps not as frequently as she expected, but I was
moving round from city to city, and sometimes her letters
were not forwarded. I was taking all kinds of jobs and
throwing them in again. Naturally I made a good deal
of money and spent it trying to make more. It was all

for Rose. I never dreamt for a moment she would . . ."
He broke off. " She sent me a cable. I had not answered
her letter. It seemed I had left California just a week
before. I didn't get the cable either till it was too late.
She had explained in the letter that her family wanted
her to marry this man, that she had not heard of me for
so long." He waved his hand. " And so on and so on.
It was her woman's craving for security. She couldn't
gamble on me, win or lose. She had to be sure of to-
morrow and the next day. I did everything I could.
I cabled. I threw in my job and rushed back to Australia.
It was too late. I had a nervous breakdown. I nearly
went mad."

He sat silent for a minute, patting Bessie's hand almost
absent-mindedly. " Never again, for Rose, for any other
woman, would I go through the sheer hell I suffered
then. It isn't worth it." He took up her hand and
examined it. " Lion cub paws," he said, almost astonished. " The same puggy look about them." He dropped
her hand and turned so that he was facing her, his eyes
very close. " Look," he said, smiling, " I'll revise the
articles of association or whatever it is you sign as mate.
I'll admit I'm all you say I am. And a bit more. I won't
offer to change. I won't promise to do anything."

" Well, where," Bessie asked weakly, " does the difference in the articles of . . . of . . ." She broke off.

" There is a difference." He spoke gently. " Look.
I give in. You can own me. See." He made a comical
gesture. " Nothing up my sleeves. All cards on the
table." He caught her hands again. " Bessie, you do
love me a little, don't you ? I know I'm a fool. I know
I'm twice your age and Ernie's right and everyone is
right except me. But you're my last hope of happiness.
You're really my mate. I don't know how the devil I'd
get on without you. Can't say any more than that, can
I ? " He had never looked younger, more amazingly,

intriguingly ugly. He knew, and she knew, that there was not a woman who could sit with him alone there under the gloom of his tall green curtains and not be in love with him.

"Well?" he asked, smiling. "Will you give me another chance?"

Bessie knew that she should have risen to her feet and said "No" in a firm voice. She tried to convince her feet and her voice that there was nothing else to do but say "No" and go down into the street, out along the gritty, dirty pavement; go home to the inevitable quarrelling; go to bed and perhaps cry a little; and get up to-morrow morning and hunt another job, her fist ready to batter the concrete face of reality, until it either gave her a living or smashed her fist flat.

And, while she was watching herself a little pityingly, saying "No" and going away from the studio for ever, she found herself returning Maurice's kisses. His smile was half cynical, half sheepish.

"Serves me damn well right," he said, "for not kissing you earlier. Resigning indeed! What an idea!"

Bessie's mind was muddled, her whole lifetime of resolute action upset. She still could not understand how, when she had decided to go, she had stayed, how he could have kept her against her will. He seemed to have scored a victory. Had he really scored a victory? He had kept her. But had she in her heart wanted to go? She could not sort out the complexities of the situation. One thing she knew: Wainwright might not be a genius at anything else, but he was a genius at kissing a girl.

"I really must do that study of you," he said presently, wiping her face-powder off his coat. "I never realized how much you resembled a lion cub until you stood there raging at me." He turned her face to the light between his two hands. "It's really most uncommon. 'Lions' I shall call it.'

"This lion needs feeding," Bessie remarked with a tired smile.

He kissed her on the tip of her nose. "Utterly prosaic," he murmured. "I don't know but what I like you better for that, kid. How much money have you got?"

"Two and seven." Bessie looked into her small purse to make sure the money was still there.

"Good." Maurice stuck on his hat at its usual careless, arrogant angle. "I have one and three until to-morrow. I know where you can get three courses for ninepence — steak and onions for a shilling. I'm hungry too." Then he put on his most didactic manner. "There is certainly a connection between hunger and love. One arouses the other. Who was it wrote a book about that?"

Bessie gathered her hat and handbag, smoothed her hair, powdered her nose and began to collect her scattered wits. "I don't know if my face is on straight," she said ruefully. "Half the complexion rubbed off on your coat."

She was still a little shy of him, a little unsure. Already the many changes of the past hour appeared far-distant, fantastic. Had he really kissed her ten minutes ago? She broke in on a rhapsody about steak and onions.

"Maurice," she asked timidly, "did you say you loved me?"

"I said I was fond of you," he responded carefully. "I said I couldn't do without you. What more do you want? Aren't you ever satisfied?"

"I just thought I'd get it straight," Bessie said humbly. "I like to know where I stand. You go so fast I'm still a bit muddled."

He squeezed her arm. "Queer little person," he said. "But delightful. You really are very, very delightful."

Bessie gave a sigh of relief. "That's the way I feel

about you too," she murmured. "So we're square, aren't we?"

But she was still not sure.

CHAPTER VIII

I

THE first effect of Bessie's new articles of agreement was, as she expressed it, that she " knocked off work to carry bricks ". Instead of leaving the studio between five and six o'clock, as she had been in the habit of doing, she now hardly ever reached home until two o'clock in the morning.

Maurice could not sleep. His nerves had reached the stage when a sound rest had become almost inconceivable, and he demanded that Bessie keep him company in his nightly rambles.

" I don't really come alive until midnight," he complained. " And then the people I want to talk to go home."

He had brought his insomnia on himself by staying out until the early hours, so that he might avoid Sam. When he did come stealthily back to his burrow, he would sit up reading and smoking cigarettes. About three or four in the morning he dropped off into a restless doze, to wake drowsy and dissipated-looking for the day's work.

He tried to persuade Bessie to sleep at the studio and keep him company ; but Bessie was firm on that point. Her morals were strictly utilitarian. She rejected the invitation as unthinkable.

" I would look a sight after I'd slept all night on that sofa," she objected. It was about one o'clock and she was beginning the nightly dispute that it was time she went home. The rather dreary club where they sat talking was showing signs of shutting up. "Besides, you don't seem to realize what you're up against in Dad. He acts like a mad bull as it is, but the first time I stayed out all night, he'd be down on you with a shot-gun."

"I can't understand the unreasonable attitude your people take up," Maurice complained fretfully. "They're positively primitive."

"Don't drink any more of that coffee," Bessie suggested. "You might at least try to sleep."

"It's all very well for you to talk about trying to sleep," Maurice snarled. "You've got the physique of a cart-horse, a home to go to and security. You must remember, Bessie, that I have no family to fall back on. I've only myself, and the constant worry of keeping my head above water. Your family don't need you at this hour of the night and I do. If you go home now, you're not doing them any good, and you're depriving me of your company."

This might sound like a just summing-up of the case to one who did not know the Drews. Bessie never could explain to Maurice that she was not leading a sheltered, comfortable life ; that, compared with her home life, his own was a refuge of calm and peace. He might need to dodge the caretaker ; but not an enraged parent, who wanted to know where you had been until two o'clock in the morning. The Drew policy of constant nagging, varied by occasional violence, demanded a tough constitution to withstand it. The more of a hell Bessie's home life became, the more she clung to Maurice as the one person who, even when he was angry, did not shout or bully her.

Maurice was unable to see that there was anything unusual in his attitude towards Bessie. Having once admitted that he was fond of her, he treated her as an equal, a companion, much as he did Ernie. He would coax Bessie out to tea with him in some cheap restaurant ; then they would put in the evening at some lecture or concert, Maurice sleeping peacefully and Bessie a monument of endurance. As soon as they emerged into the fresh air, he was active, talkative, determined to quarrel with her, make love to her, lecture her, anything to keep her beside him. They walked every water-front, every path in every park in the city.

"After midnight," Maurice maintained, " I own Sydney. I love it. When you go away from the city, there is no escaping the horrible certainty that you are in New South Wales, Australia, and you couldn't be elsewhere on earth. But all cities have a kinship. It is the mark of a civilized person to be at ease in any city after midnight. Even in this one," he added, " where there's nowhere to go and nothing to do."

If Bessie wanted to recall Wainwright, she always conjured him up as a profile with a string of street lights behind it ; a tilted hat-brim ; a stooped, rather stoutish figure, limping along in his strange boots, the same old grey muffler round his chin, a leather overcoat pulled up to his ears. He was a shabby Prince of Darkness, made up of lights broken in water ; the smell of new-cut grass in Wynyard Square ; the whisper of trees in the Domain ; the spray of the Archibald Fountain ; the façade of St. Mary's Basilica ; and the soaring fronts of floodlit buildings. Maurice came to be merged with the city ; and she could not remember him without remembering wet asphalt and the noise of trams, the quiet of wharves at night, and the black of the harbour, black like the bloom of a grape.

Night-time gave Maurice a profound pleasure because he had such a keen appreciation of shadows. Black, he contended, was not the absence of light ; it was a colour like any other colour with just as many tones. Where

other people could see only darkness and light, Maurice
Wainwright could see an infinite gradation, a subtle
interlinking of recognizable shades. He would try to
point these out to Bessie and sometimes she did compre-
hend dimly why certain curves and angles and shadows
interested him.

He told her scraps about himself, leaning over the
rails of the quay, looking into the water, or sitting on a
flight of old stone steps that he regarded as his own. His
boyhood had been spent mainly in New Zealand, where
the elder Wainwright had been a prosperous importer
with connections from Auckland to Dunedin. " I was
nearly born in the theatre," Maurice remarked one night.
" Mother was very self-willed and she would go. I almost
made my first appearance in the dress circle."

" Well, it would have been just like you," Bessie
smiled, " to do something different."

She thought with a weary yawn how she had decided,
a hundred years ago, it seemed, that by throwing in her
lot with Maurice a girl would thereby gain an adventurous
life. Night after night Bessie learnt more about the grim
underside of life, as they walked the streets, talking to
other strays from the comfortable, set world of the day.
Maurice had a flair for friendships with strange wanderers;
and Bessie unconcernedly followed him into places where
a more delicate young lady would have screamed for the
police.

She had a nodding acquaintance with any number of
night-watchmen, hamburger joints, waiters, wharfingers
and tram-guards. Tramping along beside Maurice, her
hand tucked in his pocket, holding his hand, she was
comfortably assured that he was a childish, lovable,
foolish person ; and that it was her destiny to mother
him, scold him, pet him, be close to him and protect
him. She liked the smell of his hands and his old coat.
She loved him all the more because he was getting stout

and had that round, pink tonsure in his hair. She liked kissing him. Always Bessie kissed him dutifully in return if he kissed her, and sometimes she kissed first. Very satisfactory it seemed and pleasant to be in love with Maurice ; and, almost humbly, she hoped she was doing well at it. After all, this was her first attempt, and Maurice, from all reports, had had plenty of practice. Just kissing a man, of course, was not all there was to being in love. No one brought up in Archer Street could remain in any way ignorant of the drawbacks and disadvantages of sex ; but Bessie was not interested in such aspects of the affair as a more sophisticated girl might be. Just kissing and holding hands would do very nicely, thank you, for a beginner like herself. Maurice seemed to think the same. He never displayed any fervent desire to crush her to his bosom in the manner of film heroes.

" Nice lion cub," he would say, gripping the hand so confidently resting in his ; and Bessie adored him for being kind to her, for having holes in his socks and soup stains on his waistcoats and no money. Maurice was exciting, stupid, intelligent, funny, irritating and brilliant, all at once, or one after the other.

She had a clear-eyed realization of his weaknesses and even these endeared him all the more. For one thing, Maurice would sooner have a dramatic, tempestuous quarrel than a square meal. This he found mentally bracing, an explosion of surplus irritation that did him good. He would turn on Bessie and call her everything he could think of ; and by the time he had finished with her character, it resembled nothing so much as what the moths had left of last year's woollens.

Bessie never put any zest into either the passionate tempest or the subsequent grand reunion. Quarrels saddened and hurt her ; and she accepted kisses and caresses and apologies much in the manner of a good baby who knows it has been smacked unjustly. All would be heavenly peace and affection in the studio for a day or so until Bessie might hint that a cheque should go to meet certain outstanding debts, although Wainwright had destined the money for better things, notably the Absence Register. Then the tornado would break out afresh.

"You and Hodges between you," Maurice would rage. "You're driving me mad! Mad, I tell you. I'll smash this place up with an axe and go on the dole."

For everything he always had the excuse that it was due to his nerves.

"But you can't expect to get better," Bessie pointed out despairingly, "living hand to mouth, sleeping on that couch, eating at cafés."

Under her scoldings he promised to find a boarding-house, but weeks passed and he was still living at the studio, complaining of his nerves and snapping at Bessie when she reminded him of the urgency of the housing problem. Appalled by the looming shadow of the week-end, about four o'clock on a Friday, he might run a lack-lustre eye down the "Board and Residence" column.

"This looks possible. Ring the woman, Bessie, and find out what she charges. Nothing exorbitant, mind, and tell her I can't possibly get out there before eleven to-night. If she objects, say I'm a newspaper reporter. Say anything. I'm not going to be marooned in some God-forsaken hole tossing about for hours and hours."

At two o'clock in the morning he might remember that he had a new and presumably welcoming landlady to interview. Then, on Monday, with a pathetic tale of hardship, Maurice would be back in the studio where, at least, he said, he could call his soul his own.

"It's Fate," he explained. "I was born under the wrong sort of star. I'm never fated to be popular with landladies, never to be able to live in a boarding-house. Ever studied astrology, Bess?"

"No," Bessie snapped. She was once again studying

the " Board and Residence " advertisements. If she didn't get Maurice settled into some place where he could sleep, she felt she would crack under the strain of so many late nights. " How about this ? ' Single gentleman. Pleasant, airy room. All comforts.' "

" Don't say any more. I'd get out there and find a bed that sags in the middle and jets little clouds of fluff. There's always a tram roaring under the window if they say ' Comforts '. Don't you worry. You go home to-night. I'm going out with Ernie to get a game of poker."

Bessie frowned. Maurice needed rest and Ernie was certainly not conducive to slumber. One of her first acts of aggression under the new charter had been to tongue-lash Ernie in good Archer Street style.

" And if you think," she had finished, " that this is such a good place to sleep off your beer, you can either keep your muddy boots off that sofa or stretch out on the mat where you belong."

Ernie had been in no way distressed ; he was immensely amused. " Congratulations." Then drawing Maurice aside, he shook him fervently by the hand. " When did the ceremony take place ? "

Having been vigorously sworn at and informed that there was no ceremony, nor likely to be, Ernie shook his head and declared that Maurice might as well marry her. " When a woman takes such an interest in a sofa, she is already picturing it in her front sitting-room."

The look on Maurice's face, Ernie later, for the benefit of a hilarious audience, compared with that of a hunted fawn.

All Maurice's friends, Bessie had decided, were just no good. She was in the habit of classifying people as either " good " or " no good ", though Maurice never cared how unscrupulous an acquaintance might be, as long as he was entertaining. Whether they painted or sang or conspired against the Government, or ran wine bars or grocery shops, to Bessie the gang were all " no good ". They were always talking about something, politics, psycho-analysis, sociology, platonic love or ethnology. Bessie greeted them amiably enough. She went to clubs and lectures with Maurice and mingled with his " gang " ; but carefully and politely, dodging long words as though they were bullets.

The only exception to this sweeping judgment was Esther. Bessie and Esther had been friends at sight, and if Esther used long words, at least she was willing to explain. Bessie suspected that Esther knew more than all the rest of the " gang " put together. Esther approved of Bessie as the healthiest, most direct girl she had ever met. " Why should Bessie improve her mind ? " she remarked scornfully to Wainwright. " She knows what to do by nature just the way a cat has good manners."

Maurice was pleased that Bessie should have a friend, but he felt a pang of self-pity because, while he respected Esther, she was one of the very few people he feared and avoided. Her clothes gave him the shivers. Her horrid manners made him feel that he might any moment tread on a barbed home truth. There was a good deal more Esther and less Ernie around the studio these days owing to the fact that Esther was giving a series of lectures on " The Influence of Mineral Elements on Health ". She would drop in at the studio for cups of tea ; so that Bessie and Esther had a splendid chance to probe each other's past, present and future in the way of all women who have decided to become even temporary allies.

" Esther," Bessie asked thoughtfully on one occasion, " what's a Deepus Complex ? Something about liking your father, isn't it ? "

" Well, yes and no," Esther responded learnedly. " Who's been talking about Oedipus Complexes to you ? "

" Ernie was talking to Maurice. He said I had a

Deepus Complex ; but I'm not fond of Dad. I can't stand the sight of him."

"Ernie probably meant that your not being fond of your father tended to make you fonder of Maurice," Esther replied cautiously.

"Tend is right. Hey, Esther. . . ."

"Yes ? "

"Is a Deepus Complex something awful ? "

"Oh, I don't know. Almost everyone has one."

"Maurice too ? "

"No, he's a narcissist. At least I always maintain he is. With a touch of megalomania." Esther threw her cigarette impatiently into a corner. "Why on earth do you bother wasting your time on Maurice ? I like Maurice. Always have. But he's a bundle of neuroses. Now you, I should say, have an excellent heredity, no nervous troubles, no inhibitions . . ."

"Hey, hang on a minute," Bessie demanded. "I only got one word in three. What's inhibitions ? "

"I'll give you a book on it," Esther said patiently.

"Would you say," Bessie asked next, leaning her chin on her fist, "that Maurice had inhibitions ? "

"Of course. He's wearing his nerves to bits with them. He's inhibited as far as you're concerned for one thing." Bessie was astonished. "He just treats you like a child. He doesn't realize how bad it is to be constantly courting you until the small hours of the morning and then leaving you frustrated. Both of you wearing your nerves out. Maurice is being very gentlemanly and very stupid."

All this to Bessie was as clear as globigerina ooze. She gathered, however, that she and Maurice were not proceeding along the right lines of love from the point of view of biology.

"I've been meaning to speak seriously to you for some time," Esther said severely, licking down a cigarette paper. "You may feel offended with me, but this affair

113

is not doing either of you any good."

Bessie did not reply. She was doing some heavy thinking.

"Maurice," she said that evening, as she boiled water for tea. They were eating sandwiches in the studio before going out to a meeting for the prevention of something previously unknown to Bessie. "Maurice, what is your attitude to inhibitions?"

Maurice put down his sandwich and stared at her. If his favourite lion cub had talked Latin, he could not have been more startled. "Good Lord! who's been talking to you?"

"Because," Bessie proceeded earnestly, "if you have inhibitions, whatever you do for inhibitions I'll do."

He started to laugh; then he came over and hugged her; and then went back to his chair and laughed again. "I suppose it's Esther," he said, wiping his eyes with the back of his hand. "Don't take any notice of her. I haven't got inhibitions, darling. All I need is a holiday. What else did Esther say?"

Bessie muttered something about not remembering, and Maurice gave her a suspicious glance. "Well, if it was anything about Edna," he went on sententiously, "it's a lie. Edna trapped me into it."

Bessie grunted. "She didn't say anything about any Edna."

"Oh!" Maurice raised his eyebrows and remarked acidly, "Take it from me, Esther is no authority on the subject of love. She'll spend hours telling you about your glands, if you give her half a chance, but she has fewer real feelings than a packet of tacks." He began to work up a sense of injustice against Esther. "She's a damn interfering old maid, that's all she is. Why can't she let me alone?"

"That's so," Bessie agreed warmly. And they dismissed the matter for the time being.

II

The subject reasserted itself late one Sunday afternoon when the two returned to the studio in high spirits after an all-day picnic spent rowing up Middle Harbour.

"I feel fit," Maurice exulted, thumping himself on the chest. "For the first time in months I'm beginning to feel on top gear. And when I really do strike form, young Bessie, you just watch. Why," he got out of the lift and rattled the bars on its door as though they were a cage, "I believe I'd even be able to sleep."

"I'm sunburnt," Bessie declared ruefully. "All round my shoulders and all down the back of my legs. You've no idea what it's like, Maurice."

"Haven't I?" He was full of sympathy. "Believe me, I've got the very stuff for sunburn. I thought of marketing it at one time as Wainwright's Sunburn Salve. Look, I'll put the hot-water jug on for tea, and you can get out of that damn tight frock and anoint yourself with the stuff." He rummaged in the drawers of his desk. "Here it is. I knew I had a jar left somewhere." He handed her the dubious-looking compound. "Don't spare it. You just rub it in. It will sting at first, but later on you feel the benefit."

Bessie accepted the salve resignedly and retired to the dressing-room, whence presently she emerged in her petticoat with a curtain draped modestly about her.

"Say, Maurice," she called, "did you ever try to rub something into your own back?"

"That's true," Maurice agreed. "Silly of me. No one can rub their own back. Look, I don't want my hands mucky with the stuff just now. Let's have tea and then I'll rub it for you."

They had tea, Bessie still clad in the window-curtain which Maurice maintained suited her admirably. He discoursed on Greek drapery and Spanish dancing and the art of the ballet, from which he passed lightly to the Siamese posture dancing.

"Hey," Bessie reminded him. "About my back."

"True, true. Something must be done. Where's the salve? My word, that back is a nasty bit of work. I wouldn't be surprised if it blistered."

He began energetically rubbing in the salve, but a howl from Bessie stopped him. "Not so hard, Maurice, blast you. Anyone would think you were scrubbing the floor."

"Sorry," he apologized, and very lightly, very gently, with his finger-tips, he caressed the offended area.

"I'm sorry too." Bessie was penitent at once. "I didn't mean to swear at you."

"You have a marvellous skin," he said thoughtfully. "It's so clear. I didn't realize before that you had such a beautiful skin."

"You've probably never seen so much of it," Bessie grumbled. "If it gets in the sun, it freckles. I bet my back'll be freckled right down to the waist."

"God forbid!" He ran his fingers up her spine gently.

"Don't. That tickles."

"Sorry."

Maurice resumed his labours and Bessie sat patiently on the table dangling her feet.

"Hadn't we better put on the light?" she suggested. "I don't know how you can see to rub."

"I don't need to see. I'm enjoying myself." He put one arm round her waist and sat down beside her on the table. "There's something electric in the touch of you."

Bessie was saying, "It's very probably sunburn," in a matter-of-fact tone, when Maurice kissed her very fiercely and suddenly in the hollow where her neck joined her shoulder.

"Don't," she reproved, a little breathlessly. "That makes me feel funny." It was astonishing the effect that kiss was having. It seemed to be travelling in quivers all over her. As though the little hollow in her shoulder were a pool from which ripples spread to her very toes. She turned and looked at Maurice reproachfully. "What did you want to do that for?" she complained.

His eyes were shining. "Kiss me," he said in an excited whisper. "Oh, don't sit there talking!"

He was showering her with kisses and Bessie came up for air gasping like a fish. He hugged her, his rough sleeve scraping her sunburn, his rough chin scraping her neck.

"Don't," she implored, leaning against him.

"Why not? I like it." He swept her on to his old sofa which creaked under their concerted weight.

"You are making me feel," Bessie whispered dizzily, "very . . ."

She stopped to decide just how he did make her feel. Her bones seemed to have turned to water. She could not lift her hand. All she wanted to do was to lean against him and steady her heart-beat. To lean close to him and closer so that she could feel his heart beating with a heavy thud against her own. She could not speak. His mouth on hers was throbbing, warm. All her nerves seemed to be singing together like the morning stars. She could not move, she felt sure, even if she had wanted to move. If all the mountains thundered down to crush her, she could not move. Even as she made up her mind that it was impossible, she had pushed Maurice away shyly.

"Now, why did you do that?" he asked sulkily. "Why must you spoil everything?"

"Because . . ." Bessie said, "you made me feel ashamed of myself for . . . for liking you so."

Wainwright laughed. "You are a queer person. As long as you like me, and I like you, everything's fine."

"Is it?"

She put her arms around him awkwardly and embarrassed. "You silly," Maurice said tenderly. "I wouldn't hurt a hair of your head. You're glorious. Kiss me." She kissed him softly, a small, innocent child's kiss. "Not like that. Like this." And he caught her to him savagely. "Like this, and this, and this."

At that moment someone switched on the light in the ante-room. Maurice's first instinctive move was to clap his hand over Bessie's mouth. He cursed himself for having left the door open.

"Hello," the intruder called. "What-ho within! What-ho Maurice! Bessie! Don't you try to pretend you're out."

"Damnation!" Wainwright muttered.

"It's Ernie," Bessie said, patting her hair. "It would be," she was thinking bitterly. He had dropped like ice into the bubbling effervescence of her emotions; steadied the rush of blood to her head; brought all her beautiful, quivering nerves to a standstill as if he had jammed on a brake. The shock made her almost sick.

"We weren't trying to pretend we're out," Maurice shouted defensively. They were sitting side by side on the sofa, looking very prim in the light of Maurice's reading-lamp. Ernie's eyebrows flickered humorously as he took in Bessie's curtain.

"You didn't remember you invited me to come to the meeting with you?"

"No. Did I?" Maurice asked glumly.

"Want some tea, Ernie?" Bessie's voice was cool, friendly. She might be still a whirl of clamouring nerves; but her pride was on top and in command. She had clamped a polite lid over that uproar in her blood.

"I could do with a cup." Ernie sat down. "But don't bother if you've had yours. You look particularly fetching in that curtain, Bess." Ernie was not a fool; and just then he could have kicked himself for his lack of tact.

Bessie chuckled. "My honour," she announced, "depends on a single safety-pin."

"Rather good." Ernie was pleased. "Did you think that up or pinch it from somewhere?"

Bessie was putting on the hot-water jug. "I thought it up," she said gaily. "All by myself. Did you ever have sunburn, Ernie?"

They started off for the lecture very late, Bessie and Ernie talking enough for a dozen, Wainwright somewhat abstracted and silent. He managed to draw Bessie aside for a moment while Ernie hunted for seats.

"I'm not going to put up with this sort of thing," he whispered rapidly. "And from what I know of you . . ." He looked at her wistfully. "What about you?"

Bessie hesitated. "No good getting inhibitions," she agreed gravely.

"Well, I've been thinking it out. You write and tell Esther we're coming down this week-end."

"But she's going away next week-end."

"So much the better."

"Oh! How about my family?"

"Always your damn family cropping up. Am I your family's keeper? Lie to them, murder them all off, fix it somehow. It's up to you. Are you coming?"

"I'm coming," Bessie agreed. Perhaps this peculiar craving in her blood for some other kind of life was only after all a matter of these mysterious inhibitions.

"You're a darling," Maurice said exultantly. "If Ernie wasn't waving to us, I'd kiss you here and now."

Bessie was uneasily conscious that she was not a good liar. She hated lies; she rather resented that Maurice should take it for granted that her invention of glib falsehoods was as sure as his own. However, under the spur of such an emergency, an innately truthful person will rise to heights undreamt of even by a Maurice.

CHAPTER IX

I

NOT even when they were actually on the platform waiting for the train did Bessie allow herself to think where her actions were leading her. She was inclined to be cross because Maurice was late ; and Maurice, bubbling over with good-humour, complained about her disgusting punctuality, her martyred air when a man went to get a paper and the train unfairly sneaked out while his back was turned.

"What does it matter?" he coaxed. "Yes, yes, I know it was a fast train and all the others are slow. But, even if we did miss it, I haven't forgotten anything." He had enough luggage for a European tour. "Fishing lines." He tumbled them out proudly. "Gramophone records. I know Esther has a gramophone, a good one, and I want you to hear Beethoven's Concerto. Food. Esther never has any food worth eating. Blankets, cigarettes, mosquito bane, cushions, oranges — everything. When it comes to organizing, kid, I'm recognized as an expert."

He was so young, so excited, that Bessie relented. They craned out the train window and pointed out cows and sheep to each other ; they sniffed the air rapturously.

"Breathe deeply," Maurice said encouragingly. "Doctors say you should breathe deeply at least ten times every morning."

He placed his hands on his shabby waistcoat and inflated himself, standing solemnly to attention in the middle of the swaying carriage.

"They have made some very interesting discoveries about breathing," he told Bessie. "I have been reading a book about Yoga. Getting in touch with the Infinite, the Cosmic Oneness, by breathing the right way. Most interesting."

"I thought you breathed to get some air," Bessie observed with her usual materialism.

"There you go again. You haven't read the book and yet you adopt that tone."

"What tone?"

"You think you're being ironical and sceptical."

"I don't. I just said I thought you breathed to get some air."

"Well, not according to the Yogi. I have the book with me and I'll read it to you. Listen to this. . . ."

By the time they reached the junction and commenced the long wait for their next train, Bessie knew a lot about Yoga. She was also very hungry.

"It's all very well getting in touch with the Cosmic whatsisname," she said gloomily, "but how about some food?"

"I suppose so," Maurice agreed reluctantly. He did not want to unpack supplies in the middle of a station platform, first because he was not quite sure where he had stowed everything, and secondly because he might not be able to pack them up again. "I thought we'd have lunch when we reached Esther's place. Save trouble. Could you sustain life on a meat pie?"

They bought meat pies in the main street of the junction town and wandered about gazing in uninteresting shop windows until a little motor train panted up to carry them the last stage of the journey.

"Look at it. It's the pup of the big train," Maurice exclaimed delightedly. "A one-puppy-power train. They probably have a dachshund chasing a cat over a treadmill to work it."

"Why a dachshund?"

Maurice considered a moment. "A dachshund would fit better over a treadmill."

The puppy train grunted its way out of the flat, green fields and began to climb into a congregation of cliffs where funereal expanses of grey-brown rock and scrub repeated and repeated like an attack of cosmic indigestion. It was an unsympathetic, casual country, thrown together by accident or earthquake, and covered by a dirty fleece of stringy-barks, a tree that lives in sackcloth and ashes, harsh, broken, clawing a living like a miser, clutching the earth with grey fingers. Below, a creek twisted through a broken hillside, and an isolated farm showed a glint of corrugated iron in a green hollow. Steep walls of rock stood over it like the Ten Commandments being stern to a sinner.

" This place looks like Esther," Bessie said suddenly.

" It has a certain realism." Wainwright did not care for this dreary repetition of ridges and valleys. " Iron-stone, I should say." The country looked as though the sunlight had sucked up all colours and spat them back again grey. Grey-green leaves, grey-brown rocks, smoke-coloured tree-trunks, dead sticks carpeting a gritty, grey soil.

It was three o'clock when the guard shouted at them " Here y'are. Belton View Station," and they found themselves deposited on a gravelled platform, adorned by a small weatherboard waiting-room and four insig-nificant privet trees. The station-mistress seized their tickets, locked them up in her office, and waddled across the railway line by a path, a broad, well-beaten path decorated with notices threatening dire penalties to persons thereby crossing the line. The path made straight for a general store on the main road where the metal flash of a car glancing past gave a dangerous reminder that the city was only forty miles or an hour's drive away.

" I should like to see you behind the wheel of a big car." Wainwright stared admiringly after one shining monster. "A man can never really take an objective view of a woman until he sees her at the steering-wheel of a car or on a horse."

Bessie was not interested in objective views when she was hungry. The only dwelling in sight was the general store with its gold-and-scarlet petrol bowser, its fly-spotted window and week-old newspaper placards faded by exposure. A fat dog slept across the doorstep and several local residents shared a wooden bench in the shade of the verandah.

"Air," Maurice remarked, breathing deeply. "Marvellous air. Keen, fresh, invigorating." He sounded as though he were advertising it with a large commission for every additional customer.

"I'm still hungry. I suppose the people over there would know where Esther's place is."

The loungers pondered on the whereabouts of Miss Gullick. No Miss Gullick here, they decided. The station-mistress then came to the rescue.

"They mean the queer woman, Joe. The one that lives on chooks' food and wears sandshoes."

"Oh! Her! You go across the line again, then follow the road till it goes past Chuggs' place, then down the cart track on your left till you nearly reach the creek. You can't miss it."

Maurice began to wish he had not brought so much baggage. He waited until they were out of sight of the station before he sat down to rest. He complained of a sinking pain due to despair. Bessie assured him that it was only hunger.

"We've come at least two miles already," he maintained, wiping his forehead. But he revived when they came round a bend in the road and sighted a cottage. "It might be Esther's, though it looks too comfortable."

"Probably the Chugg place," Bessie suggested.

It did not look at all like the kind of home Esther

would have. Two giant coral trees towered over a small white house, and a tall steel windmill turned lazily beside a big modern shed. Away from the house stretched vigorous rows of vegetables, neatly planted peach and plum trees with their trunks whitened, while a big poultry yard showed between the glossy green of orange trees. From the end of a paddock where someone was chopping scrub there came a whiff of burnt boughs.

"Come on," Maurice called irritably. "This must be the track we turn down."

There were two faint wheel-ruts leading into the bush and they stumbled along them, over dead twigs, loose rocks and the bed of a little dry watercourse. On the far side of this watercourse, one of the suitcases Bessie was carrying disobligingly burst open. She paused to rest, leaning against a warm stone, breathing hard and feeling slightly dizzy. Perhaps it was the air or hunger that gave her this sense of lightness and unreality. She crumpled a cluster of ti-tree leaves in her hot, dirty hand ; and they gave off a pungent odour something like pine needles plus camphor but sweeter with a tang of their own.

Maurice came hurrying back up the track, very managing and competent.

"I've found it," he encouraged, rousing Bessie to pick up the suitcase. "Lord ! what a dump ! We should have been warned."

Esther's hut stood in a clearing on a flat piece of ground from which the land sloped in a series of rocky steps and hollows to the creek below. The clearing was only a small one and the trees seemed hardly to notice it. They took it in their stride, dropping leaves and boughs about it, as if the house were a hollow log. There were two rough slip-rails instead of a gate, but it was plain that most visitors stepped through the wires of the fence.

The house had a small front verandah, two bedrooms,

a living-room and a little slip of a kitchen. The key was where Esther had placed it, under a stone.

" No wonder she's cracked, living in a place like this," Maurice grumbled. " I bet it's damp. Let's get some tea."

Bessie was staring at the trees, her hunger forgotten in a deep pleasure. The trees on the ridge had been stuggy, weatherbeaten battlers who asked for bread and were given stones. Every branch writhed its own way, developing rheumatic knobs and gnarls, while the trees themselves leaned up against the wind as if for support. They were casual in their growth and undecided in their manner of life.

But Esther's trees grew in tranquillity and leaf-mould. No axe had ever been laid to those silver pillars with branches groining over arches of air. The blue gums' great bodies, cool-veined like marble, pale grey and pastel-washed mauve, with ashes of rose and delicate green, took all the colours of a cloud. The smoky columns of the turpentine rose against the milky white of the flooded gum, while the red gum stood naked, bloodstains of old wounds upon it, the shed bark about its feet spattered as if with blood.

" Wood. That's the next thing. The joys of the simple life. And I bet Esther's axe has no edge. If you get tea ready, I'll see to water and wood." Very business-like Maurice strode over to investigate a spring behind the house. " I suppose it's all right," he ruminated. " Anyway it's too far to trudge down to the creek."

The creek was the colour of fine-cut tobacco with a gold flake in it, wide enough to flicker minute fins of silver when the faint gust struck it from the ridge, yet narrow enough to cross skipping from stone to stone.

After their meal Maurice spoke more approvingly of Esther's home. He praised the trees, quoting from the lesser known poets to the effect that trees were mysterious and good to look at. He told Bessie the names of several kinds of birds, two of them incorrectly. He insisted on going for a walk, exploring.

Already the sun was streaking the clearing with prison stripes, long slivers of light that turned the trees into bars. Maurice mentioned a set of tree studies he had made five years before ; the angles, the shots he considered you would need to get the best out of these trees. While he was talking, they came over a ledge of rock into a little pocket above the creek. Bessie stopped still, her eyes on the ground.

" Ooh ! " Her mouth pouted as though she would whistle. " Ooh ! Maurice, look ! "

" Christmas bells." Maurice smiled at her pleasure. " They are rather lovely. I've never seen them so thick."

But Bessie had never seen Christmas bells growing before. The little flames sprang up, each independently in its set of sharp, green blades. They flickered through the hollow like wildfire, so that it was hard not to tread on them. Bessie solemnly bent and rattled one of the flowers to hear the dry clack of the stamens, and that woody music gave her a sudden pang of pleasure half grief. November after November, as the gold of the year heated red, they had sprung up and she had not known, had not seen them.

There would be waratahs, Esther had said, flushed scarlet, rising curiously carved in a crown ; the Christmas bush like rubies cut into a spray of feathers ; the native roses in the shade ; the sweet boronia. All the flame of flowers November lit, but not for her. Envy of Esther caught her momentarily. To think that Esther lived in this valley and had so often described the blues and reds to the blind, the city-born and street-bound girl. " You must come and see it. If only I could coax you. . . ." And in that warren of walls Bessie had smiled politely on the enthusiast, thinking Esther a lonely, disappointed woman who put her passion into a wild hermitage, wilfully withdrawing into the desert.

Yet here was the desert flowering like paradise in a glory of red and gold. The trees, the earth, the smell of the leaves, stirred Bessie as none of Maurice's ideas, none of his talk about beauty and art had done. This place talked a language of long thirst and survival, of struggle and rain and the bite of weather. Something in her knew this language ; and the old restlessness clamoured as it had never done before — not Archer Street, not the studio — this place.

"Notice," Maurice said didactically, "how these leaves are serrated, tough, water-conserving. It's a very interesting example of adaptation to environment, Bessie, most interesting."

His voice flowed on. Bessie leant her head against the hard surface of a gum tree ; she put her arms around it, feeling the cool solidity like a stone. Maurice might talk of environment, heredity ; but they were only words. The thing that mattered was this mixture of pain and peace, this feeling of exquisite recognition of a strange place, the grasping of a meaning in life bigger than the usual worries and wants.

"Aren't you feeling well ? " Maurice asked.

"Bit tired." Bessie watched a stream of tiny black ants scuttling up the rough bark, one behind the other like people in a queue. Sydney seemed a far-away city, as fantastic as an ants' nest, a stone shell out of which she had emerged with her mind soft and blinking like something struggling up from the underground.

Maurice had grown restless. "I think we'd better be getting back," he suggested ; and Bessie followed, still in a dream, up the path towards the hut. "I don't want to miss the sunset," Maurice explained ; but the sunset was very quiet and matter-of-fact. The sky faded, the colours faded, the ants and lizards went into their holes, and the sun went into a hole between two hills.

" Well, now we've seen the sunset," Maurice announced in the tone of one who has performed an official duty, " how about lighting a fire ? "

The wood was damp and the smoke made Bessie cough. It poured out of the stove in a thick, white cloud.

" What the dickens are you doing ? " Maurice, coming into the tiny kitchen with the lamp, was nearly choked. " Why, the stuff is sopping wet and half rotten. Here, I'll get you some."

Bessie, alone in the kitchen, picked up the rejected wood penitently. She broke a piece of it and crumbled it between her finger and thumb into little yellow shreds. It gave out a smell of toadstools and damp, an interesting smell. Maurice clattered back with an armful of dry chips, brisk and efficient.

" No woman knows how to treat an axe," he grumbled. " Esther shouldn't be allowed to own one. It's years since it had an edge."

They had a leisurely meal, this time of sardines and tomatoes, lettuce, bread and butter, and tinned pineapple. All of them tasted faintly of kerosene. Maurice lit a cigarette and smiled across at Bessie.

" Why are you staring out the window ? " he asked.

" Just thinking."

Bessie was watching their reflections in the glass, dim shadows of themselves talking and eating with the stars showing through the other side. That must be how we look, she thought, to ghosts.

" Come and kiss me. I feel as though you're a million miles away." She came round and kissed him somewhat abstractedly. " What a night ! " He spoke as though he had invented it. " A night of nights. We'll remember this night when we are old, too old to be in love."

He was suddenly ardently in love with her ; then he

decided that he would not, he must not, spoil things by snatching at happiness. He would savour it slowly, leisurely, like a good wine.

" Music," he decided, going over to throw open the big window. " How calm everything is, Bessie, how spacious. Only music can ever give you the same sense of infinite splendour that such a night gives."

If I'd said that, Bessie thought, it would have sounded like acting ; but he can get away with it. He isn't self-conscious.

" Music has something," Maurice was saying, " that nothing else can offer. That was why I brought the Concerto. I felt that this night, our night, would be spoilt without it, that I must have Beethoven's Concerto or all would be ruined." He turned on her eager as a boy who has done something daring. " Darling, I got the records from a music firm on spec, and they're worth a small fortune. I told the manager I just wanted them for the week-end to see if I liked them."

" But, Maurice," Bessie was horrified, " do you mean you carted half a ton of records out here when they didn't belong to you ? "

" Nothing is too good," he replied gracefully, " to give you delight, Bessie. I would do far more." He walked over to the gramophone with the air of a king about to throw the crown jewels out of the window. He explored the gramophone. " Blast the woman ! " he exclaimed anxiously. " There are no needles."

" Oh, there must be ! " Bessie was just as eager as he that the records should be a success. She could not bear to see him disappointed. Maurice sat down, cut to the heart by the unkindness of this blow.

" I *did* want to hear the Concerto, but it can't be helped, I suppose."

" Oh yes, it can." Bessie had an inspiration. " They're sure to sell needles at the store by the railway station.

I'll just run up and get some." She felt almost a sense of escape.

" You can't. It's miles and miles."

" I'll be back in twenty minutes. What kind do you want ? "

Maurice was still standing on the doorstep protesting as she sped up the track. Dear Maurice, Bessie thought tenderly, he shall have his old Concerto. There was a cold, white half-moon pushing its way through a drift of fluff that reminded her of the feathers of white leghorn hens blown against wire netting. The dogs from the cottage on the hill barked at her as she came out on the road ; the dogs from distant farms took up the chorus ; all the way to the store she was heralded by a woofing of respectable dogs who believed that a dangerous, probably a hen-stealing stranger was abroad.

II

The little lamp-lit store sold gramophone needles.

" Though there ain't much demand for 'em now folk have these wirelesses," the old gentleman behind the counter croaked. " Seems like it was only yesterday people was payin' to go and 'ear a gramyphone. In them days the gramyphones would imitate hens and pigs in a way people thought was wonderful. Now, you wouldn't get 'em to cross the road to 'ear a gramyphone. I know me daughter-in-law won't."

He seemed willing to carry the conversation to further lengths, but Bessie breathlessly bade him good-evening and darted out of the shop.

It certainly was cold. She found herself shivering as she trotted wearily up the rise. Her legs ached, every nerve and muscle of her was tired to death. She sat down to get her breath in the same place where they had rested that afternoon, and listened to the cattle-dogs announcing her coming and the bull-frogs croaking under the paper-bark trees in the swamp. The cold, white half-moon seemed to have a mean look on its face, and it was so high up, so alone. There were black patches in the sky and light patches that looked as though the dark had been stirred round and curdled into stars. Bessie was so absorbed watching that she did not realize how long she sat until she moved and found she had become stiff.

There was a noise of something coming up the road. From the sound it might have been a very old concrete-mixer, but from the dim headlights Bessie deduced it was a car. She began to walk quickly, limping a little from a blister on her heel, hoping to reach the cart tracks before the car passed her. It was rather companionable to have it behind, a rear-guard against the black scrub; but it rattled up and overtook her at a surprising rate. Slowing down as he passed, the driver yelled :

" Want a lift ? "

" Thanks." Bessie limped up and climbed into the front seat. She would have accepted a lift in a coffin, she was so tired.

" How far y' going ? "

" To where the cart track turns off. Miss Gullick's place."

" Right."

The driver let in his clutch. From the front of the car came a rattling sound, from the back another rattling, that Bessie, peering through the dark, decided was a number of kerosene tins knocking together. A step-ladder projected over an assortment of sacks and tools.

" Just been doing a bit of a job," the driver yelled in a friendly way. " Over towards Koomong. How long you been staying with Esther ? "

" I only came to-night," Bessie replied cautiously. Deciding presently she should make conversation, she enquired above the noise of the engine and the empty tins : " What kind of a car is this ? "

" Ron Chugg," the driver said surprisingly. " I live in the stone place on the hill with me brother."

Bessie had liked the house with the coral trees. Now it gave her a real pleasure to discover its owner come friendly out of the darkness.

" I asked what kind of a car."

" Chev. Needs the pistons ground. Needs a lot of things done to it." He seemed to think her query was prompted by a real interest in cars. " Of course, she isn't much, but she gets you there." His tone was apologetic. " Me and me brother have had her that long we've practically put new parts everywhere you can put a part."

" You can drop me here," Bessie suggested, as they reached the patch of scrub where the track turned off. " You've come past your place."

" Don't matter. Take you down to the door if you like. I been meaning to come down and see Esther about that horse."

" Oh no ! " Bessie hastily slammed the car door behind her. " This will do, Mr. Chugg." It would be embarrassing if he insisted on coming in and found only Maurice. " Good night," she said fervently.

With a cheery halloo the driver backed his rattling conveyance and roared off the way he came. Bessie stumbled through the yawning blackness of the cart track, falling over the loose dirt and stones, brushing against bushes where the spiders had been busy while she was away. Across the path they had flung great clammy webs that clutched her face and sent a shiver down her back. Something black flitted past within a foot of her head and startled her. It was with a glorious relief that she saw the welcoming light shining out the front door and Maurice waiting anxiously on the step.

" I shouldn't have let you go," he said remorsefully.

" Well, you couldn't go. I'd have had you on my hands with 'flu again."

They went arm-in-arm into the dining-room and triumphantly set the Concerto whirling on its way. Bessie propped her head on her hands, her elbows on the table in a debris of sardine tins, dirty plates and cigarette ash.

" Now, just listen to this bit," she heard Maurice say. And, listening, trying to sit up straight, to be attentive, she was presently asleep where she sat. Maurice, rapt in the music, did not notice her. It did drift through his mind that she was not fidgeting. Despite the time and patience he had spent in improving Bessie's taste in music, she usually fidgeted. Rising to change the second record, Maurice turned to her for approval, and saw she had gone to sleep. Her head had sunk down on the table ; the lamp shone on her short hair.

" Poor kid," he thought. " She's worn out. How stupid of me ! "

He regarded her for a moment, the artist uppermost. She looked like a little lion asleep, funny and soft, yet alert. He felt the same tenderness for her that some people feel for small wild kittens who gallop round, pretending something is chasing them, then curl up in a ball and sleep and wake and play again. What a pity, he thought, that she must grow up. He studied her intently. It was so seldom that Bessie stayed still. She was usually doing something, trotting about, looking anxious, questioning and very responsible.

If only she realized how charming she was when she didn't worry ; dear Bessie, loyal and proud and quaint and so very young. He frowned over the thought. After all, he decided, shrugging, he was not exactly old and decrepit. He also had something to offer. But again shyness beset him. Few men, he thought, like the responsibility of being the first man a girl loves. If Bessie, for instance, had been a different kind of girl, this might have been a much more light-hearted venture. But he loved her as he had never thought to love again. I wish I could keep her always, he thought, just like that with her head beside the green lettuce and her paws folded. Then it struck him it was cruel not to send her to bed. Young things wearied out should be put to bed. The queer man had no thought in that minute that was not paternal. He had just resolved to gather her up very carefully and carry her when she stirred and yawned.

" Go on, Maurice," she murmured. " Put another record on. I was listening."

" Bed," he said.

She shook her head and woke up. " Oh," she yawned again. " Oh, yes. I meant to tell you." She blinked and rubbed her eyes. " There's only one real bed. I tested them out. Esther sleeps on a straw mattress on a bit of board." She grew shy. " Maurice, you did mean, didn't you, that we were to share the one bed ? "

He roared with laughter. " You're priceless, Bessie," he gasped. " Completely priceless."

Bessie smiled back at him, pleased that she had said something amusing. He was a completely different person from the grave, fatherly man who had looked down on her a minute before. His eyes twinkled with mischief. The youth and devilment of him were on top again.

" I suppose you think I'm a Sunday School teacher out with his favourite pupil." He touched her wrist with his fingers ; and the touch of them gave her a not un-pleasant sense of helplessness. She wanted to kiss him, to cling to him. Instead of doing either of these reason-able things, she moved away.

" I'm going to bed anyway," she said, with a forced casualness. " Put the fire out. Lock up, turn out the light."

" Don't forget to put the jug out for the milkman,"
he finished with a smile. " See, I'm domesticated
already."

He could hear her moving about in the bedroom, and
a glow of pleasure flooded him to think of her so near.
He went to the window and rested his hot forehead on
the cold pane. " This night is different," he thought,
strangely moved. " It's something I thought had passed
me for ever. It's the real thing."

" Maurice," Bessie called. " Have you put the
cat out ? "

He grinned. " Coming," he called, and blew out
the lamp.

" How do you manage to get undressed in the dark ? "
Bessie was trying to cover her nervousness.

" It's simple. You just drop your clothes on the floor.
Move over." She moved over obligingly. He tested
the bed gingerly. " I knew it." His tone was aggrieved.
" Esther bought this bed second-hand from a boarding-
house. You needn't move over as far as all that."

Bessie shyly edged nearer. Wainwright threshed about
like some large, unwieldy animal until he had settled
himself to his satisfaction. He did not like the bedclothes
tucked in at the bottom of the bed. His feet, he explained, " liked to breathe ". Bessie, who was losing her
nervousness, claimed that her own feet hated to be in a
draught, and what was the use of having bedclothes if
you only had them flapping about your knees ?

" I can see," Maurice said, " that we'll have to have
twin beds. I simply must let my feet breathe."

" I suppose they're all Yogi. Getting into touch with
the Cosmic whatsisname ? "

Maurice gave her a push. " You get over your own
side and stay there, if you're going to be smart." He
began to laugh. " I can't help feeling like the third act
of a French farce."

" Why ? "

" Oh, be quiet ! "

They were back on their old companionable footing.

" Maurice ? " Bessie asked shyly.

" Huh ? "

" Do you always wear a woollen undershirt to bed ? "

" I catch cold if I don't. You wouldn't love me if I sniffled."

She patted him cautiously as she might have patted a puppy.

" Golly," she whispered, amazed. " You have got hair on your chest."

He chuckled. " Any objections ? "

" You'd make a good doormat."

" It's a recommendation," he assured her with mock gravity. " Only the most virile lovers have hair on their chests."

He felt the little movement she made of shy withdrawal and hugged her closer.

" Oh no, you don't," he said. " You started this." The warmth of her body through her thin silk nightdress drained him of all desires except to hold her thus and feel the current of his blood cry out to her. " Love me ? " he asked.

She nodded her head vigorously in the dark.

" Well, why are you trembling, silly ? "

" It's your blasted toes breathing. I'm cold."

He knew she was only putting a brave face on things. " Silly kid," he said.

" Maurice ! "

" What ? "

" There's a big moth flopping about. Oooh ! " She sat up in bed with a start. " It's on the pillow."

Something soft and whirring hit Maurice in the eye. " Damnation ! " he spluttered.

" Light the lamp, Maurice. We can't go to sleep with

that whipping about on our faces."

He sighed wearily and padded out into the living-room to find the lamp and matches. By the time the lamp was lit he was feeling cold. He smacked the moth with a dish-cloth and succeeded, after several vain swipes, in bringing it whirring to the floor, where he finished it with a boot, and climbed glumly into bed. This time he put the lamp beside the bed.

" Now," he announced grimly, " if you want a drink of water or something to eat or a walk in the moonlight or a cold shower, tell me before I blow this light out."

Bessie had her nose buried in the pillow. She shook her head.

" All right." Maurice blew out the light and lay in the dignified attitude of a sculpture on a tomb, his hands folded across his chest. Bessie snuggled against him repentantly.

" I wish," she said, " you'd take off that woollen undershirt."

" Darn it. I catch cold, I tell you."

" Oh, Maurice, this is a special sort of night, isn't it ? Besides, I like the fur on your chest."

Maurice relented. He struggled out of the offending garment rather pleased.

" Darling." He leant over to kiss her. " Do you really love me ? "

" Uh-huh."

" You're not afraid of me now ? "

She made no reply. He buried his head in her neck and bit it gently. She smelt of eucalyptus leaves, of the smoke of the fire. He could feel the pulsing of the jugular below her ear ; and suddenly it occurred to him as extraordinary that she should be so many separable organs, that she was a million blood-vessels and nerves, a complicated web of ganglia and muscle fibre and bone. He bit her again on the neck reflectively, and as he did so, something stung his uncovered ankle. There was a faint, pernicious hum which revealed the presence of the first mosquitoes of the spring. Maurice decided grimly that if the mosquitoes were flying wolves, he would still not get up. He had set his hand to this love-making and he was not having any more interruptions.

"Mosquitoes," Bessie murmured through his kisses.

"Shut up about the mosquitoes," he said grimly. "If I can put up with them, you can." He slapped himself on the shoulder-blade.

"Let me," Bessie said solicitously. "Why, Maurice, you'll be eaten alive."

"Never mind. Kiss me and stop talking." But it was no use, he realized, to combine the bliss of love with the agony of being torn piecemeal by mosquitoes. He reached for his woollen shirt.

"Where are you going?" Bessie asked.

"I've got to get some citronella. I know I brought some."

He found his dressing-gown and lit the lamp. Bessie eyed him drowsily.

"We don't seem to be getting a fair break," she complained with a grin.

She leant on her elbow and watched Maurice rummaging through the suitcases. Naturally he had forgotten where the citronella was packed; and he had to unpack everything else before he found it. The fact that it was there restored his sense of humour. He sat down on the side of the bed and laughed, as he surveyed the contents of the suitcases scattered over the floor.

"This is the damn silliest seduction at which I have ever assisted. The thing's degenerating into slapstick."

Bessie gurgled with laughter and Maurice shook her.

"You think it's funny," he said, with mock ferocity. "Well, you won't think it's so darn funny when I really get into my stride."

She fluttered her eyelids as he smeared citronella on her face. "You can't scare me."

He blew out the light and got into bed with the deliberation of a man who feels that Fate has nothing more to offer.

"I remember Ernie swearing like a trooper when he came back from his honeymoon," he said reflectively. "It seems that Ernie and Joan went swimming the first day, and they got so raw and blistered that they couldn't bear to touch each other for the rest of the honeymoon. Now I come to think of it, this is probably happening to any number of couples who think they are being separately cursed with alligators or ants in the butter."

Bessie patted him gently. "Anyway we haven't got blisters," she reminded him.

Maurice chuckled. "You're delightful, Bessie, delightful." He kept on murmuring it between kisses. "Delightful, queer Bessie."

He must not frighten her, he kept telling himself. He must in this of all hours the most momentous of his life do nothing that in other nights would hurt to remember. The moonlight at the window, these shadows, the wide, whispering concourse of grey trees, must have no silent reproach against him. Bessie stirred in his arms, drew closer to him.

Suddenly they both started, instinctively clutched each other and glanced apprehensively upward.

"What was that?" Maurice said sharply.

"Sounded like someone chucking rocks on the roof," Bessie answered huskily. She was trembling.

From overhead came another report, a loud, clanging rattle. Bessie sat straight up in the bed.

"There's something outside," she said, horrified. "I tell you there's something outside. Listen."

"Nonsense." In spite of himself he was listening intently. They sat side by side, stiff, tense, hardly breathing. " It's nothing," he repeated presently. " Don't be silly."

" Listen."

" I can't hear a thing."

" I can. It's moving round the house. Trying to get in. Maurice, go and see ! "

For a moment Maurice was drawn into her terror, as though it were a dark mist that swam out and sucked at him. His nerves were badly on edge.

" It knows we're here."

He caught at his common sense with both hands. " Bessie," he said harshly, " you're acting like an hysterical brat."

She did not reply. She was paralysed with fear. Even as he spoke, there came again that mysterious thundering report from overhead. One must be calm, Maurice told himself, rational. Good heavens ! what did Bessie expect ? The bush woke up at night. It was alive with rustlings and creepings and small noises. But it was obvious that Bessie was not interested in love-making any longer.

" If it isn't something creeping about," she said positively, " it's Dad. You know Dad. He'd murder you if he got the chance. And he'd think this was a great bit of luck."

Maurice had never had any particular dread of Bessie's brutal parent ; but in his overwrought state the idea that the girl's father might have followed them seemed not impossible.

" There's someone breathing," Bessie asserted in a frightened whisper.

This was too much. Maurice sprang out of bed.

" Blast it ! " he growled, stumbling angrily over the scattered contents of the suitcases. He put his foot on a hairbrush and began to swear. He swore at his clothes because they were not where they ought to be on the floor. He swore at his boots ; he swore for the sheer comfort it gave him, much as a woman might weep.

" Now," he said, marching to the door, with his heavy walking-stick gripped by the ferrule, " if there *is* anyone there . . ."

He flung the door open and slammed out ferociously. The empty moonlight lay over all the clearing, presenting a simple, open face, as of an idiot. To Maurice's distorted fury it appeared to be quivering with silent laughter, a conspirator in his discomfiture. The moonlight leered like some maniac jester as its victim stamped across the chilly grass and peered into the black fringe of trees.

" Come out," he ordered, gripping his stick foolishly. " If you think I can't see you, you're mistaken."

From behind Maurice there came an unmistakable derisive snort. He spun round startled as a very old, very casual cart-horse emerged from the shadow of the house where it had been peacefully rubbing itself on the weatherboard. It began to eat grass, calmly, with a satisfied munching, wrinkling its lips away delicately from the meal and breathing like a steam-engine. If Maurice could have vented a righteous indignation and flung a brick at the horse as a symbol of that cosmic conspiracy whose fool he felt he was, he could have gone back to the hut with dignity. But his innermost self had been humiliated by a series of ridiculous incidents as insignificant as they were maddening. He had been the sport of empty inanity.

Ten minutes ago he would have cried that the gods must needs be jealous of a man who sought to fit one hour of his life like a jewel into a ring. But now the great rustle, as the night drew aside its skirts, was, he recognized, not a rustle of hurried laughter but of indifference. Could any man decree that he would spend his time as he pleased, even one hour of it ? What did it matter which specks of protoplasm mated or bred with which other specks ? All the tumult and welter of his emotion were no more than the whirr of an insect that hummed for a minute and ceased. He did not count, the place said by its silence, nothing counted in the end. He trudged slowly back towards the hut with the conviction that in some way this very ordinary stretch of earth and sky had inflicted a gruelling defeat on him.

His startling memory, sometimes so blank, at other times so brilliant, was filled with little scraps of rhyme that fluttered like the banners of a defeated army.

> Unconscious and unpassionate and still,
>   Cloud-like we lean and stare as bright leaves stare ;
> And gradually along the stranger hill,
>   Our unwalled loves thin out on vacuous air.

The chanting of the verses in his head could not turn him to defiance ; but they did straighten out a pitiful semblance of dignity. He leant heavily against the door-post, an ageing man, fattish, slightly bald, with stooped shoulders and a face sagging, loosened by overmuch emotion and ill-health. He turned and stared back at that nothingness as though he still defied it, knowing it nothing.

So now, he thought, I have been reduced to my proper level as an animal. I have had this night snatched away from me. The one perfect thing I had hoped to keep. I ought to laugh perhaps. It is better to laugh. Later I may be able to do so.

He went inside listlessly. It was not his fault, not Bessie's fault, that the high tide of his love had receded. His body was a prey to the inevitable physiological law that makes passion either a heaven or hell. He looked down at Bessie with neither mischief nor tenderness. She had wrapped herself tightly in his overcoat and gone to sleep. She lay with her head on her arm, face downward. Maurice stretched out beside her very quietly so that he would not disturb her ; and for a long time he stared at the blank square of grey emptiness, the window, as though it held all the past, the present and the future.

CHAPTER X

I

A NOISE penetrated Bessie's consciousness, a sound of fluttering and twittering and squeaking. Wainwright, who had dozed off just at dawn, muttered " Rats ", and sank into a deeper slumber. Bessie tried desperately not to wake up. She clung to the slippery edge of unconsciousness with her eyes shut. Recalling last night ; the mosquitoes ; the mysterious breathing against the wall ; Maurice, the perfect lover, swearing as he trod on a hairbrush ; she was graceless enough to grin. Then, fully awake, she decided to investigate those twitterings, and so slipped out of bed.

It was easy to do so, because Maurice, in bed, was the perfect cuckoo, only completely satisfied when he had made himself a little nest of blankets and thrust his partner on to the minimum, chilly edge of the conjugal couch. Bessie half wished he would wake up and admire her silk nightdress. It seemed a shame to bring it out on an adventure and take it home unnoticed.

The noises were definitely bird noises and they came from the next room. Standing quietly in the doorway, she observed a small, dark object, with a forked tail, shoot through the window and make for a patch of clay close to the roof. Several ugly, small nestlings held out wide beaks into which their parent snappily thrust whatever it carried.

" A swallow," Bessie told herself delightedly. Esther would have explained the difference between swifts and cliff martins and house martins, their colouring and habits, but to Bessie they were all swallows. She enjoyed this, her first bird's nest, as a country child might have enjoyed the novelty of a boat or tram. The day took on an importance with her discovery. Another small, dark bird shot in at the window and twittered to the first. They seemed to be discussing her, so Bessie stood very quiet, and presently deciding that she represented no immediate danger to clay nests or young nestlings, the birds swooped away.

Bessie glanced round at Maurice but he showed no signs of waking. He lay on his back, mouth open, snoring in an exhausted fashion. No one looks his best in such conditions ; and Maurice, Bessie noted impersonally, looked worse than anyone she had ever seen. This, strangely enough, aroused a tenderness in her, a deeper attraction, so that she shook her head impatiently. Hadn't she wasted enough time and emotion on this love business ? It was either a complete " wash-out " or else it needed a different kind of girl. Anyway, she was going to cut it right out, and she had made up her mind to have yet one more " show-down " with Maurice in which she would make this clear to him. However, that could wait.

Appraisingly she regarded the stretch of weeds, paddy's lucerne, thorn-apple, inkweed and smart-grass that had once been a ploughed field. The ground was stony and, apart from the traces of cultivation, went down to the creek in edges of rock, in dried watercourses and slopes of gritty, grey soil tangled with fallen trees and thick wattle. A person, Bessie decided, could carry rocks and build them so that the whole hillside was in time terraced in flower beds, vegetable beds, sheltered, sunny, well drained. Water ? There was the spring behind the house and surely you could get pipes to take it down-hill. She began to picture what the slope would look like if a person planted fruit trees so that they would flower here and there.

The clearing was alive with sunlight and birds and leaves. There were black-and-white birds looking like whisky advertisements and tiptoeing along on black stilt legs, making a noise like " Cool, cool ". There were silver-eyes tinkling through the bushes, while a grey bird which had been paddling its long legs in the water rose with a swish and flapped away just as Bessie reached the creek.

All the spider-webs had the light caught in their fetters ; they sagged with the weight of water-drops. The leaves of the trees glittered, the creek flashed like broken glass. A large, mud-coloured cow came deliberately slobbering down the trodden bank, and stopped to twist its tongue around a tall stalk of paspalum, then lumbered on unconcernedly. The way the cow walked was new to Bessie. It went along like a fat woman without corsets, but its hips were really quite thin and hollow. Then again, as it set its feet down, they seemed to buckle at the ankles and its udder swung about curiously, a clumsy-looking contrivance for holding milk, not half as efficient as a milk-can.

The idea of milk suggested breakfast. Perhaps along the bank whence the cow had come there might be milk in drinkable form divested of the surrounding cow. This seemed such excellent reasoning that Bessie trotted up the slope again and dug a small, competent hand into Maurice's pocket for silver.

The creek wound about in a very drunken fashion, almost as though the smell of leaves, the glittering and bubbling of birds and water-drops had set its wits whirling like the eddies under the rocks. The path along the bank was paved with grass and black mud, littered with cow manure and debris of past floods. Something inside Bessie gave a leap of joy. She stopped impulsively and pulled off her shoes, twisting her toes in the mucky pathway. That was better, much better. She watched the good black mud squelch between her toes and barely resisted the impulse to take off her tight green flowered dress and slip into the creek, flowing very green and deep under the opposite bank. But she had no bathing costume and had never swum without a bathing costume in her life.

Then it struck her that, for the first time in months, she had an opportunity to practise her whistling. This was the very morning to whistle, here was the very place, miles from anywhere. A number of birds, who had been engaged in the same sport, stopped, Bessie felt, respectfully as she whistled her best. Maurice had spent time and trouble improving Bessie's taste, but, to her, music was still a tune you could whistle. She now cheerfully fluted : " If you were the Only Girl in the World . . ."

She was so taken up with it that she came round a corner into a cow-yard before there was time to pretend that she had not been whistling. An elderly woman, with a hard, wrinkled face, was milking a cow patched red and white with little smears of red on it, as though it had rubbed against a newly painted fence. The cow's calf was fenced away in a sapling yard. The woman sat with her shiny tin bucket between her knees, and her hard, red fingers spurted the milk into the bucket in little purring jets. Bessie halted, then came nearer quietly so that she would not interrupt the woman in her interesting task, but the woman did not seem to mind. She turned to carry on a conversation, while her hands kept their automatic jerking at the cow.

" Y' livin' down this way ? " the woman called. " I ain't seen y' about before, have I ? "

" No," Bessie explained. " I'm only staying. Down

there." She pointed down the creek.

The woman was interested. " Well, now, fancy that ! They told me someone got off the train and went down to the Gullick place. Two, they said. Has Esther Gullick gone then ? "

" No, she hasn't gone." Bessie was cautious. " Only I've come. That's all."

" Oh, I thought she might 'ave moved out. When they says it was a man and a woman, I says, well, maybe they'll make something *of* the place. It's a real sin the way she don't do a hand's turn, just lets that land go to rack and ruin. 'Er brother Lester used to say to me sometimes, ' Mrs. Tracy,' 'e said, ' my sister has other work.' But I says to him, ' Nonsense, Lester, you don't call foolin' round with beetles and bugs work for a grown woman, do you ? Nor going round like a lunatic out in the bush all day ? ' Lester used to get real mad at me sometimes, but 'e knows I don't really think Esther's cracked the way some of them are. I just think maybe bein' in the sun so much and all that cleverness and all them books . . ." She broke off and inspected Bessie. " I don't s'pose Lester sent you ? "

" No, he didn't send us."

" So there was *two* of you. Are you related to the Gullicks, maybe ? "

Bessie began to feel impatient under this catechism. " No, just friends."

" Lester's the one with the business head," Mrs. Tracy went on placidly, her cheek against the cow. " You ain't met Lester ? Well, 'e's the real one of the Gullicks. No mooning about for him. He'd have that place one of the best about here if it weren't for his sister livin' in it rent-free and all. Lester can afford it, of course. 'E's got plenty, what with 'is shops selling in three suburbs." She was almost confiding in Bessie. " 'Ardware, 'e's in, and does well at it too."

Bessie decided to close the saga of the Gullick brother, Lester. "How do you do that?" she asked, pointing to the cow. "Is it hard to do?"

"Why, it's that easy a baby could milk. Ain't you ever milked?"

"I want to buy some. Could you spare a pint?"

"Why, of course. We always got more'n we need with the two cows."

Bessie was emboldened by the woman's manner. "I say," she said anxiously. "Could I have a try?"

The woman laughed. "You got to get the hang of it. It's only easy after you know how."

Bessie rested her head carefully against the rough flank of the cow, and as the cow stirred, quickly moved it away. She gingerly placed her fingers round the cow's teats and found that nothing happened, except that the cow stamped angrily.

"Look, like this." The woman showed her. "Miss . . .?"

"Bessie's my name."

"Like this, Bessie. You sort of soothe the milk down. Watch."

Bessie tried again. This time she managed to squirt milk all over her dress and sprang up dismayed.

"Look what I've done."

"Well, dear, dear, look at that," Mrs. Tracy responded in true feminine fashion to the disaster. "You wait till I finish this cow and we'll go inside and sponge it for you. Real pretty that dress is."

"It's the only one I have with me."

"Fancy that now."

By the time the milk had been decanted into the jug Bessie had brought, and her dress was sponged, and she had been presented with four new-laid eggs and a bottle of jam, Mrs. Tracy knew all about Bessie and all about the gentleman Bessie worked for, and all about the studio and her home and family, and she was almost sure she knew a Mrs. Emily Drew who used to live at Concord West and kept a dairy there who might have been Bessie's great-aunt.

" Well, fancy that now," Mrs. Tracy kept repeating. " The world's a small place, I always say."

Bessie liked Mrs. Tracy and Mr. Tracy, who, from his seat on the back door-step, grunted that the missus did enough talking for two, so he didn't need to say nuthin'. She liked the wild-looking, barefooted Tracy children who swarmed out of the house and went yelling into the undergrowth at her approach, more from mischief than any shyness. Even the four dogs, who had probably barked at her last night, sniffed her bare heels in friendly fashion.

She gathered that Mr. Tracy was a night watchman and went every evening to the city, that he had only just got the job through the intervention of a friend of his cousin's and had previously existed on the dole, child endowment, and what he could get from his patch of paddock. They offered Bessie a cup of tea, pointing out that the kettle was boiling. It was a black kettle that looked as if it was always boiling ; but Bessie decided that Maurice would be awake and wondering where she was. Laden with gifts, she departed well pleased, leaving the Tracys just as well pleased with the major scandal she had introduced into their unexciting lives.

" Fancy a nice young girl like 'er bein' there alone with a man ! "

" Yer sure the Gullick woman ain't there ? "

" Why, Joe Tracy, I seen 'er with me own eyes goin' along the road with one of them knapsacks on 'er back and a cigarette in 'er mouth as large as life Friday night. An' she ain't been back since."

Bessie was untroubled by the speculations of the Tracys. As she wandered back to the hut, she was congratulating

149

Esther on having such jolly neighbours. Bessie's mother, at Number 71, had neighbours, but you were not allowed to speak to them. Mrs. Drew knew all about her neighbours from the butcher and the grocer and the rabbit-o. She knew all about Mrs. Murphy's drunken son and Mrs. Whipple's cough. But although some neighbours in Archer Street spoke to each other, they never gave out milk and new-laid eggs.

"Look what I've got," Bessie announced, her eyes shining as she held out the four new-laid eggs to Maurice as though they were diamonds. "Some people up the creek gave them to me."

Maurice was sitting on the back door-step without his collar. He was enthusiastic about the eggs and jam.

"Splendid !" he exclaimed. "I wondered where the dickens you were, but now I forgive you." He put his arm round her waist and hugged her affectionately. "Trust you to raise a meal, even in the middle of a wilderness."

"Wilderness ?" Bessie's happiness was momentarily clouded. "Don't you like it — this place ?"

"For a change, yes. But to live here, good God, no."

Bessie looked at the sunny morning and sighed. "I can't think of anything better than living in a place like this."

"Ants, mosquitoes, flies, weeds, snails, worms, ticks and hornets, all agree with you. The place gets over-crowded with them. I prefer the comparative solitude of a city. The city is my natural habitat." He rose reluctantly. "I suppose I'll have to get some wood. Another of the pleasures of a simple life."

They neither of them wished to refer to last night. After their late breakfast Wainwright insisted on playing Beethoven's Concerto, going over and over the parts he liked best. Bessie washed up and, once, when she forgot the Concerto was being played, she whistled.

" Bessie ! "

" Huh ? " Bessie stuck her head round the cubby-hole of a kitchen. " Want something ? "

" Ssssh ! "

" Oh ! Sorry."

The Concerto went on its way without further challenge. As it concluded, Bessie came in and perched on the table shyly. She had been rehearsing what she was going to say to Maurice ; and he could tell from the look of her that she was going to deliver an ultimatum, probably unpleasant. He felt reluctant to turn the record over.

" Maurice." As the last strains died away, Bessie was ready to spring. " Maurice, about last night . . ."

" Must we hold a post-mortem ? "

" Well, it's this way. . . ." Maurice sighed resignedly and lit a cigarette. " I feel a bit of a dud at this love-making game. We don't seem to get very far. Anyway, it strikes me as a wash-out."

" Bessie," her friend said patiently, " if you had ever participated in this love-making game, as you call it, you might change your opinion. But you are simply not in the position to judge." He raised his hand as she tried to interrupt. " You are of those children who say they don't like olives. Olives are an acquired taste. And how do you know you don't like olives if you haven't tasted them ? "

Bessie grinned a vulgar, back-alley grin. " Strikes me I'll never get the chance. First it's Ernie. Then it's a horse. Next time it's sure to be something else. Look, suppose we just give it up as a bad job and get back to tors. I'll go on working in the studio and you can kiss me if you want to any time, and we'll call it quits and let it go at that."

Maurice sprang up, his mouth a tight line, his eyes narrowed. She had never seen him so raging angry before. His knuckles, when he gripped the table, were white. "Say that again," he said, in a low, strained voice.

"I don't see what you're getting so mad about," Bessie went on patiently. "If a thing doesn't work, what's the use of wasting time on it? Here's twice we've had this hoodoo on us. And it just looks as though the idea is no good. I say we might, with a bit of an effort, get back on our old footing, me working as mate, and you . . ."

"I could choke the life out of you," he raged. "You don't know what you're saying. You just don't know what you're saying, or else you're so incredibly cold that you've just been taking this as a light, girlish diversion, something to satisfy your curiosity." He looked round, his eyes blazing, for something to break. "I can't believe it. I just can't believe my ears."

Bessie was used to Maurice's rages, but she was honestly perplexed by this latest tantrum. Then it struck her that Maurice must think she didn't love him any longer.

"Don't think I'm not fond of you," she assured him. "It isn't that a bit. But it just seems a waste of time getting all stirred up when it's just as easy not to get stirred up."

"Oh, is it?" he sneered. "I suppose you think that after this I'm likely to see you come into the studio and hang up your hat and say good-morning, and just nod a cool good-morning in return."

"Why not? If I can do it, why not you?"

He almost snarled at her. "Because you're a stupid, ignorant, perverse, little hell-cat. If you were a man I'd knock you down, and, by God, if I had a horsewhip I think I'd beat you. And I'd enjoy it."

Bessie kept her temper. "If we'd made a success of this love business," she argued logically, "we might carry on with it. But I bet, if it hadn't been the horse, it would have been something else. Either I would have made a mess of things, or you would, or something." She realized that she was not being tactful. " As it is, I vote we chuck the whole idea."

" Bessie ! Will you stop talking like a putty image ? Don't you realize what you're doing to me ? " He came and gripped her shoulders with those long fingers of his in such a cruel hold that Bessie could have cried out. He swayed her to and fro as though she were a toy. " You stand there . . . Oh, what's the use ? " He turned suddenly and bitterly away. " You're just a child. Just a silly child. Go on, prattle some more."

The tears sprang to Bessie's eyes. " I don't know what you're talking about," she cried hopelessly. " Here am I trying to think what to do and you carry on like a lunatic. I love you, Maurice, I do really. I'd do anything for you. I want you to be a success. I want you to be happy, to work with you and love you and look after you. And when I try to think what's best . . ."

He roused himself from a sullen abstraction. " Keep right on talking," he said rudely. " I'm not listening, but it keeps you occupied."

Bessie wiped the tears away. She went inside to her suitcase, found her handkerchief and blew her nose. By the time she returned, Maurice had simmered down a little.

" I suppose I might have expected this after last night," he said drearily.

Bessie came over to him timidly.

" Maurice ? "

He managed to raise the ghost of a smile. " What is it, kid ? "

" Maurice, I take it all back."

He patted her soothingly. " It was my fault, kid. I shouldn't have . . ." He turned away so that she should not see his face. " I should have known better than to take you for a woman when you're only a baby."

" No," Bessie said vehemently, cut to the quick by this unwarranted insult. " No. Listen, Maurice. Suppose we have another shot at it ? I realize I'm not much good, not having any experience, but . . ."

" For God's sake shut up," he flung at her through his teeth. " The more you talk the worse it gets." Bessie was instantly quiet. After a minute he went on : " You've hurt me. Hurt me in a way I thought nothing could hurt. But I deserve it. No doubt of that. Oh, well ! " He shrugged his shoulders and looked round for the eternal cigarette. " You're right, Bessie. We'd better chuck it."

She put her arms round him and hugged him. " Look, Maurice, I'll be good. Anything you say goes with me."

He gripped her hand. " Queer little person."

" Don't say that. You can't put me in my place any longer."

He looked at her remotely. " Where is your place, Bessie ? "

" I don't know," she answered helplessly. " A fine mess I make of things."

They sat dejectedly side by side. Presently Bessie said : " I worked it out like this . . ."

" Don't," Wainwright interrupted in a tired voice, " don't start again."

" Well, I have to get it off my chest. I worked it out that if I was a real success as a love-maker you'd maybe want to marry me, and we could run the studio together."

" Eh ? "

" Well, that struck me as a good idea. I know you haven't much time for marriage, Maurice, and after all you don't know how I'd turn out. You haven't known me so long."

" It seems a hundred years. But you're right about the prejudice against marriage. I thought I told you about Rose." From the way he mentioned this, Bessie gathered that he told most young ladies about Rose sooner or later.

" Well, you've got to get married some time," she said defensively.

" Why ? "

Bessie stared at him. " Everyone does."

" There are times, Bessie, when you make me feel tired," Wainwright murmured patiently.

" Look at it this way. . . ."

" Must you go on ? "

" Oh, Maurice, give me a chance. Look at it this way. If you don't want to make it a real partnership, what's the use of fooling round with this love business ? "

" True. Very true." He leant back with his eyes closed. " But I have a headache."

" I'll get you a glass of water and an aspirin in a minute, but you've got to listen now."

" You're a predatory female, Bessie."

" I'm not. I'm thinking of looking after you, not living on you. I'm useful, aren't I ? And you've no idea how well I can cook."

" I take it you're proposing to me."

" I don't know *what* you want," Bessie exclaimed hopelessly. " I suggest we chuck love-making and just stay friends, and you go into a rage. I suggest we get married, and you go all worn and weary on me and get a headache. What *do* you want ? "

" One thing I don't want is to carry on this impossible conversation any longer."

Bessie became as grim and steely as ever Wainwright could be. " Right," she said, springing up. " That goes for me too. I'll get you a cup of tea."

She served him the tea in a silence that would have done credit to a gaoler bringing the condemned man's last meal. Maurice was lying down on the bed with his eyes closed.

" Thank you, kid," he said, as the tea arrived.

Bessie did not reply.

" For heaven's sake, sit down ! Don't stand there looking at me as though you hoped the tea would choke me."

Bessie, still with her lips tight shut, sat down on the end of the bed. Maurice regarded her humorously over the edge of the cup. " Kid," he said, in his old whimsical drawl, " you win."

Bessie continued to sit in a hostile silence.

" You're perfectly right." Maurice was penitent. " Consider yourself engaged. And as soon as I can borrow enough for a licence, darling, I'm yours."

Bessie had not moved an eyelid.

" Well ? " He reached out to touch her hand. " I haven't given you a fair deal, Bessie. You're right, but if you'll overlook it . . . what do you say ? "

Bessie snapped : " Do you want some more tea ? "

" Bessie ! " Maurice felt this was no way to receive a capitulation. " Kid, why are you acting like this ? "

She flared at him. " To-morrow you'll be going the rounds giving the impression you were trapped into something. Oh no, thank you. Being married to you would be a heavenly dream." She breathed angrily through her nose. " I don't think ! And if you believe I tried to get you to sleep with me just so I could make you marry me after . . . forget it."

" I didn't." He was on the defensive. " I never said that. Not for a minute."

" I only wanted to do what you wanted to do. And I wanted to too. I'm not pretending I didn't. But it was a case of we'd either got to go ahead or back, and marriage meant going ahead, and going back to the studio as we stand means going back."

" I agree with you," he said gravely. " I do agree with you."

" Well, I don't see where you've got any kick coming.
I put the two different ways we could go and you went
mad at me."

" I haven't your logical, impersonal outlook."

" Now you're just being sarcastic again. It makes me
want to belt the hide off you."

" I'm pleased to hear it," he grinned. " Perhaps you
know a little how I felt when you made your preposterous
suggestion that we revert to a state of platonic indifference."

Bessie sighed. " I'm getting a bit tired of talking."
She wearily snuggled down beside him.

Maurice arranged her head comfortably on his
shoulder. " I'm pleased to hear that," he repeated.
" But a little surprised. I thought you were good for
another three hours. After we are married you will
probably reach heights undreamt. The inheritance from
your mother."

" Oh, go to sleep," Bessie murmured drowsily.

He turned over to kiss her and buried his nose in her
hair and shut his eyes. They were both completely spent.
They had worn themselves out in quarrelling and were
now prepared to return to the *status quo* of affectionate
pleasure in each other's presence. In their drowsy state
the twitterings of the swallows had faded into nothingness when the door creaked and someone observed sar-
donically:

" I hate to disturb you, Maurice, but if you leave the
door open . . ."

" That will be Esther," Bessie remarked, without
moving from the comfortable place in Maurice's shoulder.

" Congratulate us, Esther," Maurice announced amiably. " We're engaged."

Esther regarded them equivocally, then took off her
glasses and wiped them.

" So I see," she said drily.

II

"I didn't think you'd be back so soon." Maurice showed a noticeable lack of enthusiasm. After all, a man ought to have a second chance to prove himself the perfect lover.

Esther, it appeared, had been camping on a favourite beach fifteen miles away.

"I came back," she explained, "because the place was infested with trippers and hikers and tents and ukeleles. I hope you've been looking after yourselves."

Bessie yawned. "We had an awful night. First, there was a moth got in and flipped all round the place . . ."

"What kind of a moth?" Esther was interested.

"Just a moth. Then the mosquitoes nearly ate us. Then a horse came and bumped itself against the side of the house." Bessie began to gurgle with laughter. She laughed until Maurice thumped her between the shoulders and commanded her to stop. "We were scared stiff. You should have heard Maurice, Esther, when he got out of bed and trod on the hairbrush."

"I have an excellent imagination," Esther said drily. She had taken from her knapsack the body of a very, very dead sea-bird. "Most unusual," she explained, "to find this particular kind of tern at this season."

Without further comment she unlocked a large cupboard in the corner of the living-room and bestowed the body on a shelf for further investigation, among nobbly chunks of rock, a collection of assorted weeds, cocoons, boxes of beetles and other naturalistic debris. Then, discovering the Concerto, she lovingly started up the gramophone and, while Bessie prepared lunch, Esther and Maurice sat smoking each other's cigarettes and disputing the rival claims of composers.

"Bessie has fallen in love with this place," Maurice mentioned. "You should have seen the way she looked at those Christmas bells yesterday afternoon. As though someone had poured a fortune at her feet."

" There is a fortune in them," Esther replied. " Ron Chugg up the road imported some seed from the United States and crossed it with his Christmas bells to get a longer stalk and bigger blooms. He sold some of the biggest for threepence each and picked seven thousand last Christmas."

Maurice was doing sums in his head. " Why don't you sell yours ? "

Esther shook her head. " Why should I ? Not in my line." She looked at Bessie. " Now, if I had someone here who cared for farming and selling the stuff . . . Anything will grow here. Fruit and vegetables bring good prices, particularly if you take a load out on the main road and sell direct to the motorists."

Bessie's eyes shone. " That would be a great idea. Wouldn't it, Maurice ? "

" It sounds ghastly. Imagine me selling cabbages to motorists." He laughed. " I always knew there was a streak of the peasant in you, kid." He got up and strolled to the door. " I'm going for a walk. Don't let me cramp your ardour for the simple life, Bessie, but our train leaves at five."

" I never knew there were places like this," Bessie said, a little wistfully. " Gee, it'd be great to come down that track and see it shining below you and say, ' That's my place.' "

Esther's face was gentle. " That's the feeling that makes a peasant turn out with a hay-fork to face machine-guns. You'd be a patriot, Bessie, if you only had the chance."

" But that's flags and bands," Bessie objected vaguely.

" Not a bit of it. Patriotism is a passion for a place."

" Like Maurice liking the city ? "

" You can't be patriotic about a city. Too many people

have their thoughts and their boot-marks all over it."

"If it wasn't for Maurice," Bessie said slowly, "I'd be saying : This is what I've been looking for and I'm staying for good." Her frank, steady gaze held Esther's determinedly.

"Why not ? "

"I'm going to marry Maurice."

Esther tapped on the table with her finger. "It's an infatuation," she said irritably. "I hoped you'd be cured of it, if you only . . ." She broke off. "Why do you think I lent you this place ? Not only because I knew you'd love it. You can't find out much about a man just working with him. You've got to live with him and have him make a pest of himself. Of course," she admitted liberally, "you don't have to live with Maurice to know he's a pest. But I hoped . . ."

"I'm going to marry him all the same."

"My good girl, you're mad. He isn't the marrying kind. He's a monk."

Bessie looked surprised.

"He's a monk, I tell you," Esther repeated irritably. "The civilization of cities is breeding a new race of monks who have none of the original religious drive towards chastity, but are just incapable of facing the responsibilities of marriage. They're incapable of adjusting themselves to the more complex life of monogamy, because they have been brought up in an environment that unfits them for it, a life of slight social contacts, of mass amusements, of selfish and easy satisfactions. Men ! " She flicked her fingers contemptuously.

They were silent for a while. This was the first time Esther had made such a speech to Bessie. Her words were usually dry and few.

"Well, I'm going to marry Maurice," Bessie reiterated slowly.

"Uh-huh." Esther had recovered her good-humour.

" All I hope is that your infants turn out like him. Serve you right."

Bessie grinned. " Thanks again," she said, and they began to feel on better terms.

With her usual shrewd sense, Esther had long ago realized that she was lonely and in Bessie she had found someone whose outlook approximated almost to her own in its disregard for social formulas. Bessie did not fit into any clique, but stood on her own worth as an individual, firm in her faith that work counted more than words, eager to learn but not to accept ideas ready-made. She was so healthy, so devoid of moral judgments, so comfortably adaptable, so unspoilt by over-education. In Esther's eyes Bessie's main fault was her foolish addiction to Maurice, her unswerving decision to remake him and push him into a mould for which he was never meant.

" Only fools and fanatics," Esther said half wistfully, " never change their minds."

Maurice came across the paddock shouting and waving his arms excitedly. " Bessie ! Esther ! I've got the scheme of the century. I'm going to revolutionize the outback." He sank gasping into a chair. " It came to me in a flash. Just like that ! Inspiration ! I was down there beside the creek — don't clear the things away, Bessie. I want another cup of tea — and a cow came down to drink, and I began to think how plentiful water was here and how they pump it in droughts. And then it flashed into my mind : Why not make the animals pump their own water ? " He began to draw on the back of an envelope. " You'd have to build a runway like this, so that when your sheep or cattle approached the dam they'd have to walk along a moving belt connected . . . here . . . and here . . . with the pumping apparatus there, and as they walk along, they turn this, and this, so by the time they reach the tank they've pumped a gallon or so of water."

" Not bad," Esther said tolerantly, " but uneconomical."

" What do you mean ? Uneconomical ? The exigencies of the small farmer . . ."

" I think it's wonderful," Bessie declared loyally, frowning at Esther.

" Have it your own way." Esther decided that you could never reason with a woman who felt maternally about a man.

Late in the afternoon Bessie and Wainwright departed, Maurice insisting that it was essential that he should consult an engineer friend of his that night about the details of the new invention. Esther waved good-bye from the doorway to her two guests.

" Don't forget," she called to Bessie. " Any time you want to come down, just come."

Maurice's indignant back, the set of his shoulders, boded ill for Bessie when he should be out of earshot. He was already framing a choice selection of the things he wished Bessie to hear about Esther, and " frustrated spinster " and " vinegarish shrew " were not the worst of them.

Esther, turning back into the darkened house, paused thoughtfully, then, lighting the lamp, she went over and unlocked the cupboard. The rather noisome sea-bird she brought over to the table, settling happily to an inspection of certain wing markings, certain peculiarities of the beak that had interested her.

Presently she sat back and wiped her glasses. An almost childish wonder was on her hard, tight-skinned face, an expression of simple pleasure that made her in that instant curiously akin to Bessie. Just that same worshipful look that Bessie had first given the studio when it began to blossom in its green silk and theatrical grandeur. Then the look changed to one of intense concentration. She reached for paper and a fountain-pen and began to take notes. Outside the old horse cropped gluttonously at the long grass beside the house ; a possum scuttered chattering across the roof. Esther noticed them no more than she did the perfume of the sea-bird, its all too obvious state of disrepair. Late into the night she wrote on and on.

CHAPTER XI

I

THE studio seemed shabbier, more flamboyantly theatrical after Esther's hut. Dust had settled on it while Bessie was away, and as she cleaned, the disloyal thought strayed into her mind that soap and water constituted her only contribution to the taste in which the place was furnished. Maurice had built it as a shell for himself, a shell that fitted his personality. Wherever Maurice went he altered surroundings to suit himself or wrecked them. That was why he could never fit into a boarding-house, why he had been so uneasy in a strong-willed place like Esther's. Maurice was a charge of dynamite smashing the atoms of things into other shapes than they were meant to be. He had smashed her into another shape than she had intended, into the shape of his shadow. She moved, as he moved, through a welter of restless plans. They were all around her like a heaving sea.

One plan was fixed, however, for Maurice was wholly in earnest, wholly taken up with the idea of marriage.

" We'll get a flat," he said warmly, " at King's Cross. It's so Continental, so full of interesting people and un-usual little shops. I like the colour and gaiety of the street stalls and the cafés. What d'you say ? "

" How about a cottage ? " Bessie asked. " With perhaps a bit of a garden where I could grow vegetables."

Wainwright regarded her frowning. " You've had this craze for vegetables ever since you came back from Esther's horrid little hut. Of course I can see your ideals are still those of Archer Street." He was deliberately cruel. " I could always spend my afternoons mowing the lawn of some hovel in a row of similar hovels with a hideous uniformity of squalor. . . . Don't make me writhe ! "

Bessie accepted the rebuke, feeling that it was well merited. She had regretted the suggestion the instant it was made and would have done anything to recall it. But lately, almost in spite of herself, she found herself reading such items as " Root Crops " and " Pruning Notes " ; and the idea of being out of the city, out in the open, now the weather was growing so warm, overcame her almost like a homesickness. To be cooped up in a flat, listening to intellectual conversations for the rest of her life, running errands, forming an audience, a competent background for Maurice ! Little by little the prospect of marriage was tinged by a smothered disloyalty. Was there any real difference after all between working competently in a factory, marrying the foreman, and putting in the rest of your life getting meals in a cottage ; and working in a studio, marrying your boss, and living in a flat ? Then she remembered that it was she who had offered to marry Maurice. He had not offered to marry her. As she had made the proposal, she ought to stand by it.

Perhaps this inner rebellion was more than anything due to Bessie's astonished discovery that Maurice took for granted that she would stay home after they were married. Bessie had pictured herself coming in to the studio every day with Maurice and going home to keep house at night. Marriage to her meant extra work. She had seen too much of it in Archer Street to regard it in any other light, and had honestly considered that she was making Maurice a good offer when she proposed to him, an offer that showed a keen interest in his welfare.

But Maurice had waved his hands, as though he were wafting a set of gossamer difficulties from his path. " One's wife," he asserted, " must be a jewel in a guarded casket."

" How do you get that way ? " Bessie was indignant. " I don't show any signs of just sitting about. Not if I can help it."

" I spoke metaphorically." Maurice, after dinner, was apt to speak metaphorically. It was the sign of a satisfied digestion. " To come home to a woman, fragrant, gracious, charming, after a day of toil, is surely one of the most pleasurable of life's rewards."

Bessie grunted rebelliously.

" I am old-fashioned," Maurice continued, rather charmed with himself in the role of the hard business man who has yet kept his illusions. " I am old-fashioned in the sense that I feel a man's home should be a place apart. He should, as it were, drink from a hidden spring."

" You try and find a hidden spring in King's Cross," Bessie replied grimly, from a bitter experience of the " To Let " columns. She did not really believe that Maurice would maintain this attitude that " a woman's place was the home " ; but she would not put it past him to try. Sometimes she suspected that Maurice was a little resentful of her efficiency in small matters, that he would like to slop about the studio in a big way, undismayed by neatly filed bills with their innocent little faces staring up at him from the desk where Bessie had arranged them.

On their return from the hut, their first impulse to rush off and be married at once had been chilled by the problem : " How do you go about it ? "

" There are legal formalities," Maurice explained, with a wave of his hand. " Legal formalities. Papers to sign."

The very thought of signing papers quenched their ardour.

" Suppose we say we'll get married on the 1st of next month," Maurice proposed, as October, then November, went past and they still remained single.

Bessie agreed, because she was rather tired of talking about this wedding. " We'll need some money," she advised cautiously. " You can't run a furnished flat on nothing."

" I had decided to make provision for contingencies." Maurice resented this implied doubt of his practical ability. " I suggest we set aside a wedding fund and add to it each week."

Bessie looked at him admiringly. " Oh, Maurice, that's a great idea ! "

" We're not doing so badly." Maurice straightened his shoulders and registered modest pride, ignoring the large pile of bills, all, as usual, neatly filed. " I actually paid two weeks' back rent this week. Old Fullman nearly burst into tears of gratitude, poor man."

" And Maurice," Bessie hesitated, " I haven't told my family about . . . us. Now that we are going to be married next month, do you think I should tell them ? "

" Must you ? " Maurice looked glum. " Couldn't you leave it until it's too late for them to be demonstrative? "

" Well, I guess they'd feel relieved," Bessie objected sturdily. " I ought to let them enjoy themselves at least that much."

" Have it your own way." Maurice raised his hand. " But, I beg of you, restrain them from any idea of visitings and junketings and gruesomeness in the form of kitchen teas."

He fully expected an effusive welcome from Bessie's degraded relations. Never having any reason to dislike himself, he could not realize the ungovernable hatred the Drew family harboured.

" They're likely to carry on a treat," Bessie prophesied with more truth than she knew.

The Drew family had settled into a philosophical attitude towards Bessie, her employment and her employer, on the principle that if Bessie hadn't gone to the bad, she'd had plenty of opportunity. In any case, there were so many interesting domestic storms rolling over the horizon. Bessie had sunk in a much less important position in the war annals of the tribe since George hit his father over the head with a plate and Beryl had taken up with a bookmaker's clerk. In fact, Bessie had even settled appeals on nice points of conduct, such as her father's habit of spitting prune stones on the floor, on the grounds that " she mixed with these silvertails and ought to know ".

When Bessie broke the news that she was about to marry her employer, an awful silence descended on her relatives assembled. Immediately they sprang to the conclusion that Bessie was going to have a baby, something they had suspected all along. Their impulse was to sally out in a body and tear her scoundrelly betrayer apart.

" Disgusting, I call it," Beryl said, with a superior lift of the eyebrow. " An old man like him."

" I told you you'd get yourself into trouble," Mrs. Drew shrilled. " But you wouldn't take any notice, not you."

Bessie ground her teeth. It was no use arguing ; that only made matters worse. She rose from the table in the midst of their reproaches. " You give me a pain," she raged, as she slammed out the door. " This is the last time I ever tell you any of my business. From now on I'm through."

" I'll go in there and break his neck," she heard her father booming behind her ; but the threat carried little weight. On a number of previous occasions Mr. Drew had threatened murder with not even a black eye as the outcome.

Bessie tramped angrily into the backyard, down to the privet tree beside the tool-shed. It was a scrawny little privet, very ill-used ; but it had nevertheless a showing of white, feathery flowers very pleasant to beetles. Bessie was very hungry and very angry and, as she raged up and down the little strip of yard, it seemed to her that the whole world was full of stupidity and misunderstanding. Why couldn't people recognize that there was such a thing as a working partnership between a man and a woman ? Maurice had brains and personality, while she had a certain business capacity. Why not combine forces, particularly as she and Maurice were so much in love ? She felt very cold and virtuous when she thought of her evil-minded family imputing all kinds of offensive motives to a sensible life partnership. Then she had the grace to smile, as she reflected what a shindy there would be if ever they found out about her week-end with Maurice. Rendered a little more tolerant by her hunger and the thought that this subject for a lovely row had been withheld from her family, Bessie trotted back into the house, her small, snub nose very much in the air.

Her family was by this time involved in a bitter argument as to which church was to have the privilege of marrying Bessie. In the distant past she had attended a Methodist, a Presbyterian and a Foursquare Gospel Sunday school. She had also attended a convent school for several terms because an aunt insisted that this would teach her to speak nicely. Bessie's religion, owing to this mixture, was of the vaguest and most comfortable kind, and her prospective husband, as far as she knew, would have raised his eyebrows at the mention of a church, but her parents, Bessie found to her surprise, were showing symptoms of deep religious bigotry.

" Mr. Hawkins of the Methodists did Cousin Jane and

I'd like to see 'im do Bessie," Mrs. Drew declared. " You can't beat a real solid Methodist wedding."

Mr. Drew pounded on the table with his fist. " I've got the say in this house," he thundered. " And I say she's going to be done by that Presbyterian whatsisname that christened her. If he christened her, 'e's got a right to her, ain't 'e ? "

Bessie strolled over to the dresser and helped herself to some custard and jelly.

" I remember when I had 'em christened," Mr. Drew rumbled. " I was coming home with the parson on the tram one night. Real nice feller 'e was too. Didn't mind a bit that I'd had a few at the pub, and we got talkin' about christenings and that, and I says to 'im : 'Well, it can't do 'em any harm and I've got a batch of kids at home. If you like to come up an' christen 'em, I wouldn't put nothing in your way.' An' he come." He turned to Beryl for support. " You remember that, don't you, Beryl ? Bessie wouldn't be old enough to remember but he come up and done you all together."

Beryl shrugged her shoulders huffily. Her young man had not as yet mentioned the possibilities of matrimony.

" She's too young," she said. " You got to get your family's consent under twenty-one."

Bill Drew's face lit up. He smote the table delightedly. " You hit the nail on the head that time ! So she has. You hear that ? " He turned on Bessie. " You try an' get married, see, without me letting you, and I'll pretty soon show you what's what. The hide of a kid like you comin' home and saying she's goin' to get married. Like fun you are. And when you do, it's going to be at the Presbyterians, an' I'm goin' to be there to see it done proper."

Bessie was in a bad mood. " O.K.," she said nastily. " You stop me getting married and I'll have twins and you'll have to explain me to the neighbours." And having collected enough food to stay her, she fled, leaving an alarmed debate to break out afresh as to whether she was just being a "poisonous little nark" or really meant it.

"Anyway she ain't goin' to get married," Bill Drew announced deliberately. "I'm not givin' my consent to her marryin' that slimy snake, not if I know it. I'll go and knock his face off first."

"You have your tea," Mrs. Drew sighed wearily. "And hold your noise. Bessie's one you can't roar at. She'll get her own way or bust."

The truth of this statement was so obvious that none of Bessie's family felt like denying it. Ever since she had been a solid, rather grumpy child, Bessie had had her own way. There was little likelihood that in a matter of marriage she would reverse all previous form.

II

The 1st of December was so manifestly unsuitable for the wedding, owing to a press of work and trouble with the developing, that Maurice and Bessie decided to put it off until after Christmas. There would be a lull in the portrait business after Christmas. Maurice had singed off his eyebrows experimenting with some new kind of magnesium powder, and was working with much pain and difficulty. Impossible in such circumstances to distract a man's mind by marriage. "Besides," he pointed out hopefully, "look how the fund's mounting up."

Maurice was so interested in the marriage fund that Bessie had difficulty in restraining him from diverting the petty cash to it. Maurice always concentrated heart and soul on whatever he was doing, and the marriage fund was his toy for the moment.

Bessie was rather relieved that the wedding was postponed. Flats were scarce and Maurice had been dissatisfied with the three she had selected for his inspection.

" We are not asking for anything palatial." He elevated his partially grown eyebrows over the best of the flats. " But one does require a modicum of quiet and comfort."

They had not broken into the marriage fund, except on three occasions when money was short and pressing bills had to be paid. Both of them regarded it honourably as a pledge of good intentions ; and the studio continued to muddle along in a way that fretted Bessie's orderly nature. She never interfered with what Maurice called " finance ", although now and again she would mention that some more than ordinarily exasperating bill might be met.

About the middle of December, Ernie came wildly into the studio with two hatless and collarless youths, at the sight of whom Bessie immediately stiffened.

" Maurice is out," she exclaimed, automatically making a spring for the door of the studio.

" Oh no, he's not." Ernie got there first and flung the door open. " Hey, Morrie, George and Bert want to see you. They're in a hole."

George and Bert looked as though they had newly emerged from a hole, a deep, very grimy hole. Bessie had suffered from the George-Bert combination before. They lived by painting pictures on the walls of any café which would feed them at so many meals per fresco. One trusting entrepreneur, who was about to open a large restaurant, had actually engaged George and Bert to paint scenes from Shakespeare around his walls, but made the fatal mistake of paying them in advance. Naturally the café opened without George or Bert or the scenes from Shakespeare. When the two appeared, unrepentant but with a beautiful hangover, the proprietor set up a tariff of so much per robe, so much per figure, and an extra threepence for every square yard of background. This was the way you had to treat George and Bert to bring out the best in them.

Bessie could hear snatches of loud and heated argument behind the green curtain.

"You fellows," Wainwright complained, "seem to think one is made of money. I tell you I can't possibly do it. You go and see Bessie."

"Not on your life," Ernie replied firmly. "She's got a heart like a bank door-step. Now come on, Morrie. It's only until the end of the month. They have to have their fares and a clean collar each. Morrie, old man, you wouldn't let a friend down."

From what Bessie could gather, George and Bert were urgently needed in Melbourne to help found an association of Writers and Artists of the Red Dawn, or some similar-sounding body, and they needed their fares.

"Bessie," Wainwright called feebly; and Bessie bounded in like a young terrier.

"Since when," she demanded, her hands on her hips, "have you mob got so feeble you can't walk ? "

They eyed her sullenly.

"If you want to get to Melbourne," Bessie went on wrathfully, "why don't you do what Alice and Joan did — walk on your feet."

"That may be all right for Alice and Joan," George said in a bored voice. "They were looking for work. But Bert and I are delegates. Besides the conference opens in three days, and it's a matter of five hundred miles."

"Alice and Joan got there in three days with lifts."

"Now you keep out of this, young Bessie," Ernie ordered. "This is an important event in the history of Australian culture, and George and Bert must be there to represent the artists of Sydney."

"How about you ? "

"I have already borrowed my fare," Ernie answered

virtuously. He massaged Maurice's sleeve. " How about it, old chap ? "

Wainwright was shaking his head uncertainly. " I can't, can I, Bessie ? "

" I can't stop you," Bessie replied very quietly. " It's your money, but at the same time, I'm asking you not to."

" There you are," Ernie exulted. " She's not stopping you."

" I'm telling you — no." She turned on her heel. If he does give those little wretches any money, she thought, I'm through with him.

It came as no surprise, however, when ten minutes later Ernie, George and Bert swooped past with triumphant smiles on their faces. Her heart was hot, not against them, for they were acting in the manner natural to them, but against Maurice who should have known better.

Maurice avoided her eye, avoided any occasion for speech. He knew Bessie's views on George and Bert, and when he appeared late in the afternoon with a bunch of roses and set them propitiatingly on her desk, she realized that even his rudimentary conscience was aroused. Bessie did not really appreciate roses, regarding them as a waste of money. She liked buttercups, but no one had ever discovered how much she liked buttercups.

" How much did you lend them ? " she asked, without glancing up ; and Maurice answered like a guilty schoolboy :

" Seven pounds. Really, I couldn't see them left."

Late in the afternoon was their time for any quarrelling or rejoicing. There was usually half an hour to spare between the last sitting and the closing of the studio, though sometimes if Wainwright was going out to pick up extra money photographing a dance or conference, they would rush off to tea and then back to the studio to get everything ready.

This evening, there was nothing to restrain Bessie from expressing her disapproval ; but she shrugged her shoulders, a gesture that, with so much else, she was acquiring from her fiancé. What was the use of talking ? She put the roses in water and set them in the studio. Maurice watched her sulkily. They both knew that only from the marriage fund could seven pounds be conjured on the spur of the moment, and it was her trust fund as well as his. Maurice had been so sure that he could win her round, so certain that although she might be angry he could smooth everything over, that he became as indignant as any other man who has a grievance against a girl. He assumed an air of deliberate provocation.

" I suppose you wish to imply that your proprietorial rights have been infringed ? "

Bessie refused to flare up at him. " Are you going to the club to-night ? " she countered. It was a very shabby club, boasting a poker machine and a chef whose speciality was dandelion salad. Wainwright's " gang " hung around the club almost as persistently as the odour of coffee and dish-washing.

" No," Wainwright answered, and then to be annoying, he added, " I think I'll take Lucy to the pictures."

Lucy was a very plump model with an easy laugh and gold-filled teeth. Wainwright was doing a series of advertisements for a firm which sold electric cleaners ; and photographs of Lucy posing soulfully with the cleaner formed, as he said, " a pleasant break from dowagers ".

Bessie shrugged again and disappeared into the dressing-room to arrange her hat.

" I wish you wouldn't sulk." He tried a wistful tone as she emerged.

" Good night." She walked towards the door without looking at him.

" Bessie," he called. " Bessie, don't be so damnably righteous." He caught her by the arm. " God ! you're enough to make a man want to thrash you."

Bessie lifted her eyebrows. Meanly, she had all his weapons against him. "Poise?" she said, far too cuttingly for one so young. "One requires poise."

"Oh, rub it in," Maurice stormed. "Put on the injured proprietress act. Of course, everything I do I have to account to you. I suppose you believe this place would go to pieces without you? The trouble with you is that you're a born boss, and get this straight, so am I."

"Really?" Bessie asked in the same cool voice. It stung him like a nettle-rash.

"Don't be so artificial," he almost yelled at her. "What is all the scene you're creating? All over nothing. Just because I had to do the only thing possible for George and Bert."

Bessie was provocatively silent, regarding him as though he were some curious exhibit behind bars. Maurice lost all remnants of self-control.

"Oh, you . . ." he stuttered, "you little . . ."

"See you to-morrow," Bessie responded indifferently.

She was feeling far from indifferent. If she chose to quarrel with him now, they would call each other all the names they knew, and then make it up, as they had done so often before. Bessie, however, was a little weary of the same old reconciliation scene.

Next morning Wainwright was chilly, polite, hard. He worked furiously. They spoke as little as possible and no reference was made to the plans for being married at the end of the week. Wainwright was indignant and hurt. That this girl should behave as though she were married to him already, assume rights over him, and, into the bargain, treat him as though *he* were the child and she the experienced business head, was more than any man could endure.

This business of addressing Bessie with chilly politeness could not go on. He would have it out with her. But first he took his troubles to Ernie who was preparing to depart south, the preparations consisting of packing a clean shirt and his favourite mauve tie. Ernie had often endured Maurice " grieving on his shoulder " before, but he had heard so much about Bessie that he was heartily sick of the subject.

" Well, either marry her," he advised irritably, after an hour and a half's analysis of Bessie's failings, " and get it over. Or cut her out and shut up."

" I've often wondered if Bessie has a cold nature," Wainwright brooded, with the painful relish of a man removing the bandage from the wound. " One would never have classed her as a passionate type, but do you think, Ernie, that this preoccupation with trivial tasks, all this bustling restlessness, is rather more a sign of a cold, surface nature than of adolescent frustration ? "

Ernie grunted. He knew when Maurice launched on a psychological monologue that he never went away until one in the morning ; and for once Ernie wanted to sleep ; he would be sitting up in the train all night.

" I'll tell you what," he snapped. " If you're still mucking about on the edge, put your clothes on and go home. The water's wet. Trouble with you is you've got to talk and talk and talk until you're bored with a thing before you start it."

Wainwright paid no attention to interruptions.

" It would be an explanation," he said lingeringly. " All these months she's shown not the slightest sign of passion, of anything more than affection. A cold nature . . ."

" All right," Ernie snapped. " Ask for your ring back and be done with it."

Wainwright smote himself on the brow. " Good Lord ! I suppose I should have bought her a ring. It *is* usual. I never thought of it." He brightened. " Still, she isn't the type of girl to worry over a trifle like that.

I have been far too occupied with major matters. But it's an idea."

" What is ? "

" Buying her a ring."

" Then after all this whining and howling," Ernie asked ferociously, " you're going on with it ? "

Wainwright looked surprised. " Why not ? "

" After the things you said about her I should think . . ."

Wainwright drew himself up virtuously. " I have to discuss my affairs with someone, and, at the moment, Bessie herself is about as easy to approach as the Himalayas. However, I shall buy her an engagement ring . . . as soon as I have enough money for the deposit."

" Oh, get out ! " Ernie exclaimed wearily. " You make me tired. Don't come to me when it turns out a flop. She isn't marrying you, she's marrying the studio."

" Do you think so ? " Wainwright started all over again to outline for Ernie's benefit the course of events which had led up to his acceptance as a prospective spouse. Ernie wondered why he did not hit Maurice on the head with a rock and get peace that way. If he did, Maurice, when he regained consciousness, would want to discuss the impulses and repressions that had led Ernie to knock him out. Thank God, Ernie reminded himself fervently, young Bessie would be taking Maurice off his hands. But, and this was a depressing thought, the marriage would wear off in a year or so, and he would have Maurice back again, moaning about another girl. He regarded his friend curiously.

" It's a damn mystery to me," he observed, " why women rush you as though you'd been marked down from three shillings to two and elevenpence ha'penny. Should have thought young Bessie would have had more sense."

Maurice might have paid a deposit on a ring had

not the idea been clean driven from his head by a letter which came from Melbourne after Ernie and other delegates to the Writers and Artists of the Red Dawn descended on that unconscious city.

"There's a chap here from Adelaide," Ernie wrote, "with pots of money and, I think, slightly cracked. I was telling him about your fool tin Register and laughing like hell, but he seems to think there's something in it. Wants to transpose the idea to a kind of factory bundy, so watch your step. He's coming over to Sydney, so I thought I'd tip you off. As I said before, he's slightly cracked. You should have heard the speech he made at the first session. Sheer tripe. Luv. Ernie."

This missive acted like a stingray flung into the zoo fishpond. It galvanized Maurice until he was rushing up and down on the red and green triangles leaving footprints on them as though they were the sands of time.

"I don't know whether the fellow's going to steal my patent or whether he wants to buy me out," he moaned excitedly. "Bessie, send an urgent telegram to Ernie, 'What do you mean? Be clear. Imperative you wire me details.' Well, go on, send it."

Bessie was still waiting. "I will when you give me Ernie's address," she observed coldly.

Wainwright rushed to his desk in search for the letter, and naturally the letter was written on the back of an agenda paper, and there was no address. "He doesn't say." Maurice was depressed and then excited again. "But wait! They must be holding this conference in some hall or other. Let me think." He pounded his forehead. "No, they were keeping the address secret. That, of course, means that only a couple of hundred people know. Who was that girl Ernie's been tagging round with lately? The blonde?"

"Doris," Bessie replied, still cold.

"What's her address?"

" I don't know."

" Well, ring up someone and find out."

" Forget about it," Bessie advised, " until Ernie comes back. He'll be here in a few days."

All Wainwright's smouldering exasperation flared out at her. " Yes, yes, of course. Let a fortune slip through my fingers without even closing them. One would think you . . ." He broke off fuming. " I believe it would make you completely happy to see me sticking on here turning out hack photographs of fool females. You don't care if the Absence Register never comes good. You simply don't care, God damn it ! A ball and chain ! That's all you are, a damn, obstructive, hindering, snooping, wet blanket of a girl. You'd ruin any man's zest and enthusiasm with your lukewarm sabotage. Oh, I know you think you're a pillar of society, but you're not. You're the kind of woman that sends men mad. Mad ! From sheer boredom. Makes them blow their brains out."

Bessie was unmoved. She had heard it all before. " If you tell me who to ring to get Doris's address, I'll ring them."

Her lover gave an inhuman scream. " Get out of here ! " He collapsed on a chair breathing heavily. " Get out of my sight. I'll have a stroke or something." Bessie walked away behind the cubicles. " Where are you going ? " he howled. " Just when I want you, dammit ! "

Bessie came out with her hat and bag. " If you want me, I'll be down at Esther's."

" That's it ! Desert me just when I need you most ! That's a woman all over. Clear out when you're needed. It's what I might have expected."

" You can send me a wire if you want me." Bessie was unmoved. " I've worked for over a year without a holiday and I'm going to take one until after the New Year. And I want some peace to think things out. If you like to come down any week-end, Esther won't mind. Miss Simons can do my work here."

"Quite so," Wainwright agreed with a sneering courtesy. "I trust you have a pleasant holiday. And, no doubt, you'll have more congenial company than Esther's."

"What d'you mean?"

Wainwright smiled nastily. "Oh, but do not ask me to believe that you are just intending to grow vegetables. I am afraid it would strain my credulity. After all, I am sorry I do not afford sufficient gratification for your adolescent lust. No doubt someone younger, more vigorous than myself . . ."

The door slammed behind Bessie, and Wainwright drew his hands down his face sadly, slowly, as though he were wiping away invisible tears. In that moment he looked a very old man.

"I might," he murmured, "have bought her that ring, poor kid." Then he smiled rather wretchedly. "Anyway, what would I do with the thing now she's gone off in a temper?"

He pondered a little whether he should have spoken so nastily to Bessie; but, after all, he had said so many worse things to her that his closing effort had been comparatively mild. In fact, much less than she deserved, going off like that. If there was one thing he hated, it was a woman who could not control her temper. She would get over it. He would send a repentant telegram, a telegram every day for a week, and then, at the week-end, he would sweep down and bring her back. Or, perhaps, a little brutality might stand him in better stead. Anyway, blast the girl, he couldn't worry about her now; he must find out Ernie's address somehow. If he pulled off a scoop with the Absence Register, she would be a little more respectful.

He paced up and down uncertainly, unable to decide

whether he was most annoyed with Bessie or excited about the Absence Register. Behind him on the floor his foot-marks assumed an intricate pattern superimposed upon the red, black and green triangles. There was no one to erase those marks, no Bessie to come forward with a mop in some slack moment, cautiously lest a customer appear, quickly applying polish and vanishing again leaving a shining expanse. Up and down Maurice tramped, up and down.

CHAPTER XII

I

From her first day at the hut Bessie's eagerness to be up and doing was, as Esther said, "most disturbing". That the ground was baked hard as a brick, and the only spade a lamentable affair held together by one nail, did not deter her in the least.

Esther had a routine that varied little. She rose, drank a glass of sour milk, ate a plate of some breakfast food that tasted like assorted pebbles, and, if the day was sunny, lay down behind the house to bask. A long tramp in the bush, or a swim, might replace a round of the haunts of various insect and animal pensioners. In the afternoon Esther wrote or examined specimens or worked at problems of diet deficiency or pigmentation. Most of her thinking, she maintained, was done while she basked.

Bessie was a reluctant basker. She abandoned her clothing with the air of a drowning man giving away a life-belt ; and when a telegraph messenger, bringing a propitiatory telegram from Maurice, made a sudden appearance, Bessie flashed under the house like a centipede, leaving Esther in a tattered old dressing-gown to deal with the lad.

Despite protests from Esther, the guest spent her first two days scrubbing out the hut, and when she had finished scrubbing, she took a sack and industriously carted manure from the surrounding scrub, getting quite a sizeable pile in one corner of the paddock. Then she cleared the first of what she claimed would be a row of vegetable beds, marking off on a piece of notepaper a complete design for the replanting and cultivation of every inch of land except that on which the hut stood ; even that Bessie eyed speculatively with a hint that mushrooms grew in dark places under houses.

" There are mice living under the house," Esther objected. " You let them alone." She eyed Bessie amusedly. " I'm going to Central Australia in a couple of months to study aspects of dehydration and, unless you stay and look after it, everything will be weeds by the time I get back."

Bessie shook her head firmly. " If I get the place shipshape, you can easily get someone to mind it. There's lots of chaps I know, artists, who would come down here and do a bit of weeding and painting and thank heaven for the chance."

She had not decided whether she would stay permanently or only for three weeks' holiday. It would depend on Maurice.

" I don't want," Esther complained, " a man, even an artist, messing about my hut. If you stay, that's different."

They argued for the first three days, but agreed finally to leave any decisions for a week or so.

" I'm going to get some chickens," Esther said, with superb cunning, " and a goat." She knew Bessie. Give Bessie some solid, tangible object and she would be happy. " If you'll only let that spade alone, I can get Ron Chugg to come down and plough the whole paddock up in half a day."

"Ron Chugg?" Bessie was interested. "That was the chap who gave me a lift."

"Probably. He rears poultry and plays a good game of chess. Ever played chess, Bessie? I'll teach you."

Bessie had hoped to save Esther the trouble of housework and cooking. She had pictured herself as the tactful buffer between a genius and the hard toil of life. But in Esther's hut everything was so simple that it did not need cleaning or tidying ; and the meals did not need cooking because they were all raw vegetables and black bread that kept a week. Occasionally potatoes or pumpkin might be boiled, but one meal followed another as a succession of grated carrots and shredded cabbage, or grated beetroot and tomatoes. Garlic there was, and salad oil. But food was no problem. Esther's only vices were tea, coffee and tobacco ; and in these she revelled with a fearful sense of their unhealthy and devitalizing effects, attempting to harrow Bessie's soul with descriptions of what such drugs would do to her inside.

This lack of indoor occupation left Bessie free to tidy the paddock, and before she had been there a day the place began to look different, less a happy home for weeds and bits of rusty wire. She cleared away rubbish and nettles and old bottles. She made a beautiful bonfire of burnable odds and ends while Esther watched her pathetically, forbearing to point out that Bessie was disturbing the homes of any number of privileged inhabitants under those old tins. If it was a choice, Esther decided, between keeping Bessie and her rare collection of living centipedes and beetles, then Bessie won hands down. Bessie was willing to learn to play chess, and that counted for more than all the beetles ever hatched.

"Tomorrow," Bessie said, standing in the dusk in the doorway and peering out at the paddock, as though daring it to deny her statement, "tomorrow I'll really set about work."

This prickly heat of activity, this restless desire to do something, was only the surface covering of a loneliness and unhappiness, a painful longing for Maurice. Bessie knew that when she went to bed, she would, as she had done the night before, begin to cry in the dark hopelessly. But while Esther was there, she would put a brave face on things. Maurice must make up his mind to take business seriously or she would quit for good. That was the ultimatum. And she would stand by it. In the meantime she would teach this pocket wilderness to respect a capable farmer who had been studying the planting notes in the daily papers for months.

"You go ahead and enjoy yourself," Esther declared. "Work till your bones fall apart if you want to. You can dig up every square inch of it and welcome."

Next morning they were basking after breakfast when another obstacle to honest toil appeared in the person of Bessie's father who arrived with a roar in a large red lorry. When Esther peered under the house and announced that a big truck was negotiating the track, Bessie, remembering she had left a note with her address, said thoughtfully :

"That'll be Dad."

The thundering on the front door was enough to knock it down.

"Yes, that's him," Bessie decided.

"Well, go and open the door."

There was no need. Bessie's parent, hearing voices, had charged round the side of the hut, letting out a bellow of triumph as he came.

"So there you are," he howled, bearing down on Bessie. "I've got you, have I ! You wait." He transferred his attention momentarily to the red truck which was still panting heavily at the gate. "Right-o, Joe," he roared. "You can be on your way. Thanks for the lift."

"O.K., Bill." His confrère put his foot on the accelerator and Bill watched him back up the path.

"So you thought you'd cleared out?" He turned on Bessie again. "I'll give you the biggest hidin' you ever had."

"Sit down, Mr. Drew." Esther indicated the back door-step. "Bessie, get your father a cup of tea. I don't think we've met before?"

Bill Drew glared at her. "We have not," he shouted. "An' what's more, I don't want to meet you, whoever you are, encouragin' my girl away from home, lurin' 'er down here. Where is 'e? Where's that Wainwright?"

"Trot along and get your father a cup of tea, Bess," Esther admonished. "Will you have something to eat, Mr. Drew? I'm Esther Gullick."

"No, thanks." Bessie's parent was still hostile. "I had me breakfast. Lost me a day's work she has. I says to old Sam, the boss : 'Sam, if you want me to work late Christmas Eve, I want to-day off.' 'Without pay,' 'e says, 'Bill, and I wouldn't do it but as a favour to you.' *He* knew the trouble I was 'aving with 'er. 'E knew she'd cleared out from home. 'Put 'er in a gaol,' 'e says, 'one of these girls' gaols, and then she won't be no trouble.' Chased her all over the country. . . ." From a shout Bill Drew was dying down to an indignant rumble. "Leaves a note, see? Just clears out without sayin' a word." He felt that his rage was ebbing and endeavoured to stir it again. "When I get hold of that . . ."

"Mr. Wainwright isn't here." Esther cut through a flow of unusual adjectives.

"Oh no!" Mr. Drew responded with fine scorn. "Oh no, 'e wouldn't be. Wherever I find trouble, I know that smarmy bastard's at the bottom of it. You can't kid me she didn't clear off because of 'im."

"Bessie came down for a holiday with me." Esther drew her wrap about her scrawny frame. "Sit down, Mr. Drew. You're keeping the sunlight off me." Bessie's parent moved with surprising docility to the back step. "I didn't think Bessie was really accomplishing anything in that studio and I persuaded her to come down here."

They eyed each other carefully, Bill Drew with a lowering bull glare and behind it a doubt that all was as simple as he had seen it. He began to moderate his tone.

"She just takes her own way," he complained. "Her mother's nigh off 'er head worryin' and I ain't much better meself. It ain't no use talkin' to her, see? We tried everything. I've belted her and roared at her and she just takes not a bit of notice." A tone of reluctant pride crept into his voice. "No affection, that's her."

"It serves you right." Esther's voice was friendly. "If you will treat a grown-up girl the way a baby shouldn't be treated, you can't expect her to fall on your neck. You'll never do any good by violence."

"I didn't do nothin' violent," Bill Drew objected, on the defensive. "I wasted the whole afternoon yesterday goin' in to see that bloody Wainwright. Smarmy and polite 'e was, enough to make you kill 'im. 'I ain't seen 'er,' 'e says, raisin' 'is eyebrows at me. 'I do not know if she still considers herself in my employ. As you know,' 'e says, 'Bessie and I had certain plans.' 'Plans,' I says, 'plans! You're full of plans, nothin' but creepin' and crawlin' and plannin' and plottin' . . .'"

"Tea," his daughter said from the step above him. Bessie had put on the grim, wary look that she reserved for dealings with members of her family.

Her parent turned and surveyed her.

"What the hell you doin' here anyway?" he demanded.

Bessie set down the tray. "I'm going to make this

place into a farm. Esther puts up the capital, I put up the labour. She's a kind of Hodges and I'm Maurice."

The name inflamed her parent's mind once more. "Maurice! That damn Maurice! I'll give him Maurice, the dance you've led me."

"Bessie's being here has nothing to do with Maurice," Esther cut in, a trifle bored. "He doesn't really like the idea."

Bill Drew glanced suspiciously from one to the other. "That true?" he asked, after a moment's silence.

Bessie nodded carelessly. "Well, why the hell couldn't you have said so?" her father complained. "Draggin' me down here, losin' me a day's work, losin' your mother and me our sleep, worryin' your brothers and sister."

"Like hell," Bessie retorted heartlessly. "Here, drink your tea."

Bill Drew accepted the cup as though it contained arsenic and blew in it thoughtfully.

"What did you say you was doing down here?" he enquired.

"She came for a three weeks' holiday," Esther explained, in the loud, clear tones she used for lecturing. "But I'm trying to persuade her to stay permanently. If she cares to convert this land into a vegetable garden and fowl-run, I will supply the money for the seeds and wire netting and so forth. If there are any profits, we split them fifty-fifty. Fair enough?"

"I'm lookin' for the catch in it," Mr. Drew rumbled.

"There isn't any catch." Bessie took up Esther's patient, reasonable manner. "I just thought it would do me good and we might make some money out of it."

Despite his obstinate dislike of altering a viewpoint, Bill Drew could not but be struck by any scheme which removed his daughter from the vicinity of his prospective son-in-law. Such a scheme was likely to take on a certain intrinsic beauty in his mind apart from any material advantages.

" You ain't getting no wages ? " he demanded.

" I don't know if Maurice is still paying me," Bessie replied honestly. " I came away without asking."

Bill Drew became more friendly at this further evidence of a rift between Bessie and her lover.

" Well, seein' Miss . . . Gullick, wasn't it, miss ? Seein' she's so good to have you here, I ain't goin' to have you depending on her for everything. I can see she's been good to you and I ain't goin' to have her think your family won't do the right thing too. While you're here, Bess, I'll see to it that you get ten shillings a week." He looked a little shamefaced. " I'm glad to see you tryin' to make a fresh start." He gave Esther a broad, bloodshot wink that said louder than words : " You keep her out of his reach and I'll do my part."

It was a friendly, obvious wink, and Esther returned it good-naturedly. As for Bessie, she was so astonished that she stood looking at her father with her mouth open. She knew what ten shillings meant for him. It was the difference between little comforts and a deprivation of tobacco, tram-fares and drinks. She was touched by this rather pathetic paternal attempt to set the ruined daughter on the right path.

She was saying, " No, thank you, Dad, I don't really . . ." when Esther cut in blandly and accepted the offer.

" It will give Bessie a sense of liberty," Esther remarked, like a welfare officer discussing some case with a famous philanthropist, " and that's very important."

" It is that," Bill Drew beamed. He was drawn to Esther as a sensible, nice-spoken woman who seemed to understand what a trouble he had had with Bessie. From the poor look of her she would probably be glad that Bessie would have ten shillings a week for her very own.

He rose up and snarled at his daughter : " Well, see you behave yourself, that's all. Don't let me hear you've been goin' behind Miss Gullick's back and seein' that feller again."

" I don't want you to think I'm dictating to Bessie," Esther told him. " As a matter of fact I've invited Maurice down for this week-end. Bessie's affairs are her own business."

For a moment it seemed that Bessie's father was going to have a fit. " I knew there was a catch in it," he raved. " So that's the game, is it ? Sneaking away down here to live with that cow ? "

" Don't be silly," Esther said sharply. " If Bessie wanted to live with Maurice, she could do it much more conveniently in the city. A man with your blood-pressure should be more careful. Maurice isn't worth a seizure, and if you're not careful, you'll do yourself serious harm. You don't realize how it affects you to get into a rage or you wouldn't do it. Bessie, give your father that spade and take him over where you want the vegetable bed. If he doesn't work off some of the adrenalin in him, he'll be ill."

Bessie regarded her parent sullenly. It was her spade, her vegetable bed, and she didn't want him interfering. However, she handed him the tool without a word. The elder Drew was so nonplussed that he stood looking at the spade like a dazed man. Argument with Esther had no pleasure in it. He wanted to thresh out this matter of Bessie and Wainwright ; but some glimmering of sense kept him silent.

" It will do you good, Mr. Drew, and it will help Bessie," Esther went on tranquilly. " I'd help too, but, thank heaven, there isn't another spade."

Bessie's father was recovering. He rattled the spade contemptuously. " Don't call this a spade, do you ? "

" A bloody shovel then," Esther suggested amiably.

" Here, gimme the axe." He beckoned his daughter.
" I'll fit the handle in proper." When he saw the axe,
he snorted again. " I'd better fix that first."

" By all means," Esther agreed. " And why not take
off your shirt and get some sun while you do it ? "

" No, thanks," Mr. Drew growled, almost fearfully.

When he had detached the axe-head from the haft,
he decided to heat it, and built himself a fire.

" What did y' say you was goin' to plant ? " he
demanded.

" Corn," Bessie responded promptly.

" That just shows what a fat lot you know," her parent
sneered. " Potatoes'd do splendid this kind of soil. I
was talkin' to a chap who drives a big Dodge for Simpson's
down at the markets, and 'e tells me potatoes are going
sky-high. Can't get enough of them. Then you could
plant a side crop of onions or maybe beets."

" Rock-melons and pumpkins." Bessie's jaw had set
firm. " You can sell them any time."

" Yeah. But look what you got to spend on super-
phosphate," her father contended. " Hens is a good
thing. I can see that. But this melon business, you just
waste your time."

Bessie stared at him with puzzled surprise. " What do
you know about it ? "

" A hell of a damn sight more'n you do. I s'pose you
think I was born in Redfern like your mother. Why, your
gran'pa had a farm up Gloucester until I was twelve and
then he had a greengrocer shop out Waverley. Never
did no good after 'e left the country. As a kid, there
wasn't nothin' I didn't know about 'orses and cows
and crops."

" You never told me," Bessie murmured thoughtfully.

" Only *one* of the things you don't know," her father
snarled. But it was a defensive snarl. He was trying to
improvise a pair of tongs to draw out the axe-head.

" See if you can find a hammer."

Esther basked, respectably, in her swimming costume, while Bessie and her father toiled. There was a smile on Esther's face as she heard Mr. Drew instructing his daughter how to dig. Bill Drew was enjoying himself. He wanted to be an offended parent ; but he had a whole day and a chance to show Bessie just how much more he knew than she did. Mighty clever she'd thought herself, hadn't she ? Mighty smart, working in a place that called itself a studio. But he'd show her she didn't know anything about farms. At lunch, Bill Drew was good-humoured for almost the first time in Bessie's memory.

" I brought me own," he announced, refusing the proffered lettuce and onion ; and produced a pile of the thick cut sandwiches on which Mrs. Drew reared her family. Bessie regarded them wistfully. Grated vegetables were not her favourite food and those stodgy hunks of bread and butter made Bessie's mouth water.

" White bread ! " Esther exclaimed disgustedly. She proceeded to lecture Bessie's father on the foolishness of eating white bread, giving a brief résumé of a talk on diet she was preparing for a broadcasting station. By the time she had finished with the subject, Mr. Drew had eaten all but two of the sandwiches and those Bessie had appropriated.

" I dunno," he rumbled propitiatingly. " I guess different kinds of stomachs like different things." He was not going to risk quarrelling with Esther again. He had once had an aunt called Esther who had spanked him when he was a small boy.

Queerly enough, Bill Drew was not feeling worried any more. Whenever he saw Bessie in the flesh, looking chunky and square-jawed and self-reliant, he somehow felt it was not much good worrying.

" What am I supposed to tell your mother ? " he demanded.

" Just what I told her. That I'm due for a holiday and I'm staying here."

" O.K." Bill Drew rose heavily. " I s'pose I better be going."

" Why ? " Esther asked. " Aren't you going to finish that vegetable bed ? "

Bill Drew hesitated. " Might as well," he muttered.

Between them he and Bessie dug a sizeable patch of dark-brown earth and, with an old broken-toothed rake, levelled it.

" I always wanted a place like this," Bessie's father admitted rather shamefacedly. " But of course your mother wouldn't leave Redfern where she was brought up. She don't like being away from the city." He wiped the sweat off his forehead. " That Miss Gullick's a nice woman, ain't she ? "

" She is."

Bill Drew settled to his spade. " Well, that's about the first thing in years," he mumbled, " that you and me think the same about."

Esther came to the kitchen door. She had been writing busily all the afternoon. " You'd better stay to tea, Mr. Drew," she called.

Bessie's parent hesitated and looked towards his daughter. " I guess you've had about enough of me for one day," he muttered.

" Not at all." Esther could be very pleasant when she liked. " We're very happy to have you any time you care to come."

Bessie followed them gloomily into the house. It was all very well for Esther to invite the visitor to stay to tea, but he wasn't Esther's father. To Esther he was just another interesting specimen ; she had not seen him at the top of his form. Wait until he went into his usual nightly rage and began to pound the table.

However, Bill Drew showed no signs of working himself into a rage. Esther had mentioned the timber of the North Coast and Bessie's father was a mine of information on the subject although he had left the Coast at the age of twelve.

" Your Uncle Jim was a timber-getter," he told Bessie, " and what he didn't know about trees wasn't worth knowing."

From the subject of trees they progressed to timber-getters and timber camps, then to the songs the timber-getters sang. Bessie discovered that she had not heard her father talk before. At home he was sullen and morose. He conversed only with his mates at work, regarding his family as a burden ; but Esther was an interesting, nice woman, if a bit of a terror and scrawny-looking. He wanted to show Esther that he could give that Wainwright a few points, if he got the chance.

To tell the truth, Esther was far more interested in Bill Drew's talk than she had ever been in Maurice's, because Bill Drew knew a side of life that was new to her, the life of the wharves and warehouses and factories, the life of a truck-driver.

Presently Bill Drew discovered that Esther knew songs he had not heard since he was a boy, so they sang them untunefully.

" It's years since I sang," Bessie's father announced. " Ours was a great family for music. There was Bessie's uncle who was on at the Tivoli as a Whistling Wonder turn. Real popular he was. I used to sing bass meself when I was bit younger."

" I daresay Bessie inherits her love of music from you," Esther remarked, ignoring the suspicious look Bessie gave her.

" She does that," Bill Drew admitted. " Did you ever know a song called ' Good Company ', Miss Gullick ? "

" Esther," his hostess prompted. " Yes, it's a great song."

"That used to be one of me best," Bessie's parent said, with a simple pride. "How about giving it a go, Esther?"

"Sure," Esther agreed. Her rather cracked voice rose with Bessie's and Bill Drew's.

A curious picture they made sitting round the table singing by the light of the kerosene lamp :

> "I know not, I care not, where fortune may be :
> But I know I'm in excellent company . . ."

bellowed Bessie's father.

He drew in a deep breath. "I haven't sung for that long," he maintained, "that I almost forget how." He turned to Bessie. "Your mother an' me used to sing at the piano. We 'ad a piano when we was first married, but things was terrible tough and we 'ad to sell it. Your mother used to miss not havin' it, but I always told her we couldn't pay off another in a lifetime."

Somehow, with her feelings quickened by the loss of Maurice, Bessie had a sudden sympathy for her father and mother. They liked music, and they had done without it for nearly twenty years. What a difference it might have made to her mother if she had had that piano! Surely some of Mrs. Drew's bitterness could be traced to such deprivations.

"'Course she finally got the wireless when the children grew up," Mr. Drew rumbled on. "But it ain't the same hearin' someone sing to doin' it yourself." He heaved a deep sigh. "Well, I guess I better be goin', but I must say I've enjoyed to-day. Now you remember to do what Miss Gullick tells you, Bess, and don't let's hear any more about this Wainwright feller." It was his last plea. "Thanks, Miss Gullick, I've 'ad a real good time."

Esther repeated her invitation to come again. "And bring Mrs. Drew," she added.

Bessie's father hesitated. " I don't get much time, but maybe . . . some week-end." He turned to Bessie with his old ferocity. " Potatoes," he snarled. " You hear ? And onions as a side crop. I'll be out to see how they're comin' on."

II

Next morning Bessie awoke bad-tempered. Sour milk and bran for breakfast did not improve her.

" It's your liver," Esther reproved. " All due to the resentment you were showing your father yesterday."

" Well, what right's he got to come and spoil things ? Him and his potatoes."

" It was a good idea. Lie down and relax, can't you ? "

" He's had that backyard for fifteen years," Bessie was still brooding over her father, " and he hasn't grown as much as a blade of grass. Even as a kid, when I started a flower bed, he put ashes in it."

" Does a garden good to put ashes in it."

Finding Esther unsympathetic, Bessie lay down on the blanket spread in the grass and surveyed herself critically. Her fair skin was taking on a pink tinge. Esther claimed it would bake a beautiful even brown with a little care and olive oil. Bessie refused the olive oil because it made her feel messy. She stretched out cautiously with her head on her arms. Presently she began to feel better. Either the sour milk had subsided into her indignant digestive system or her mental unrest was lulled. She was even beginning to feel drowsy ; the sunlight was a red coal on each eyelid, so she turned over.

" Hey ! "

Bessie, caught off her guard, started and looked round.

" It's a man by the fence," she told Esther. " I've a good mind to tell him what I think of him."

" I can't see without my glasses," Esther complained.

But Bessie had already caught up the blanket and, draped in it, was striding ferociously over the paddock. The intruder awaited her coming, leaning placidly on a post.

"What do you mean?" she shouted at him. "Sneaking along the fence like that? You get away from here. It's private."

"I'm Ron Chugg." The stranger removed his hat.

"I don't care who you are," Bessie replied ferociously. "You can't come butting in here."

The stranger looked perplexed. He was a lean, shabby young man with a two days' growth of beard. "I come to do the ploughing. Esther sent a note. I called so she could get in some clothes."

Bessie began to be mollified. "Just so long," she said loftily, "as you don't make a habit of it." She stalked off to the house, the blanket trailing ludicrously behind her. There she stayed, pretending that the kitchen needed sweeping. Outside, the slow drawl of Mr. Chugg joined Esther's sharper voice as they discussed the ploughing.

"Bessie," Esther called, "do you remember where your father said we ought to put the fowl-run?"

"Down the end of the paddock."

"Well, one of us," Esther complained, "will have to go and show Ron what needs to be ploughed."

"I've put pegs in." Bessie appeared at the back door like a suspicious ant at the entrance to its mound. She glared at Mr. Chugg, as the intruder turned to bring his plough from the cart which he had driven quietly along a bush track by a short cut from his own house.

"Don't get so hot under the collar, lamb," Esther pleaded. "He doesn't care twopence if you were wearing nothing but a blanket."

"Yes, but *I* care." Bessie tramped indignantly over to her vegetable bed. Yesterday she had begun bringing burnt leaves and loam from the creek edge, dumping them in the turned earth. It seemed senseless to stay indoors and register disapproval when there was this interesting job to be done. So pouncing on her bucket and shovel, she climbed through the fence. Esther resumed her basking. Esther would give no active assistance to the civilizing of the paddocks. She had the same attitude to digging that Maurice had to filing bills. It was an unnecessary evil.

Digging soothed Bessie's ruffled feelings and presently she began to whistle absent-mindedly, bubbling out notes with the rich, happy unconsciousness of the creek running over its rocks.

" You cert'ny can whistle," the ploughman called to her in a friendly way, as he turned his horse.

Bessie scowled at him and went hot. He might have thought she was whistling for his benefit. Cheek ! She dug in silence, making frequent journeys into the bush for loads of manure and black leaf-mould.

" It's lunch-time," Esther called. " Come and get it."

Bessie and Ron Chugg met at the back door. He drew aside politely to let her pass, his hat in his hand. He had black hair and more perspiration on his forehead than Bessie had seen on anyone before. His brow was startlingly white where the hat covered it — the little drops of moisture ranged along it looking cool rather than hot, clean rather than dirty. It was as though he had emerged from a shower, wet but shining.

Ron talked with Esther about neighbours and cows and the need for rain. " Only a drop the other night and things are still too dry. You want to put a fire-break round your fence, Esther. It's going to be a great season for bush fires."

" You and Bessie can do it," Esther suggested. " You haven't met Bessie, have you, Ron ? "

The two glanced at one another appraisingly.

" You gave me a lift one night," Bessie said sullenly.

" Oh ! was that you ? " Ron Chugg asked, with a smile that made Bessie feel as though she were blushing down to the tip of her toes. " I remember. You and an old gentleman came down one week-end. While Esther was away."

Bessie could have annihilated him. How dare he call Maurice an old gentleman ! A man with a name like Chugg to patronize anyone !

" And how do you like Esther's food ? " Ron Chugg drawled.

He was eating the same thick sandwiches of bread and meat that Bessie's father preferred, and the sight of them made her feel that she had not been fed for days. It was all very well for Esther to live on pumpkin and grated carrot, when she did nothing but bask ; but Bessie had been reared on meat. She looked at her plate so mournfully that Ron Chugg smiled again with a little wrinkling of the corners of his eyes that made his ordinary face look lively and pleasant.

" I like it," Bessie answered snappily. She and Esther were having a raw egg each, beaten and spread over bananas with a little chopped cabbage.

" By the way, Ron," Esther suggested. " Do you know if the Tracys still want to sell that goat ? "

" They don't like goats, Esther. Cows are their mark, now they're coming up in the world."

" Well, see if you can get it for me for ten shillings. If they know I want it, they're sure to put the price up."

" Right-o, Esther. And about this fire-break. If you want it done, I'll bring the brother down. It's a job for two."

" Bessie could help you."

Ron Chugg's eyes swept Bessie again in unspoken comment. " Right-o," he drawled again. " But I can easy get the brother."

" What brother ? " Bessie asked in a hostile tone.

" Why, my brother." He opened his eyes wide. " Who else would I be getting ? He's off this morning doing a bit of pea-picking for old Sam Leonard."

" Ron and his brother live by themselves," Esther explained maliciously. " They don't really approve of women."

Ron remained politely silent.

Bessie turned to Esther. " A lot of that type about," she said nastily. " Getting to be quite a fashionable pose. Maurice thinks he's a woman-hater, you know."

Ron Chugg did not seem disturbed. " Who's Maurice ? " he asked Esther.

Bessie snapped : " The elderly gentleman you spoke of. I'm engaged to him." That, she thought, ought to make him feel he wasn't so clever. But nothing apparently disturbed the equanimity of Mr. Chugg.

" He's too old," he said reflectively, " for a very young girl like you."

This, Bessie decided, was just too much. First, this impolite young man had walked quietly to the fence when she had no clothes on. Then he had doubted she was capable of burning a fire-break ; and on top of it had said that Maurice was " too old ", and she, who felt at least a hundred, was " a very young girl ".

While Esther and Ron lit cigarettes and discussed the price of eggs and the Egg Board, Bessie simmered indignantly. She was out digging her imposing vegetable patch by the time Ron Chugg strolled good-humouredly down the yard.

" Well, what about this fire-break, Bessie ? " he began easily.

" My name's Drew," Bessie said menacingly, " Miss Drew."

He stared at her, perplexed, as though it was just dawning on him that she was annoyed.

" All right," he murmured ; and walked over to survey the blackberry bushes and nettles which had formed a thicket around the fence-posts. " All you got to do," he drawled, " is to stand by with a bucket in case the posts catch."

While Bessie went to fill the bucket, he lit the bushes in several places. A yellow flame ran along the fence with a crackling sound and a puff of blue smoke.

" She's dry all right," Ron Chugg said thoughtfully, pushing his old felt hat back on his forehead. He glanced critically at the scrub. " I wouldn't like to see a decent-sized blaze come through here." He had obviously forgotten he was in disgrace. " I've seen it come down from Beckham's Hill like a . . ." he stopped for a word, " like a racehorse." He glanced at the house critically. " That tank don't hold much. The place'd go up in about five minutes."

Bessie flung her bucket of water. " The post's caught," she cried.

It was fun beating out the fire when it spread, hitting the little yellow tongues with green boughs. Ron Chugg smiled at her.

" You wait till you see a real fire. Come from Sydney, don't you ? "

" Yes."

" I thought so."

Bessie had recovered her temper. It was such a waste of time to be out of humour with this long, slouching man. Of course he was rude ; but had she not been so nervy and angry, she would have treated him tolerantly, as she treated Maurice's friends.

" Esther said you reared ducks," she mentioned, as they rested, very dirty, by the blackened stretch of fence when the fire was finally beaten out.

" Hens are no good," Ron told her briefly. " Ducks do well."

" Oh ? " Bessie was learning something.

" The only thing about ducks "—his face lit up when
he mentioned them—" is that they're hard to rear. Me
and the brother are practically the only people round
here can rear ducklings. Do you know how we did it ? "

Bessie was interested. " How ? "

" We sang to them." He looked down at her gravely.
" People think ducks are just ducks, but they're very
nervy, they are. Sensitive. Me and the brother had
been having a bit of a tough spin. It looked as though
we'd have to go back on the relief. But I said to the
brother : ' No, we'll get some ducklings.' Now when they
come out of the incubator," he paused impressively,
" most people just let 'em sink or swim. They think
they've done enough hatching them. But it's *after* the
hatchin' you got to watch 'em." He paused again.
" Me and the brother had 'em in the house with us, by
the fire, and nights we'd sit and sing to 'em and they'd
sit up happy as a lot of kids."

The idea of this tall youth and his brother solemnly
singing to several hundred ducklings around the fire
tickled Bessie's fancy.

" We didn't lose one." He was not boastful. It was
a statement of fact.

Bessie regarded Ron Chugg with a new respect. " How
do you hatch the eggs ? " she asked.

They sat down on a log and she listened with her chin
on her fist, while he described his home-made incubator
and brooder. He spoke in a quiet, drawling voice, using
his hands occasionally to show her the measurements.
They were dirty hands, calloused, loose-jointed, with
chipped nails and grained knuckles. Bessie inwardly
compared them with Maurice's hands, quick, white,
always moving and changing. Here were hands that lay
steady. Deliberate hands.

" Then you take your red flannel, or sacking, if you

like, and tack it down the length," Ron Chugg finished his description of the hatcher.

" I don't suppose I could make one," Bessie reflected gloomily. " We haven't a saw."

Ron Chugg grinned. " If that's all that's stopping you, you can have ours." He glanced at her. " Ever used a saw ? " Bessie shook her head. " Well, I'll tell you what. If you like to come over sometime, when you've nothing better to do, I've got some bits of board, and I'll give you a hand with it."

Nothing he could have said would have done more to establish him in Bessie's good graces. " Oh ! that'd be great ! " Then she drew into her shell again. " I'd be taking up your time. Thanks all the same."

" Don't worry. Me and the brother take it in turns to stay home."

Bessie shook her head. " First I've got to get up a chicken-run. Esther's going to write to her brother to send the wire." She turned her green eyes on him again enquiringly. " Do you know how to put up chicken-runs ? "

He smiled. " I ought to."

" Have you time," she hesitated to ask the favour, " to tell me about it ? "

Ron found Bessie interesting. Most girls would be only too pleased to accept an offer of help ; but Bessie wanted to know how to do things for herself. He refrained from pointing out that to build a chicken-run was far beyond her strength. They paced out the proposed run and Ron Chugg calculated with a stub of pencil how much corrugated iron and netting and cement would be needed. It seemed to Bessie an enormous, a depressing total.

" How much would it cost ? " she asked in a hushed voice. He told her. Bessie shook her head. If Esther's brother were a millionaire, it would not be right to have him pay such a sum on the chance of rearing a few chickens. She heaved a sigh. " I'll concentrate on the vegetables. Then, if we make any money, we can put it into fowls."

Ron scratched his chin thoughtfully. " You know," he said, " there's nothing to stop you buying a few day-old chicks and building a little yard for them, and letting them run loose and scratch all day. Mrs. Tracy might let you have a dozen or so."

They were becoming almost confidential.

" Do you think when you ask her about the goat, you could see about the chickens ? Would you ? "

" Sure." He looked down at her benevolently. " I'll come down on Saturday and give you a hand putting up a little run for them."

" Don't bother," Bessie said hastily. " It's very good of you." From the first night when he gave that lift, he had shown a tendency to visit the hut at inopportune times. Then Esther had not been home, now he wanted to come just when Maurice was about. And Maurice was so miserably jealous. Why, she could hardly exchange a word even with Ernie without Maurice glaring at her.

" That's all right. I'll be down." Ron Chugg did not take the hint. " Tell Esther I'll bring the goat at the same time."

Because the girl seemed so anxious he should not come, he felt all the more disposed to do so. There had been a good deal of talk in the small settlement about Bessie ; and some of it naturally enough had reached his ears. He had imagined her as a sophisticated, permanent-waved, young lady ; but she looked small and independent, as she stood there in her faded dungarees and old sandshoes. She had a red handkerchief of Esther's tied round her head in a most unbecoming fashion. Her nose was shiny and a big smear of black dust streaked the side of her face where she had wiped it with her hand.

After he had gone, Bessie returned to what Esther called her " mud pies ". She dismissed Ron Chugg from her mind and concentrated on getting out stones from the next patch of ground which she had set aside for carrots and radishes and spinach. Already her life in the studio seemed far away, faded and dull. From it she had emerged into this exciting, purposeful place where life had a clear-cut edge, a crisp, enlivening colour. There were no subtleties, no half-truths to perplex her, but a deep-toned murmur of demands and duties coming like bees laden with honey. There was the buying of seeds and plants, the problem of water, weeding, drainage. And presently there would be the goat, the chickens.

She drew a deep breath of joy and relief. Sooner or later she would go back to the studio ; but while she was here, she would work, so that even when she was gone, Esther could enjoy the fruits of her labour. Struck by a new idea she straightened her back and gazed thoughtfully at the kitchen door. A grape-vine trellis ! Of course. And maybe she could get some passion-fruit vines and plant them. She would ask Ron Chugg.

All the sky had taken on a pink flush, deepening to mauve and green and gold. There were no clouds and it was very still. She leant on her spade and, just as the sky had flooded with colour, so she felt herself flooded and filled with peace such as she had never known before : a peace so deep that it came near to reverence. There was nothing in the whole world but this peace, this clear, immeasurable depth where every happiness blended into one. She stood there leaning on her spade, so long that when Esther looked from the window, Bessie's solitary figure, and even the red handkerchief, were dull against the broken earth and the wall of darkening trees.

CHAPTER XIII

MAURICE had half a mind not to accept Esther's invitation to stay the week-end. He compromised by arriving four hours later than he had said he would, driving in a taxi from the junction station instead of taking the connecting train. As he bumped royally along the cart track, he was at peace with the world and very pleased with himself. He had on his new suit, he had just had a Turkish bath, and he looked very distinguished. Also he was laden with presents : a bunch of roses for Bessie, chocolates, gramophone records, a patent rubber pillow, cigarettes, salted peanuts and an electric torch.

" Hey, how much more of this is there ? " the driver asked glumly.

" Here's the place." Maurice got out, over-tipped the man from force of habit, and turned to meet the glad rush of welcome.

For all the disturbance his entrance made in the sylvan setting, he might have been a nut dropped from a tree. At the far end of the paddock, two figures, one in dirty dungarees and the other in a pair of shorts and nothing else, were bending over a hole in the ground. As the shorter figure straightened, he saw a flash of red handkerchief and knew it for Bessie.

" Hoy ! " he shouted, waving the roses ; and Bessie dutifully rushed up and kissed him and led him into the kitchen. She was brown, mud-splashed and rather grubby ; and he had been picturing her waiting at the gate, fresh and sweet, longing for his advent. His high spirits were checked, annoyance clouded his brow.

" Esther will make you some tea," Bessie told him hurriedly, affectionately. " And then you can get straight into some old clothes. You don't mind if I go back and help Ron Chugg, do you ? I'm holding the post for him."

She sped away, leaving the mortified Maurice to Esther's care without even giving him a chance to bestow his largesse. He turned on Esther tight-lipped.

" Just who is that yokel ? " he asked, biting out each word as though it were a separate insult.

" He's helping Bessie build a chicken-house," Esther explained. " And a shed for the goat." She yawned. " Terrific the energy they put into it. Suppose I should give them a hand, but my conscience doesn't really worry me."

She regarded Maurice benevolently. Resentment and jealousy quivered out of him like a heat-wave from a hot road.

" If those are the only clothes you brought, I can lend you some old trousers of Lester's." She added maliciously : " You can carry stones. That was supposed to be my job."

Maurice swallowed. " Thank you," he said, " but I feel more like tea."

Esther brought him some. " You always time yourself splendidly," she remarked.

" I can see that." He scowled out the window at Bessie and the far-too-helpful lout in the shorts. The best plan, Maurice decided, was certainly not to compete in any trials of muscular strength. Certainly not. He would stay polished, urbane, dignified. Perhaps, if he were to stroll down and see what they were doing, direct them, use his mechanical genius for their benefit, Bessie might realize that it was not necessary to be covered with mud in order to count in the world.

By the time he had finished his tea and lit a cigarette, Maurice was feeling better ; and he picked his way towards the toilers over the ploughed earth, not exactly strolling perhaps, but still dignified.

"And what is it going to be, Bessie?" he asked jovially, as they paused to wipe their faces. There were rolls of wire netting lying about and several saplings with the bark peeled off.

Bessie launched into a description of the completed chicken-run and goat-shed that made it sound like an annexe to Heaven. "It's going to be marvellous," she finished modestly. "And the best part about it is that it won't cost anything except the wire netting. This is Mr. Chugg's free afternoon."

"Hmmm." Maurice glanced at the drooping figure of Mr. Chugg. "A splendid way to spend it. Out of doors in God's great spaces."

Ron Chugg grinned. If this chap didn't like him, the grin said plainly, he could do the other thing.

"Come on, Bess." The free labour took up its crowbar. "Hold the thing straight this time."

"Want a job, Maurice?" Bessie asked. She beamed at him affectionately, and, behind Mr. Chugg's back, made a movement with her mouth to blow him a kiss. Maurice raised his eyebrows, and sensing that something was wrong, Bessie immediately became solicitous.

"Aren't you feeling well?" she asked anxiously.

Maurice played up to the suggestion. "It's nothing. Just a headache. I've had a pretty hard week." He drew himself up, a man who did not let his secret pains and aches bother him. "I'll join you as soon as I've changed and you can put me to hard labour."

Bessie's solicitude increased. "I don't think you'd better, Maurice. Suppose you just sit in the shade."

"It's nothing at all."

"I forbid you," Bessie said warmly, "to lift a hand. You mustn't get yourself overheated."

"Nonsense."

"You know it's true. I'll have you down with 'flu."

The object of all this care was beginning to be

annoyed with her for overdoing it. Ron Chugg's back was politely blank and expressionless.

" Don't be silly," Maurice said irritably. His previous decision to be aloof and dignified was entirely reversed by Bessie's anxiety. He strode angrily across the vegetable bed unmindful of Bessie's shouted warnings. She watched him go with the old nervous frown between her brows.

" He does such silly things," she said aloud. " You see. He'll want to cut down all the trees and build the shed all by himself, and he'll knock himself to pieces doing it."

It had been on the tip of Ron's tongue to ask if Maurice had always been delicate but he considerately refrained. Sure enough, Maurice came charging back in a dirty old pair of trousers and a torn shirt and proceeded to be the life and soul of the party. He swung the axe gallantly. He dug like a mole. He stretched netting and hammered nails. He did six men's work, flinging orders and directions about as if they were chips flying from the axe. He told stories of the days when he had worked his passage on a timber boat to America ; and Ron Chugg plodded along in his wake, taking no notice of orders.

Bessie was tremendously happy. She had no idea of the tempest brewing under all this industry. Maurice, she felt, was enjoying himself ; and, actually, he was, but that did not stop him from turning over in his mind certain pertinent remarks which he intended to direct to Bessie just as soon as this Chugg fellow had betaken himself elsewhere.

When Mr. Chugg finally collected his tools and departed with a promise to bring the chickens on Monday, Bessie flung her arms round Maurice's neck and hugged him.

" I've missed you," she declared fervently. " I've missed you dreadfully. But as long as I know you're all right and the studio is all right, I try not to be lonely."

" So I see." Now that there was no longer any need to act for the gallery, Maurice could allow his disapproval to show. " So I see," he repeated.

Bessie gave him another hug. " Don't be cranky," she reproved. " Ron Chugg came in to help of his own free will because he's interested in chicken-houses. Now don't start thinking I'm in love with a long streak like him, because I'm not."

Maurice was not lightly mollified ; but he found himself answering questions and listening to the absorbing details of the rhubarb planting and the making of the vegetable beds, in an almost amiable mood. It was good to have Bessie petting him and fussing round him and tenderly insisting that he lie down before tea to lose his headache.

" And everything is really going well at the studio ? " Bessie asked for the fourth time, as she sat at his feet.

" Oh, quite."

" How is Hodges ? Did Mrs. Cummings call for that sitting ? No, I thought she wouldn't. I bet she rang up at the last moment. Did you get Miss Simons to do the receptions or did you get Doris in ? "

" Neither," Maurice replied silkily. He knew that Bessie was half hoping he would ask her to come back, and pride forbade that he should. He had a much better plan. He would make her plead to come back before he was through. " As it happened, the day you decided to take offence at nothing, Jenny Evison happened to be passing, and, seeing what a fix I was in, she kindly offered to give me a hand, just for the time being."

Bessie sat very still. Her pride was as large as Maurice's. If he thought she was going to fly back just because he blackmailed her with the presence of Jenny, he was wrong. If Maurice wanted Jenny Evison in the studio, he could have her. She stiffened.

" That's a great idea. She can keep the job."

" Don't be silly," Maurice said affably. " Jenny is no earthly use. She's just taken over for the time being because I sacked Billy Raine-Smith."

Bessie gasped. " You sacked her ! Oh, Maurice ! Whatever for ? "

Maurice raised his eyebrows. " Don't look so tragic, Bessie. The woman was becoming far too patronizing, and besides she drinks heavily." He looked away from Bessie, unwilling to meet her eyes. " For some time I have felt that I would do well to break into advertising more. This society ramp sickens me. I'm doing a series of machine posters for the A.B.M. Company. There's really more money in it."

Bessie was doubtful but willing to be convinced. " Then you won't be needing a receptionist ? " she asked.

" I need a secretary. And," he added reproachfully, " the position of wife is still vacant."

Bessie began to make excuses. " Now that I've committed Esther to this expense, I'd feel rotten leaving her before I've got things straight. I know she doesn't care twopence and the vegetables'll never be a handicap. . . ."

" You stay another couple of weeks and then think again," Maurice told her kindly. " I realize that the novelty has captured you. It was only to be expected. I didn't want you to feel I was dragging you back." He regarded her with a fatherly benevolence. " One recognizes that the young must be allowed a time of scampering and indecision. Sport about, my child, play with your Ron Chugg, plant your chickweed or whatever it is, and then when you are quite tired of it, perhaps you won't look so unkindly on your stupid old Maurice." The role of a paternal, world-weary sage was very becoming. " I can wait, my dear. I want you to have all the experiences. The little lion must make its own kill and do its own stalking. Very well. I am content." He lay back looking noble.

There was a discrepancy, Bessie considered, between the world-weary Maurice and the Maurice who had given Jenny her job. If he didn't want Bessie back, why did he mention that Jenny was on the premises? Maurice must like to worry her. However, it was no use wrangling about it. If Maurice wanted to leave the situation indefinite, that suited her, and she added mentally, " down to the ground ".

Maurice was developing a bad cold. Over tea he made painful efforts to disguise his misery, but he sneezed into his lettuce and mopped his streaming eyes.

" You always eat too much," Esther pointed out helpfully. " If you'd only fast for a week, Maurice, you'd lose pounds and the cold into the bargain. It's suicide to eat when you're sick. And besides all that fat is a handicap. The lean animal is the healthy animal."

Maurice muttered something about not being in danger from over-eating while he stayed at the hut. They were feasting on carrots, lettuce and pumpkin, with oranges to follow. He resented Esther's reference to his fat.

" The daily strain of one's job leaves little time for healthful exercise," Maurice complained. " I agree with you, Esther, that city life is unhealthy. But what is one to do? Economics, you know, the necessity of bread and butter."

Esther snorted. " Too much bread and butter is your trouble, Maurice. A little more bran and roughage would tone up your bowels immensely."

Maurice was outraged. His bowels were private property and Esther, he felt, almost laid herself open to arrest for trespass. Her remark was in the very worst taste, the type of remark that one expected from Esther. He raised his eyebrows and turned to Bessie.

" I suppose you have been following the situation in Europe? We," he always referred to his friends as

" we ", much as though they were an international board
of administration, " we have come to the conclusion that
there are likely to be serious developments, very serious
indeed." Maurice sneezed again piteously.

" Where are you going to sleep ? " Esther asked briskly.
" That's the next serious situation. I said you could
have my bed but Bessie says you can sleep in hers. Of
course you can always sleep on the floor."

" Not with that cold," Bessie put in quickly.

Maurice gave her a grateful glance.

" Well, my only stipulation," Esther proceeded cheerfully, " is that you don't creak. I have a low imagination."

If the lettuce had choked Esther, Maurice would have
watched the death agonies with pleasure. He had never
felt more miserably virtuous. He sneezed again reprovingly.

" You'd better go straight to bed," Bessie advised.
" I'll get you a hot-water bottle. Have you one, Esther ? "

" What would I be doing with a hot-water bottle ? "
Esther asked. " Do I live in a boarding-house ? "

" Well, I'll warm a brick. And, at least, I can get
Maurice a hot lemon drink."

" No, no," Maurice protested feebly ; but he was
hustled off to bed and fussed over.

" You're worn out." Bessie was all sympathy. " Poor
darling."

Had Maurice been ardent, he would probably have
met with no corresponding glow ; but because he was
miserable and sniffly, Bessie brooded over him in a passion
of maternal tenderness.

" I don't want you to catch this thing," he croaked.
" It looks like being virulent. Sorry."

" Oh, that's nothing," Bessie assured him, soothing
his burning brow. " Now, you just drink this nice lemon
drink and don't worry." She squeezed his hand. " I
love you just the same."

As she tiptoed out, she gathered up some spare cushions.

"Poor lamb," she whispered to Esther. "I won't disturb him. I guess I'll just sleep here on the floor." It could not be, she reasoned, harder than Esther's straw palliasse nor any colder than sharing the edge of blanket that Maurice left over.

"Bessie!" Maurice's voice called plaintively.

"Yes, darling?"

"Turn off that tap, would you? It's dripping."

"Yes, darling." Bessie tiptoed into the kitchen. "He does *overdo* things," she confided to Esther, as she creaked in again. "To-morrow he'll just have to sit in the sun and read. He needs a complete rest."

"Nothing like an occasional visitor to liven things up," Esther commented unkindly.

CHAPTER XIV

I

BESSIE had expected to lead a remote, hard-working life with only Esther for company. Rather to her regret, visitors descended at frequent intervals, most regular among them being Esther's brother, a quiet, bespectacled man with grey hair, whose interests appeared to be mainly scriptural. He liked Bessie because she listened so attentively to his summing-up of the situation caused by the intervention of the Vatican in world affairs. Perhaps because his sister never heeded his warnings of Popish plots, he took a peculiar pleasure in Bessie's society. Esther's scepticism had pained him ever since he was converted to one of the more ferocious evangelical movements, and the fact that Bessie had once attended the Foursquare Gospel Sunday School formed, as he said, " a bond ". Bessie could have ordered several miles of wire netting and charged it to him. For the first time in years he agreed with Esther. They both felt that Bessie was " a fine type of girl ".

On Boxing Day Bessie's family descended on the hut. They stood about awkwardly trying to make conversation, while Bill Drew in a flannel singlet and old trousers performed prodigies of strength erecting the shed for the goat. Maurice also signified his intention of gracing the place with his presence over Christmas, but his influenza kept him in the city.

" We might put up a dormitory as soon as you finish the goat-shed," Esther observed pessimistically.

On week-days the most constant visitor was Ron Chugg. He was always calling to put in a fence-post or to see how the chickens were doing or to consult about the goat ; if he was not there during the day, he would appear in the evening. He sat and chopped at a piece of wood or mended something that needed mending, being, as he said, " a poor hand at talk ". He was loquacious compared with his brother, who, on Bessie's third visit to the stone cottage on the hill, ventured to ask what she thought of the weather. Bessie liked the Chuggs for their silences as she liked the Chugg cottage because it was built of stone. Her first impulse had been to scrub it, but that would have looked like an insult to Ron and his brother, so she regretfully abandoned the idea. The Chuggs might be efficient out of doors but . their living quarters were sadly neglected.

" Mother used to look after things in the house," Ron explained, " and since she died we ain't had much time to pretty it up."

Bessie glanced from the bachelor litter of old matchboxes and boots to the picture of " The Stag at Bay " over the smoke-blackened mantelpiece.

" That ought to come down," she said decisively.

Ron looked surprised. " Why ? " he asked.

Bessie shook her head sternly. She had learnt from Maurice that a Stag at Bay was a horror unmentionable. Whenever " the gang " had wished to disparage an artist friend, they always referred to him as " One of the Stag at Bay School ".

" It's wrong artistically," Bessie told Ron gravely.

" Well, it ain't done much harm that I can see." Ron studied the picture, surprised. He had a quiet respect for Bessie's opinions.

Next time she strolled up, the Stag at Bay was gone.

" It's bush-fire weather,'' Ron remarked more than once, sniffing almost as though he could smell smoke. And, indeed, the days had become so blazing hot that even Esther lay in the shade, and Bessie was forced to get up at dawn and rest during the middle of the day, watering the plants in the evening. She carried heavy buckets from the sadly depleted creek and discussed with Ron Chugg a scheme for a primitive irrigation system.

By this time Bessie had heard so much about bush fires that when reports came in of blazes on the far side of the hills at Peterman and Creedy's Crossing, she felt relieved the wind was blowing the other way.

" After all it wouldn't come across the creek," she remarked hopefully.

" You ain't seen the bush fires we have here," Ron answered. " The Costers, over next to Tracy's place, were burnt out year before last. All the other side of the creek is Crown land for miles and miles. Just thick bush. Once she starts, she takes some stopping."

Bessie considered he was unduly pessimistic.

" You're sure you'll be all right by yourself ? " Esther asked. She was going away for a week's conference ; and Bessie assured her that there was no need to worry.

She was quite capable of looking after the place until its owner returned.

"If Maurice wants me," she added, "I can always travel in and back by train." She made a face. "Not that he shows much sign of it."

Maurice had shown no pressing eagerness to have Bessie back in the studio, and this made Bessie a little heart-sick. She worried about the studio and Maurice's influenza, and was not reassured by news that Jenny was dosing him with warm rum.

"Anyway you won't be lonely," Esther pointed out maliciously as she packed her haversack. Esther never carried a suitcase, never stayed at a hotel, so her preparations were comparatively simple. "If I know anything, Ron Chugg will be on the mat every evening. He's doing his best to lure you away from me."

"Don't be silly." Bessie tried to look stern.

"Well, you don't think he comes down night after night for the pleasure of my conversation. He's a nice boy."

"And that's about all. There are hundreds of nice boys about. What of it?"

"Don't you like him?"

"Of course. But he just sits. Or else he wants to be doing something. You can see through him like a hole in a wall."

"And you like them to keep you guessing? The whirlwind lover, eh?"

Bessie nodded. "Maurice never just sits."

"Unless he's confined to his bed with influenza," Esther said wickedly. "At least Ron doesn't ask for a wet nurse."

"Ron could ask for a wet nurse," Bessie responded firmly, "or any other sort of nurse and it wouldn't matter to me."

She was more and more lonely for Maurice, a possibility that Maurice had foreseen. The Friday Esther set out, Bessie walked in the blinding heat to the little post-office-cum-store and sent a telegram that was as near capitulation as she could make it : " If not doing anything come week-end. Bush fires about. Bessie."

She awaited an answer hopefully but it was not until Monday that the reply came : " Sorry. Had important engagement."

It was so hot the air seemed full of invisible flames. The heat quivered from the baked ground and Bessie's vegetables lay over limp and shrivelled. Bessie was almost as depressed as they were. A lump rose in her throat when she thought of Maurice denying her unspoken appeal. The heat made her nerves jump, and at the end of the day she was exhausted. She tried to read Esther's books, but found she could not concentrate on *Cephalaspid Ostracoderms*. A restlessness, almost a fear, seized her. She was waiting for something. The trees, the air, seemed to be waiting. The suspense made her grateful for the presence of the silent Ron Chugg.

He would appear on the door-step each evening, his hat in his hand, politely expecting to be asked in, and he was not disappointed. He might not talk much but it was marvellous the things he could find to do. Bessie could not but realize that there was an intimacy growing up between them. They would sit on the kitchen door-step and slap at the mosquitoes and listen to the gramophone, or sometimes Bessie would whistle for the visitor. Ron Chugg was one of the few people who appreciated Bessie's whistling, and he could not have chosen an easier way to her heart. Little by little she lost the habit of talking to him. Ron could express his thoughts without words, and once you fell into the way of it, it was quite easy. He would glance at her shyly, cautiously, and he did not need to amplify what his eyes were saying.

Bessie often broke into conversation by way of building

an artificial barrier between them. She found herself
putting on little airs, talking about the people she knew
in the city, as though she would explain to him that she
was unapproachable, and this she did in self-defence,
talking quickly, almost chattering, while he sat mono-
syllabic, shut in his own queer dignity and purposefulness.

Ron Chugg did not need to state his intentions towards
Bessie in words. It never occurred to her that it was at
all unusual to stay at the hut by herself. If Esther did,
why shouldn't she? The whole neighbourhood knew
that Ron was " going with the fast piece from Sydney
who was staying with the mad woman ". They were of
the opinion that it was a scandal and they said so. Ron
himself and his brother had, in their wordless way, already
settled which room Bessie was to inhabit; and James
Chugg had looked thoughtfully in Ron's presence at the
whitewash brush, thereby declaring his intention of kal-
somining the house as a wedding present.

It is very hard to repel a man who has made up his
mind, and Ron had made up his mind about Bessie.
The fact that Bessie's mind was made up in the opposite
direction disturbed him not in the least. He regarded
Wainwright as a clever man but old. Bessie was sorry
for Ron Chugg. She felt that she should refuse him but
he did not give the chance. She tried to disillusion him,
to force on him the conviction that she was a bad woman.
Ron had been religiously brought up, and perhaps, she
thought, he might be so shocked that he would be checked
in his course, if she made some casual reference to the
week-end she and Maurice had spent together in the hut.

Ron Chugg glanced at her shrewdly. " Well, I haven't
been such a Holy Willy myself," he drawled; and Bessie
gave up trying to impress him with her sophistication and
general decadence.

An acrid, leaden-coloured haze lay over the hills and
blurred the heat of the day; the nights were stifling.

Bessie was relieved to think that Esther would soon be back. Esther was to return on Friday; and on Wednesday night Ron came down with the report that bush fires were burning on the far side of the ridge.

Together they crossed the creek and started up the same rocky path that Bessie had taken with Maurice on the day they had first visited the hut. The whiff of smoke was stronger on the ridge, as though the shaggy stretch of country gave out a smell of sweat. Against the thick darkness points of yellow moved and flickered intermittently. The hills were lit into a ghastly semblance of streets, mile after mile, like the windows of dwellings in a city, not of men, but devils. The fire was too far off for the watchers to hear the crackling as the flames flared into the dead wood.

Ron Chugg, watching those lights, said in a loud voice that startled the girl beside him : " Ever seen Hell ? " He flung out his arm. " There she is."

Bessie was silent. The sight of those flames oppressed her. I have made such a mess of things, she was thinking miserably, just the way a boy starts a bush fire. I have started something and I don't know how to get out of it.

In his everyday voice Mr. Chugg drawled : " Ain't much to worry about unless we get a wind this way — a westerly."

They sat down on a rock and watched the fires in silence.

An impulse seized Bessie to speak out her troubles. " I started something — like this, and I just don't know how it's going to end. It's this way, Ron. I was working in a biscuit factory when Maurice came and took a room at our place. He was sick, and I thought it was only square to look after him. Well, he started a portrait studio and I touched him for a job. One thing led to another and we thought we'd get married. I'm fond of him and he's fond of me, but we fight all the time, and somehow — Oh, I don't know. He's letting the business go to ruin, staying up all hours of the night. I'm just giving him a chance to see how he gets on, but I'm worrying all the time."

Ron Chugg said thoughtfully : " Sounds like those problems they write about to the papers and a woman gets a fat salary advising what to do. Strikes me I'm not the one to say."

" Why ? " Bessie asked wilfully, knowing what he would say, yet wanting him to say it.

" Because I guess I'd rather you stayed here. The brother says I can do what I like and I guess you know what I'd like."

Bessie would not reply. After a pause, her escort added : " If you don't get a good crop, you can always plant something else."

Bessie shook her head. " What I start I like to finish. I sort of promised I'd stick by and be a mate to Maurice and I'm not going back on that. Let him go ahead and do what he likes and, when he mucks things up, I'll be there waiting to give a hand."

" You're a mug," Mr. Chugg said ; but his tone was not altogether reproving.

" I dunno. I've been having a great time here." Bessie sighed. " About the best time in my life. Oh, well," she turned to go back, " I guess it'll sort itself out."

" How about me ? " Ron Chugg asked. " Don't I get a look in ? "

Bessie shook her head. " You'll always be standing on your own feet. You don't need anybody."

" Sure I do," he said breathlessly. " I need you bad. So does the brother. He said the other evening you weren't one of these gabblers."

Bessie grinned in the dark. " Did he ? Gee, that's a compliment from James." Her tone softened. " You're a nice boy, Ron, but you're just a boy."

"I'm twenty-four," he said sullenly.

"And I'm a hundred," Bessie responded wearily. "Come on, let's go back."

She could see Ron taking some kind of momentous decision and guessed it was the usual one ; when he suddenly swung her into his arms and attempted to kiss her, she said nastily : "Cut it out. I was trained in Redfern."

They turned their back on the bush fires ; Bessie stumbling ahead, not sure whether to be vexed or to dismiss the incident ; the crestfallen Mr. Chugg following humbly in the rear, not presuming to offer his arm.

II

On the whole Bessie felt kindly to Ron for his ill-advised gesture. It was the sort of thing she might have tried herself if she had been a man, and she bore no malice.

The incident was completely wiped from her mind by an urgent telegram which arrived from Maurice next morning. Automatically Bessie counted the words and decided she could have sent it for a shilling.

"Need your presence every passing hour. Crisis of worst possible description. Demand you come back immediately. At once if not sooner. Desperate situation."

Bessie sped up the road to the Chugg homestead, hardly waiting to change into her city clothes. James Chugg, immobile in the doorway, was contemplating the thick grey haze.

"I've got to go to town," Bessie gasped. "If I shouldn't be back tonight, would you ask Ron to feed the chickens and milk the goat for me ? "

James jerked his head. "Wind's wrong way. Westerly."

Bessie paled. "Oh ! " She paused, undecided. "You mean . . . the fire's coming ? "

James nodded. He eyed her kindly. "Tracys are

moving their stuff. Not over-much time."

Bessie stood biting her lip, trying to make up her mind. She could not disregard Maurice's command ; on the other hand, could she leave all her labour, the hut itself, to go up in smoke unguarded ? Could she do anything if she stayed ?

She looked up at James. " What are *you* going to do ? "

" Burn a break," James said. " Soon's Ron comes back."

. " Will that be any good ? "

" Might. Might not. 'Pends how the wind is. Comes forty miles an hour sometimes. Jumps a hundred feet."

Bessie clenched her fists. Her jaw tightened. She couldn't go. She couldn't leave. Esther had given the hut in her charge, and while it did not matter to Esther if the hut burned, it would matter to Bessie. She could not just walk out and leave it.

" I've had an urgent telegram," she said desolately. " I have to go."

Maurice came first. She had promised to be his mate.

She ran all the way to the station, the sweat damp on her best city dress. In her mind there flashed pictures of the poor goat crying to be let loose, roasting alive ; Esther's hut alight, her beloved microscope locked in the cupboard unwitting of its terrible end ; all Esther's notes and papers ; and Bessie's own vegetables. By the time she reached the city, she was pale and wide-eyed. The tram could not go fast enough. The lift deliberately loitered on its way to the top floor, and Sam, the caretaker, noticing her impatience, gave her a sour smile.

" You're a stranger, Miss Drew," he said far too pleasantly. He jerked his thumb upwards. " Didn't hear about *him* ? "

" Mr. Wainwright ? What about him ? "

" He's in jile," Sam announced with pleasure. " And the right place too. I always said that's where 'e'd land."

Bessie rushed into the studio. A hasty glance showed no one there. The tall green curtains swayed in a dignified way, as though they would draw a veil, if they could, over the scene of disorder. The beautiful green and white studio was a wreck. What furniture remained was piled against one wall. The pictures were lying in a heap on the table. The telephone was gone, the period chairs and tapestries had vanished. The floor was a pattern of boot-marks ; the ante-room was stripped of everything except one chair on which lay a half-eaten cheese sandwich. A hasty tour of the expanse behind the cubicles showed that Mr. Montgomery's office furniture had also departed.

Bessie swept the cheese sandwich from the solitary chair and sat down and nursed her head. There was no note, no explanation except Sam's horrible words. Miss Simons was not in her cubicle. Bessie waited but nothing happened. She continued to wait and found her thoughts veering restlessly from the mysterious disaster which had befallen her betrothed, to the goat and the unprotected chickens and the advancing menace, a crackling chorus to Ron's remark, " Ever seen Hell ? There it is." She had half a mind to catch the next train back.

Bessie had been waiting half an hour when Ernie tramped in unconcernedly and greeted her : " Well, well, hello, Bessie. What do you think of your boy friend ? Huh ? "

Bessie could have shaken him for being so cheerful. " Where is everybody ? " she demanded. " What has happened ? What's going on ? "

Ernie sat down on the table and answered concisely : " Maurice was sold up over a bill he owed, a bill for storage. Jenny is probably up at the police station trying to persuade Maurice to be bailed out or else she's in court. I'm looking after the studio. Just dashed out for a quick one, that's all."

" What's this about Maurice being sold up ? "

Ernie raised his eyebrow. " Old news. Storage people put the bailiff in. Quite a decent chap. Maurice and I taught him to play three-handed whist. We managed to smuggle some of the things out and bought a few of the others. Then, to add to the gaiety, Maurice goes berserk and tries to choke Hodges. He might have known Hodges would give him in charge. He met Hodges in Pitt Street and tried to choke him. Can't say I blame Maurice myself. But he should have let himself be bailed out. Just sulking. That's all it is."

Bessie tried to sort this out. " Start at the beginning," she begged. " How long ago did all this happen ? You know I've been away."

Ernie looked severe. " I must say we've all thought it was a rotten deal you gave poor old Morrie," he reproved. " I stuck up for you. Said you weren't to know they'd put the bailiff in for refusing to pay for the storage of those rugs. Maurice told them in court it was a manifest injustice. Now I remember it, he didn't want you to know anything. Said he would have everything right by the time you came back from Esther's. Silly idea, but I can't blame him, the way you nagged. Of course, knocking Hodges rather upset things."

" When was that ? "

" Saturday." Ernie was surprised. " I thought you at least knew that."

" Go on," Bessie urged wearily. " Go on."

" Well, Maurice is very upset about it. He refused to be bailed out and he says he doesn't care if he gets five years."

Bessie produced her telegram. " Do you know anything about this ? "

Ernie nodded. " I told him to get you back. Thought you might persuade him to have some sense." He rose to go. " Jenny'll be back soon. I don't suppose you

224

mind keeping an eye on the joint ? No sense in two of us wasting our time here." He glanced round the studio and gave her a smile as he disappeared. " Place's a bit unkempt. Needs your hand."

Bessie sat down heavily. She should have been passionately sorry for Maurice ; but instead she was only apathetic. If there had been something for her to do, she might have felt better ; but to be called to sit in the ruins seemed pointless and annoying. She was still sitting in the ante-room with the cheese sandwich at her feet when Jenny hurried in, flushed, voluble, full of explanations. Jenny was triumphantly the Valkyrie who had picked the hero out of the battle, even if she did not know what to do with him.

She had been hoping for an interview with Bessie in which she could tell the girl certain things for her own good. She had even rehearsed what she was going to say : " I think, Bessie, you have been a little too credulous about Maurice's intentions." Perhaps she might pat Bessie's hand. " I'm older than you are, my dear, and I have often thought someone should tell you not to take Maurice's romantic impulses too seriously. . . ."

But the look of Bessie, as usual, set Jenny on edge. What use was good advice to a girl so stolid and self-sufficient ?

" Of course there is nothing you can actually *do*," she began tartly. " But Maurice seemed to want you here."

" Where is he ? "

Jenny's tone took on the hush of one summoning relations to the death-bed. " I drove him straight to my flat. Luckily Clare, my sister, is away. I insisted that he should lie down and have a *complete* rest. After all he's been through . . ."

" It doesn't seem much of an idea," Bessie growled, " leaving this place open with all the mess lying round as an advertisement."

" Really ! " Jenny was indignant. " I can't be expected to do *everything*. You go off and leave Maurice in the lurch for a month, and then come back and complain because the bailiff and the auctioneer haven't kept the place spotless."

Bessie cut in abruptly : " I don't quite get the strength of this Angel of Mercy stunt. Did you put Maurice up to sacking Billy Raine-Smith ? He'd never have done it by himself. And I bet you had the bright idea that Maurice could specialize in advertising."

" I introduced him to a friend of mine," Jenny said icily, " the director of Universal Milk Distributors, and Maurice was given the handling of the posters for the More Milk Campaign. If that is a crime . . . Anyway, I'd like to know what right you have to sit there catechizing me ? "

" Skip it," Bessie said moodily. What was the use of talking to Jenny ? She rose and kicked the cheese sandwich under the table. " Tell Maurice I'm going back to help fight a bush fire. There's nothing I can do here."

" I think you might at least stay and mind the place. . . ."

" Shut it up," Bessie suggested heartlessly. " Maurice has his excuse to quit. He brought this on himself, every bit of it. Tell him the marriage is still on if he wants it. I guess the family will take us in till I can find a job, and then we'll get a furnished room somewhere." She looked at Jenny sturdily. " If you've got a better suggestion, let's have it."

" You're a peculiar girl," Jenny said with distaste. " Disposing of the world as if it were second-hand." This was her chance for that acid maternal speech. " I am a good deal older than you . . ."

" And a damn sight sillier." Bessie adopted something of her father's pugnacity. " Fussing over Maurice like a hen with one chick. Ernie could have bailed him out or he could have stayed where he was to cool down. Maurice just loves a fuss the way a kid does. If he'd paid the stupid bill for the rugs instead of going hysterical about it . . ."

Jenny was very angry indeed. The Valkyrie needed only armour and a winged helmet to go into battle ; but arguing with Bessie was like stubbing your toe on a rock. Jenny decided to be icy, a great lady reproving a gutter child.

" Of course, to your realistic outlook, the sensitivity of a man like Maurice would be inexplicable." A grim smile flickered on Bessie's face for a moment. " It has been obvious to Us All," Jenny swept on grandly. " Steering Maurice into a marriage which would hamper his whole career ! The absolute crudity of the whole affair is laughable."

Bessie was not really listening. The trains, she thought, ran every few minutes past the hour. A quarter of an hour to the station by tram . . .

" What time is it ? " she demanded.

Jenny was taken aback. " It's a quarter to twelve."

" 'Struth ! " Bessie jumped up. She turned on Jenny determinedly. " Look here. If you can get Maurice to America, big ideas, Absence Register and all, I'll chuck him. What d'you say ? "

Jenny's mouth opened. " Upon my word," she said indignantly. " Who are *you* to dispose of . . ."

Bessie was irritated. " Now be sensible. I've been thinking a lot about Maurice. He doesn't need a mate. He needs some money. Have you got any ? That's all I'm asking."

Jenny thought. It was no time to palter. " Yes," she replied coldly. " I think I could put Maurice beyond reach of any economic embarrassment, if that's what you mean."

"Good. I thought you'd have a few pounds stowed in the sock." Bessie shrugged her shoulders in that characteristic way she had caught from Maurice. "You're right. He'd be a wash-out as a husband. Too much temperament, bless him. Now, remember, I'm leaving him to you in my will. He's yours. Tell him I've quit. Anything you like." She had an inspiration. "Tell him I'm going to marry Ron Chugg."

"Chugg?"

"Chugg is the name." She turned resolutely to the door. "Good-bye. I'd get him to America if I were you. Never do any good here."

She was gone. One minute she was there, self-reliant, concentrated ; the next, there was nothing but the cheese sandwich lying under the empty chair. Jenny stood dismayed. If Bessie had hurled a hand grenade instead of this decision, she could not have been more shattering. What would Maurice say? He would blame the poor Valkyrie ; he would say that she had driven Bessie away and would rush after Bessie, forgetting all, the studio and herself. Tears came to Jenny's eyes as she thought of the position in which she had been placed.

"The little wretch," she said brokenly. "Oh dear!"

Outside the studio Bessie paused for a moment, then started towards the Quay at a pace that caused people to turn and watch her. She flew down Pitt Street running like a professional. Esther's brother, of Gullick & Co., Ironmongers and Hardware, was only a few blocks away. If only she could see Lester and convince him that he must drive her back! They could be there long before the train. Oh, he must!

Bessie panted into the office and clamoured her way to its chief with desperate assurances of the urgency of her mission. Lester rose and shook hands, adjusting his pince-nez surprisedly.

"It's the bush fire," Bessie gasped. "Esther's away."

"Dear me, Bessie, you *have* been running. Miss Stokes, will you bring a glass of water? Now tell me what it is, Bessie."

"The bush fire," Bessie gasped out more collectedly. "On the mountains. We need everyone we can to beat it out. Would you please drive me back, quickly, as fast as ever you can? And bring everyone you can spare. Oh, please, Mr. Gullick. There's all Esther's notes, and the poor goat. . . ."

"What are you doing down here?"

"I had to come. Please don't wait to ask. If we don't get there in time . . ."

Lester Gullick patted her hand soothingly. "Now, don't excite yourself, Bessie. My sister's notes, a few yards of wire netting and a tumble-down weatherboard shanty. Really, it isn't worth worrying about. Esther won't mind. It's unfortunate, of course, but the place is worth very little. One of my least profitable investments. It may develop into something approaching a real-estate value in twenty years' time, but it's too far from the city to subdivide. It's a good thing there's nobody there, though, of course, I'm sorry you wasted so much work on those vegetables."

Bessie was staring at him dazedly. "But it's *your* place. You own it. You wouldn't let it burn, Mr. Gullick, not without . . . without . . . raising a hand?"

"Don't you worry any more. I'm sorry your holiday has been spoilt by this fire but I'm glad you came back to Sydney. I didn't like Esther leaving you. I should have worried at the idea of your being there alone."

Bessie rose. "I'll have to go. Good-bye."

"Stay and have lunch with me."

"I can just catch the train," Bessie muttered distractedly. "I'm taking a taxi."

She rushed down the stairs. I'm taking a taxi to the station, she repeated to herself. It always emphasized to

Bessie the greatness of a crisis to take a taxi. She had just enough money of the housekeeping fund Esther had left. But the train had to be caught. If the hut burned, she would never forgive herself, she thought fiercely. It might be Lester's hut financially, but spiritually it was Bessie's. "Patriotism," Esther had called it. "The emotion that makes a peasant turn out with a hay-fork to face machine-guns." If she had to do it alone, Bessie would be waiting for that bush fire with a green bough in her hand.

III

There was just a hope of saving the place. Had it been in its original condition, housing Esther's wild live-stock under heaps of dead leaves and bushes, there would have been no hope. But the ploughed land all round the house, the fact that Bessie had cleared and planted the slope to the creek, gave the weatherboard hut in the middle a fighting chance. With a little luck and not too fierce a westerly, it might survive.

Bessie peered from the train window, sick at heart, ready to cry at each halt and delay, each leisurely pause at little stations. When the guard remarked: "There's a lot of bush fires burning in these gullies," Bessie could have choked him for his indifference.

At the station the smoke was strong in the air. The store was deserted, a bad sign. They were all away helping neighbours further towards the fire. Before the train had stopped Bessie was running up the platform, racing across the line, her heart pounding madly as she set out for the hut. It was a long, weary walk at the best of times ; it was worse for running, but with pain-fully distended lungs Bessie ran all the way. Sometimes she would fall into a gasping trot only to put on another burst of speed as she prayed : "Let me only get there before the fire. Let it not have happened." Bessie usually disapproved of praying. She hardly knew she was doing it.

There was smoke eddying towards her, the sound of the shouts of men. She met one of them coming up the track.

" Ron Chugg and the others are burning a fire-break on top of the ridge to go round Tracy's place and yours and their own."

The audacity of the thing halted Bessie in her tracks. Fire-breaks around a fence she understood ; but to burn a whole ridge, that was tremendous.

" How many are there ? "

" Tracy and his kids, and Ron and his brother and a couple from the store."

" Where's the fire ? "

" She's only five mile or so away and coming strong."

Even if they burned their fire-break, they would still have to stand by to see that the fire did not creep in at the sides. On a scorching day hot enough to burn you without any help from the fire, they had been beating and fighting since she left. A deep sense of her desertion came over Bessie, a contempt for herself that flung her down the track at a headlong pace.

Mr. Tracy and the lad from the store were arguing as she panted up.

" We should've tried to stop it at the creek," Mr. Tracy argued. " We'd been on a better wicket then."

" Yeah ? With all that thick stuff along the bank waiting for the chance to go up. Like fun."

From the ridge the view of the fire was alarming. Like a morning mist the smoke came rolling up the valley, first thin, then eddying higher until it blotted out the opposite hill.

" Come on, get going. Clear this stuff."

They fell to again like madmen, burning and beating,

the boys ready along the bank of the creek to stifle any dangerous leapage.

"She's coming fast," Mr. Tracy muttered, wiping the sweat off his brow as he contemplated a roaring bonfire of dead bush and leaves. "She ain't far off now." When Mr. Tracy really swung into action, he could do four men's work.

They toiled along the top of the ridge, blackened, blistered, coughing in the smoke, their eyes streaming tears from reddened lids. The break would have to run the full length of a curved line round Tracy's, the hut and the Chugg property.

From the top of the ridge to the creek was a matter of two hundred yards : an ambitious fire-break with little time to make it and a danger that some stray spark would prove as dangerous as the greater fire rolling up behind them. It was a faint hope, but the only hope for two families standing to lose everything they possessed. As for Bessie, she worked with the tenacity, the grim determination of a woman who had given up every other aim in life. A shout from the boys, and she and James were rushing down the slope over the burnt ground to where the fire had leapt the creek and was blazing in a patch of dead brushwood. Stopping to snatch a mouthful of water flavoured with cinders, they began their flailing at the yellow harvest of flames.

The side of the ridge was now smoking in half a dozen places ; the fires were cracking down it with eager beaters dodging carefully round. It was too big a job for a handful of people ; and, with a gulp of anxiety, Bessie realized that the greater fire was driving up on them, the mist was rising rapidly. Could they keep their own fire under control and yet extend it to protect the three farms in a sufficient sweep of blackened, cleared ground ? Might not a spark from their own fire light the opposite flank of the ridge where stood the hut and, higher up, the

Chugg farm ? Tracy's round the creek was in a safer position, as the fire must go through Chugg's and Esther's property to reach it.

Coughing and choking, her eyebrows singed, her shoes hot and baking, her throat dry and parched, Bessie raced up the height again. It was a monumental job they had set themselves ; a job for a gang of trained forestry men, not the awkward little band of beaters blistering themselves unnecessarily in the holocaust. Each had under his charge a section of the break. If it got out of hand, the others were to be called upon, but only as a last resource.

The sparse stringy-barks on top of the ridge, the stony ground, were in favour of the beaters. Here and there a dead tree began to glow into a red-hot lump ; but the dead leaves, the sticks, were carefully watched.

" It's the sparks jumping the creek we've got to look out for," Ron muttered to Bessie. " Lucky the wind ain't high."

The wind was increasing however. The choking, thickening smoke from the advancing fury blinded them with its hot breath.

" She's over," one of the Tracy boys howled, and Bessie raced along the creek bank to attack a patch of dead leaves which had burst into a blaze.

One minute there was only the white choking smoke, then suddenly in the dead leaves a little devilish flame, running ahead, danced up ; and then other spikes of fire sprang from the ground like her Christmas bells, while Bessie's green bough rose and fell, threshing them into a blackened quiescence.

As Bessie worked monotonously, automatically, her thoughts were not on the fire. They had settled into a timeless contemplation, emotionless, ruthless, of her life, her plans, her very existence. Without her volition this detached part of her was making up its mind, summarizing, setting fact against fact. Like the bush fire she fought, her thoughts blackened and blighted all they touched ; but with the promise that from these cinders new plans might rise.

She had been a fool, was the first conclusion. A fool who went blindly from the biscuit factory and Archer Street to the studio and a round of futile activities. Her life had been full of mental lies, half of them the result of her home, half of Maurice's snobbery. Her mind took the decision calmly : Maurice was a snob, an upholder of small values.

He had taught her that clothes counted ; that money counted ; the people you knew counted. He had encouraged her to tell lies, to be selfish. But, worst of all, there was the example of poor Maurice always telling lies to himself ; never finding himself out ; revelling in a self-imposed martyrdom ; wrapping himself in his own esteem. To live with him was to live with a walking lie.

To live in Archer Street was to live in a lie ; for the poverty, the bitterness and stupidity of Archer Street were just not necessary — she saw that now. To go back to Archer Street and all it meant ; to get some hot, hurried job as a waitress, a factory hand, was to slip into a hole between lumps of brick and mortar, to bury yourself for ever. To go back to Maurice was to return to an emotional and mental insecurity, living the shadow of Maurice's life, feeding on the husks of a prodigal's habits.

It was not Maurice's spendthrift poverty that frightened her ; Bessie had always been without money, had grown used to it. But the way Maurice threw his emotions around, the way he wallowed and gloried in his emotions, was frightening. Now she must make the decision : either to go back loyally to Maurice and spend her life thwarting and annoying him, having her own nerves ground to a sharp edge by his conceits ; or to betray him basely in his hour of need for his own good. The knot had to be cut or tied tighter. To compromise, to linger and defer : that was Maurice's way. She had followed it when she was uncertain, when she did not know what she wanted.

Now she knew what she wanted. She had found the life, the place that had been meant for her : the place that gave tranquillity and clarity of mind even in the midst of fire and disaster. It was not her reason told her this, but something deeper, something that sang " Never to go away, never to go away, to live, to live, never to go away " with every blow of the draggled bough.

Bessie wiped her stinging eyes and stood trembling with weariness, her knees failing under her. Her mind went on tirelessly reasoning for all that her body ached and sagged. To love a place was somehow cleaner than to love a person. In time you might identify a person with a place as she identified Maurice with the city. But there was a joy in seeing plants take water from you, in turning soil, in aching labour, in rest, in the loneliness and calm of trees. Maurice would never be happy in the mountains and she could never, never live in the city again.

Having arrived at this statement of fact, Bessie took one more desperate, weary swipe at the patch of scorched bush and pitched sideways on to the smoking ground into a blackness of complete unconsciousness, so deep that she did not realize her eyebrows, her hair, were singeing ; that had she not been snatched up, she would have smoked like the soles of her own shoes.

CHAPTER XV

I

MAURICE did not really swing into action until the following day. He had spent the evening of the bush fire at the club, receiving condolences from fellows who were inclined to treat him as a hero. It was something to be a man of iron determination and relentless will who, when outraged by a partner bent on disclaiming all liabilities, responsibilities and deficits, slugged that partner in the public street and squashed his loathly straw boater.

"An eyesore the thing was," one club member remarked. "You performed a public service, old man."

But all congratulations rang hollow without Bessie. The horrible ache of her absence, the astonishing, mystifying message she had left, occupied Maurice's mind to the exclusion of all else. He looked in at the studio next morning languidly and decided that only a Turkish bath would clear his brain. That took him most of the morning and he seized on Ernie and dragged him off to lunch, pouring out his troubles with a dramatic power surprising in one who confessed himself " completely crushed, dazed with the shock into a state of imbecility ".

"Of course it isn't true," he kept repeating. "But the fact that she could heartlessly leave a message like that when she knew I depended on her, is beyond my comprehension. It's the callousness of it."

"You don't think there's anything in this Chugg rumour then ? " Ernie was interested. His regard for Bessie had risen. The girl had some sense after all. He had always suspected it.

"There is and there isn't. She has probably been carrying on some kind of an affair, but I don't for a minute believe it's serious."

" Then what are you worrying about, blast you, if she isn't going to marry the bloke ? "

" It's the heartlessness of it at such a time. As to the Chugg episode," Maurice proceeded to contradict himself, "that is proved fact. I knew it," he said brokenly, " I knew it all along. I told you from the first, Ernie, that she was only going down to Esther's because she had struck up an understanding with the post-digging yokel. Good God ! the ignominy of it ! To crash this on me when she knew I was snowed under with other troubles ! The base, deceitful, little . . ." The tears began to run down his face and fell into the dandelion salad he was eating for lunch. " The only woman I ever really loved ! "

" For God's sake pull yourself together ! " Ernie snarled. " Do you want all the rest of the gang to see you in this mess ? " Maurice's habit of weeping in public had always filled Ernie with horror ; and the club was the last place in which to weep while eating.

" I can't help it," Maurice murmured. " I am completely overcome. The only woman I ever really loved."

Twenty years of Rose, Ernie thought gloomily, and now, I suppose, there will be twenty years of Bessie ; and he will be able to tell a succession of girls about his broken heart.

" You're well rid of her," he consoled. " She never was so beautiful that the sunbeams followed her round. I always told you, didn't I, that she'd skid off with someone else ? You're damn lucky it happened before you'd made even a worse ass of yourself about her."

" You don't understand." Maurice lifted a mouthful of salad, the tears still running down his face. " Bessie meant all the world to me. I don't believe for a minute she realized what she was saying— But to leave such a message at such a time. The shock of it has stunned me completely."

Ernie moaned, not in sympathy, but with self-pity.

"I'll be getting along," he said hurriedly. "Got to see a chap. . . ."

"Did I ever tell you about the week-end we spent together?"

"Yes, you did — often."

Maurice gripped him by the arm. "Wait!" he said dramatically. "Wait! It's all coming back to me. I said then . . ."

"Listen, Morrie . . ."

"I said then there was something of the peasant about her. That was intuition, sheer intuition. And it is the gross type of this Chugg swine that attracts the peasant in her. He is so completely rural. He fits the kind of hovel, the kind of dull existence Bessie hankers after."

"Well, why not let her have it? Why not just . . ."

"Let me get this clear." Maurice pushed the salad to one side. "There are obviously two conflicting tendencies in Bessie. The one which brings out her better nature, the one that I have roused, and a lower, earthier streak . . ."

"I have to see old Joe Adams. You know Joe, Morrie? I simply must see him about the meeting on the 10th. It's important, Morrie."

"You can spare a minute to come back to the studio, Ernie. I want to show you something. I feel you will understand . . ." He seized his hat.

"We'll tell Louis to tick it up," Ernie said casually. "He'll let it wait until next week. D'you owe him much, Morrie?"

"Only about two pounds." Maurice had just borrowed five pounds from Jenny, but he felt it would be injudicious to allow either Ernie or Louis to know this.

"Well, I owe him more than that, so he can charge it to you. Come on, dammit, if you've got to get whatever it is off your chest, I suppose I'll have to put up with you." He seized Maurice by the arm and lugged him into the hall. " And no more of this damn howling, hear me ? "

The studio was as Bessie had seen it the day before, only more dejected if anything.

" I suppose Jenny's having lunch too," Maurice said indifferently. " I should have invited her, but I didn't feel quite in the mood for Jenny."

He led Ernie to one of the cubicles and pointed to a square object neatly wrapped. He lifted the cover.

" Look ! " Maurice stood back dramatically. " I made it for Bessie. I spent my spare time when I could have been at the club, when I could have been forgetting my worries, my economic instability . . ." He broke off, the tears beginning again. " A labour of love — for her."

" What the hell is it ? " Ernie cocked one eyebrow enquiringly.

" It's a chicken-brooder," Maurice explained. He lifted the sacking to show the little strips of flannel. " I was keeping it for a surprise. And now she does this to me and it's all wasted."

" You're a bloody mug," Ernie said harshly. " You always have been a bloody mug about women, Maurice. Take 'em and leave 'em, that's my motto. You'll get over it."

" I still feel," Maurice was determined to extract the last ounce from the situation, " that there has been a misunderstanding somewhere. I don't know where. At first I thought Jenny was lying, but she really isn't a good liar ; and where would she have got the name Chugg if not from Bessie ? No, it all fits in. It's too obviously true."

" Well, there's nothing you can do about it."

" I can go to her, implore her to be reasonable. I can humiliate myself. I can convince her she must come back."

" You can do nothing of the sort," Ernie snarled. " The trouble with you is your damn vanity. You just have to get that girl back on principle or, if you don't, you'll make all our lives a misery. I know you, Maurice. The fish that got away is always bigger than the one you caught. If you hadn't made a mess of things when you went skylarking together that time at Esther's, none of this would have happened. You would have got fed up with the kid and passed on to someone else. But just because . . ."

" Nothing of the kind. The way I feel towards Bessie is different. She is worth any sacrifice, any trouble."

" Maurice ! " Jenny had returned, rather breathlessly. " Oh ! there you are."

Ernie, seeing a chance of escape, leapt at it. " Well, I'll drop in and see how things are some time, Morrie," he said breezily. " So long."

" Bessie hasn't been here again, has she ? " Jenny asked, half hopefully, half fearfully. She had learnt a lesson from Bessie. Perhaps Jenny was too old to change now, but it struck her that being a lady had disadvantages.

" The whole thing is ghastly." Maurice was not sure whether to be dramatic or pathetic. He tugged the lock of hair which should have hidden but did not hide his bald patch. " Have you ever noticed the way everything happens at once, Jen ? You can't smash one plate without the salad bowl and a cup smashing too ? "

Jenny nodded sympathetically. " What are you going to do now, Morrie ? " She had been asking that at intervals for days.

" God knows." If Maurice knew, he did not feel inclined to confide in Jenny. She was being very noble and anxious to cancel her engagement in Melbourne to help him through this crisis.

" You go off to Melbourne, Jenny," he said wearily. " I'll be perfectly right. I'll just go out and get Bessie from that hole of Esther's and start building afresh." He passed his hand wearily over his brow. " Building afresh," he murmured. "All that pain and effort gone for nothing. Oh, well!" He gave a pitifully brave smile. "I suppose it's just luck or Fate or something that downs a man."

"Poor old Morrie." She put her rather plump white hand on his shoulder. "Why don't you leave all this and take on the idea of being my press-agent?"

Maurice patted the hand that lay on his shoulder. "Dear Jen," he murmured. "Always so solid, a true friend. But I suppose," again that weary little smile, "that one has one's pride."

"You do make me so angry, Maurice." Jenny's tone was plaintive. "Honestly, I wouldn't be a bit surprised if you were heading for a nervous breakdown. Why can't you be sensible and leave this miserable business? You know you hate it, and what's the use of carrying on with something you hate?"

"True," he murmured abstractedly. "True." He was still patting that plump white hand. "But there are . . . loyalties."

"You and your pride and loyalties," Jenny said bluntly. "You're only thinking of Bessie and she only thinks of herself." Again that plump white hand descended maternally on his shoulder. "I hope to see you in America when I go over next year. If you would only . . ."

"Jenny," this time he squeezed her hand, "you're a darling. But never, never could one allow oneself to form a parasitic growth on someone else's reputation."

"You could make a reputation of your own. You need leisure and money to do the things you could do."

Maurice cast a glance round the studio and was depressed by the prospect. "I suppose I'd better get a man to clean up this place and put the furniture back. I haven't the heart myself." There was a knock at the door. "That will be Fullman wanting to know when I can move out. Well, I won't move, and that's all about it, it doesn't matter how urgent he gets."

II

Discussing Bessie with Ernie and Jenny was one thing ; making an assault on Esther's stronghold and having it out with Bessie was quite another.

There was a hoodoo on the place. Every time he went down there something unpleasant happened. Had Maurice been superstitious he would have crossed his fingers.

The thought of the dreary walk from the station deterred him ; but he was determined to make the journey. It was a late, leisurely train he caught that evening ; and he travelled with the gloomy and sinister grandeur of one from whom Fate's blows rebound. Nothing now, he felt, had power to hurt him. He would overlook Bessie's selfishness and coldness of heart ; he would forgive her ; but he could not forget that in his hour of need she had deserted him. He would take her back but it would be a long, long time before she regained her old place in his regard.

From the evidence about him on his walk to the hut he concluded that there really had been a fire. The whole area looked and smelt abominable. However, the hillside on which the hut stood appeared, as far as he could judge in the dark, to be unscathed. The hut door was open and he paused in it melodramatically. Bessie, he was surprised to observe, had lost her eyebrows. What was left of her hair was covered by a red handkerchief ; and without her eyebrows, Wainwright reflected, Bessie looked more like a peasant than ever. Her companion, the loathsome Chugg, was also showing signs of wear and tear ; but *his* burns Maurice was able to regard with equanimity.

The two were playing chess by the light of the lamp, and they looked up rather surprised, but without any of the guilt Maurice anticipated.

" And so I find you ! " Maurice paused to note the effect. Bessie did not jump up to welcome him ; she did not rush forward joyously as of old.

" I'm glad you've come, Maurice." She turned to Ron. " Now, maybe, I'll get a straight story of what happened to the studio."

Maurice remained standing in the doorway like a figure of doom. He was not going to have his entrance spoiled. " What is all this," he demanded, " about you being about to marry someone else ? "

This time he succeeded in disconcerting Bessie. " Nothing of the sort," she said hastily.

" You didn't tell Jenny you were about to marry this — " he jerked his head at her chess partner, " this . . . gentleman ? "

The gentleman in question was regarding Bessie intently.

" You've got it all wrong," Bessie hastened to explain. " Sit down, Maurice, and don't look so dramatic." She turned appealingly to Ron. " You shove off home like a good scout and let me sort this out."

Very slowly and deliberately Mr. Chugg shook his head. " I'm in on this." He sat like a rock. " What was that about marryin' me ? "

Bessie cursed under her breath. This was one of those situations Maurice loved, a chance to demand explanations, to be aggrieved, to fly into a passion, perhaps to do as he had done with Hodges, giving a display of the man tried beyond his patience and gone berserk. If Maurice attempted to blacken Ron's eye, he would find it a very different proposition from blackening Hodges'. Bessie could not imagine Ron calling for the police. He looked quite capable of tearing Maurice apart.

" I am still waiting, Bessie," Maurice's voice was chilly, " for an explanation."

" So'm I." Ron Chugg was enjoying himself.

" Well, you won't get one," Bessie retorted sulkily. She was exhausted and in no mood to struggle against Maurice.

" Bessie," Maurice tried pained reproach, " kid, do you think this is fair ? "

" I don't know about it being fair," Bessie faced him determinedly, " but if you're going to yell for explanations and stand there looking like a storm at sea, you can go to the devil."

Maurice's usual course, in the face of such stubborn unreason, would have been to call Bessie all the unpleasant names he could remember, but the presence of Ron Chugg spoilt his vocabulary. Bessie never took offence when abused, but there was no saying that Ron Chugg might not become incensed at some of the visitor's pet phrases. Maurice therefore created a diversion.

" Where is Esther ? " he demanded.

" She'll be back to-morrow. She's away at a bugging conference."

That was quite enough to give Maurice his opening. He flashed into it brilliantly.

" So ! " He raised his eyebrows. " Very pretty. Esther has left you here, presumably by yourself, for how long did you say ? "

" What's up with you ? You know the way Esther's always going off somewhere. She's going to Central Australia in a couple of months."

" And I presume you will stay and entertain visitors in her absence ? " Maurice was beginning to be very nasty indeed. " I trust it is worth your while ? Much more lucrative than working in the city. So much a night of chess lessons, shall we say ? "

Ron was beginning to be annoyed, but Bessie jerked

him back to his seat with a glance that said : " You let me handle this."

" Now don't be silly, Maurice," she said quietly and reasonably. " I asked you out last week-end and you didn't choose to come. If you had come out then and told me all about that silly business of the bailiff, I might have come back at once. But no, you didn't say a word."

Bessie had found a weak point for attack, but before she could seize her advantage, Maurice leapt in again.

" I should have been sorry to spoil your charming tête-à-tête. I can see I had good reason for my suspicion that it was not Esther's company you were seeking. Oh no ! Fresh fields and pastures new ! Any pretext, any pretext whatever, will serve a cunning woman. . . ." Had they been alone, he probably would have said " treacherous bitch ", but the presence of Ron was hampering him.

Bessie was exasperated. She hated Maurice's method of innuendo.

" While I have been fighting, struggling," his mood of self-pity and indignation deepened, " to stem the financial troubles that threatened to break up all our hopes, *you* have been engaged in dalliance with someone you obviously decided was nearer your intellectual and moral level. Really . . ."

Ron did not know what dalliance meant, but it sounded nasty. He stuck out his jaw. " You lay off it," he ordered. " You stop chucking hints about and spit it out straight or not at all."

Maurice ignored Ron Chugg superbly. As far as he was concerned, his manner said, the yokel had ceased to exist. The discussion was between himself and Bessie.

" Consider the thing from only one angle," he urged, " from that of public decency. I have a certain standing, a reputation, to consider. I cannot allow your name to be coupled with low gossip, scandal. Do you think I want people to know that while I was slaving in the city endeavouring to make enough money to marry the woman of my choice, she had crept away to an isolated spot where she could entertain her paramours in secret? Ordinary, common decency, Bessie, at least, should have restrained you. I must say I am disgusted, not only by your inordinate selfishness and conceit, but by your lack of all moral scruples. To come down here to live with a man furtively disgusts all the best in civilized persons. . . ."

Bessie was watching this display of virtuous indignation with a detached curiosity. It had never occurred to her before that there was any resemblance between Maurice and her father. She had previously taken Maurice's lectures as her due. Now, however, when he let loose on moral tone, there was, despite the difference in wording, a similarity of outlook between Maurice and her parent : the same harping on what people thought, the same snobbish regard for reputation, the same imputation of evil motives.

Ron was getting restive. He looked calculatingly from Maurice's face to his own nobbly fist, as if measuring the impact. " How about me knocking him cold ? " he suggested, in the middle of Maurice's eloquence. Ernie had often had the same impulse to stop that flow of reason with a well-delivered left, and Ernie had endured it for years.

Bessie shook her head silently and once more Ron relapsed into a stifled resentment.

" I can only attribute your behaviour to your physiology," Maurice was saying. " Naturally, having gone too far and wishing to cover your conduct with a seeming but over-hasty propriety, you now inform me through a third party that you are going to marry this man." He paused on his climax. " I demand the truth. Is that or is that not your intention ? "

"No," Bessie said clearly. "I'm not going to marry Ron, and I'm not going to marry you, not if you were the last man in the world."

"Well, at least we know where we stand." Maurice again got into his stride. "I take it that to lie to me, to deceive and plot for no earthly reason that I can see . . ."

"I just wanted to end it quick, that's all. I didn't think it was a fair deal marrying you, and I thought you'd be less likely to make a fuss about it, if you thought I was marrying someone. I might have known," Bessie admitted resignedly, "that you'd make a fuss anyway."

"Oh no ! Oh dear me, no ! " Maurice was fiercely dramatic. "A man centres his life in one woman, plans, dreams, works to build his whole career to suit her whims ; but to say one word against a base and treacherous betrayal, when he sees his life crashing to the ground in ruins — that would be an impertinence." He quivered with fury. "Shall I tell you what I think of you ? "

"I thought you had," Bessie sighed wearily. Maurice, she remembered, always wore down her resistance in the end. He talked and talked until people got so tired that they were ready to give him anything for a little peace. A nagger, Bessie thought suddenly, Maurice once said *I* was a nagger. Huh !

"I can see it all now," Maurice swept on. "All that talk about being a mate, a partner, standing staunchly beside me — I should have known what kind of female you were, only seizing the main chance, ready to clutch at any man who would provide you with money or security, dropping him if something better turned up. A gold-digger ! A thieving, clutching, scheming, selfish female in search of a good provider. I trust, oh, I do firmly trust, that you realize your own ignominious and filthy betrayal of all that womanhood has been thought to mean by people who have not had any experience of you." This was Maurice at his best, but Ron was definitely getting out of hand.

" Hey ! " he shouted loudly, " I'll give you a belt over the ear if you don't shut up."

" I don't doubt you would try." Maurice swung round on him. " The only reasoning of which your type is capable is violence, and violence, to the civilized person, is beneath contempt, with those who use it. Certainly, by all means, use your thug tactics to silence my justifiable observations on your lady friend's methods. By all means use force to silence reason. But do not think by those means to silence your own conscience, if you have any conscience buried in the muddled depths of what goes under the courtesy title of your nature. You, a thick-headed lout, a goat-tending rural slug, what can you understand of ordinary, civilized conduct ? "

Ron did not mind Maurice's attacking him, but he objected to Bessie's being abused. Bessie, on the other hand, was used to Maurice calling her names, but she did not like his turning on Ron Chugg who had done nothing, she felt, to deserve it.

" You leave Ron alone," she said firmly. " He's done nothing."

" I'm sure of it. He hasn't the ability, but you might inspire him at least to promiscuity. I am deeply grateful," Maurice took a deep breath, " deeply grateful to you, Bessie, for all you have done for *me*. You have given me a valuable lesson. From this time on I will act selfishly, greedily, with no care for a soul in the world. I will learn to distrust all women, now that the one woman whom I had ever loved has so filthily shown me what she can do in the way of treachery and deceit. I will use others for my ends and throw them aside. I will lie, owe debts of honour that I do not pay, break promises. I will be utterly unscrupulous. Oh ! I will, be sure, profit by your inspiration and help . . . soul-mate ! "

Tears sprang into Maurice's eyes as he contemplated his forlorn future as a Timon of Athens (revised version). He would go to America with Jenny, become rich, famous, esteemed, but always, always, those about him would know that a hidden canker, bravely concealed, was warping his native nobility. And then, the sadness of it all overcame him. Anger and righteousness did not seem to be having any effect on Bessie. She was lost to all decent feeling. But one thing had never failed to bring her to her senses. Pathos ! Maurice sat down and cried.

He might not have resorted to this in the presence of Ron Chugg, had he not felt that desperate measures were necessary. He was not in any way self-conscious about weeping. Many a time before he had resorted to tears when Bessie proved recalcitrant. Besides it did him good. It was a relief. He had worn himself out being angry.

" Bessie ! " he sobbed brokenly. " Bessie ! To think you would do this to me ! After all you have been to me ! "

Bessie, he was pleased to note, reacted immediately. It did not matter that she had so often accused him of turning on tears for his own ends, using them as a weapon. She was immediately at his side, murmuring endearing words, hugging him tenderly.

" There, there," she comforted. " Don't, please, Maurice. Please ! Look, I'm sorry I've been horrid to you. I didn't mean it, really. I didn't. Now stop and I'll do anything you like."

Ron Chugg watched this reunion with the greatest indignation. Maurice's sobs did not move him to sympathetic tenderness. On the contrary, he felt that his rival was taking a low-down, unfair advantage. Ron Chugg was incapable of bursting into tears and had not done so since he was a small boy. To hear Bessie cooing to the sufferer who, a minute ago, had been tearing her character to shreds, seemed to him the limit of unreason.

" Hey ! " he protested indignantly. " Hey, go easy."

Bessie looked up from her mothering. " You run along, Ron," she said gently. " I'll talk to Maurice and everything will be all right."

" I won't run along. And everything'll *not* be all right. Twistin' you round his finger ! Gee ! I thought you'd got more backbone than that."

Maurice allowed himself to be mopped up and took no notice of the scorn of Mr. Chugg. " My dear," he murmured brokenly. " Say it is all a mistake. Say it is all a horrible nightmare, and that you still love me."

" Of course I do. But, Maurice . . ."

" My darling, then nothing in the world matters except that." He rose majestically but rather tear-sodden. " Come ! "

" What do you mean ? " Bessie asked dubiously.

" I forgive you. Not another word will I ever utter about this . . . this . . . lapse. I will never reproach you. Only come now, away from here for ever."

" I can't just clear out and let Esther find the place empty," Bessie explained reasonably. " Look, Maurice, when Esther comes back to-morrow, I'll tell her you need me in the studio and I can't," she sighed involuntarily, " stay here and raise ducks after all."

" Do you think," Maurice said with a sniff, " that I'm going to leave you here with that low-down swine lurking about till all hours of the morning ? I insist that you come away with me now." He drew himself up. " Now or never. Make your choice."

" Well, I can't just clear out to-night, and that's all about it. For one thing, I'm too tired. You don't seem to realize there's been a fire."

Maurice said splendidly : " Then, darling, I will remain here. Yes, yes, I'm sorry. I can see I have been wrong — selfish. I'll stay."

" You can't do that either," Bessie amended hastily.

She was conscious of a silent howl of protest from Mr. Chugg. " I'd sooner be by myself, thanks all the same." Men, she thought, were a nuisance, always complicating simple things. Why couldn't Maurice be sensible ? From the look of Ron Chugg he was not going to be sensible either.

" I would prefer to stay here," Maurice said thoughtfully. " I didn't tell you, Bessie, but Fullman has proved himself a snake, a reptile of the same breed as Sam. During the time of The Trouble the man actually called in a lock-maker and put a new lock on the front door. A lock," he added with virtuous indignation, " to which I have been unable to obtain a duplicate key."

" Well, where are you staying now ? "

" For the time being," Maurice admitted, " until finances adjust themselves, I have accepted the hospitality of Jenny and her sister Clare."

" Oh-ho ! " Bessie said indignantly. " And Clare's away. Jenny told me that yesterday. A nice one you are to come out and put that What-will-people-think stuff over me ! And I take it, this Come-let-us-walk-into-the-night takes us both back to Jenny's flat ? "

" No." Maurice was dignified. " Not at all. If you prefer it, I will take you to any hotel you choose." He remembered that he still had sufficient of Jenny's five pounds.

" Huh ! Look, Maurice, you trot back to town and I'll show up to-morrow at the studio just as soon as I fix everything with Esther. Can't say fairer than that, can I ? "

" I will not agree," Maurice said, " to my prospective wife staying alone in the vicinity of a potential menace of this man's type."

Bessie almost yelled : " But I'm not your prospective wife. Get that straight. I wouldn't marry you, Maurice," she searched for a word, " not for quids."

Maurice sat down and took up the discussion tenaciously. "You said you loved me, didn't you ? Just a moment ago ? "

" I think you're a darling, but I'd go mad if I married you. I think Ron's a darling." She loyally included the third member of the party. " But I wouldn't marry him either. I want to be left alone. I've only got one life, haven't I ? I want to find out what suits me and do it. I like being out here raising vegetables, but since I told you I'd stick by the studio, I will. Get it straight, the marriage is off — permanently and completely."

" In that case," Maurice folded his arms, " I will stay here and endeavour to persuade you that you are wrong."

From behind them came a deep growl. " So will I," said Mr. Chugg. " She said she was goin' to marry me ? All right, I've got a right to sit in on this. You stay, we all stay."

Maurice sat down on the most comfortable chair. " I don't care how long it takes," he declared, " to thrash this thing out. I shall stay all night."

" So'll I."

The situation was becoming ridiculous. " Well, you won't mind," Bessie said, " if I *don't* stay ? "

" If you go, I come with you," Maurice maintained.

" Oh, hell ! " Bessie was so tired she ached, and here were these two keeping her from the sound, restful sleep that alone she craved. " Go and play somewhere else," she commanded fretfully.

It was a deadlock. They just sat, and at sitting, while Ron was the more solid and rock-like, Maurice was the more restless and disturbing. Fervently Bessie wished that Esther with her ironic, dry humour had been there to send them away. This comes, Bessie thought with a rueful grin, of being an unprotected girl living alone. She couldn't go and sleep in the bush ; it was burnt black, all hot and smoking. She couldn't leave the place deserted with Esther returning tomorrow. She couldn't stay there with two infuriated males ready to fly at each other's throats.

" Ron," she said suddenly, " will you do me a favour ? "

Ron's expression acknowledged complete willingness to sacrifice life and limb.

" Then see Maurice to the station and go straight home yourself."

" Right-o." Ron rose as aggressively as he had sat down. He jerked a thumb menacingly at Maurice. " Home ! Do you want to go on your feet or will I knock you out and carry you ? " He advanced with a purpose.

Maurice stood up also. " Bessie ! " His tone was distressed. " My dear girl, this is impossible."

" I'm not having you stay all night," Bessie declared, then added drily : " I've got my reputation to consider. What there is left of it."

" If you insist on my going, remember I shall not return. I shall not have anything further to do with you, and you need not think to come into the studio to-morrow. I cannot have my feelings trifled with in this way."

" Hooray ! " Bessie murmured unfeelingly.

" I am going," Maurice said with dignity, " and one last word . . ."

" Come on," Ron said grimly. " You heard what she said."

" How do I know you're not coming back here as soon as I am out of the way ? "

" You don't," Ron admitted. " But you hear her say she don't want me. That's enough, isn't it ? " He turned to Bessie. " G'night, Bess."

" Good night," Maurice said superbly. " And good-bye." He did not really mean it ; but it allowed him to turn and stalk out into the darkness with the attentive

Mr. Chugg at his heels. Maurice had every intention, as soon as he shook Ron Chugg off, of returning and finishing the discussion ; but, from the look of Ron, not only would he see Maurice to the train, but he would wait several trains to make sure he did not come back.

Bessie watched them go with relief. The room seemed to have more air in it after their departure. She felt freer, happier, but so tired she could not think. One thing she did know, she was quit of Maurice and glad of it. She wanted to stay here with Esther and learn about planting fruit trees and making jam and selling eggs. She was not in love with Maurice, nor with Ron Chugg. She was in love with Esther's barren little bit of land and this disreputable weatherboard hut. Time enough later to settle in her mind whether she wanted to marry anyone.

Bessie had been lying in bed for some time, restful, relaxed, when it struck her that the silence of the bush, a dead silence broken only by a rustling stir, was disturbed by a curious intermittent noise. It became apparent when she reluctantly dragged herself to the window, that the siege had not been lifted. Ron Chugg and Maurice were standing by the slip-rails talking and Maurice had not troubled to lower his voice. This affront made her angrier than anything that had happened. How dare they hang about the place !

" You go away," she ordered indignantly. " Both of you. D'you hear me ? "

They heard her. Their voices dwindled up the track, and were hushed in the solemn, moonlit peace, leaving Bessie to return to her solitary couch.

She stretched herself with a luxurious sigh, pleasurably conscious that had Maurice stayed and worn down her resistance, she would now be occupying the cold outer edge of the same bed, sleeping humbly on whatever left-over portion Maurice allowed. It might be selfish, but it was very pleasant to have a bed all to yourself and not be sharing it with a sister or a man, very pleasant to have solitude and time to think out what you wanted to do with your life. Very pleasant not to share your life and live on the left-over edge of it.

THE END

www.ingramcontent.com/pod-product-compliance
Lightning Source LLC
Chambersburg PA
CBHW050024180626
46810CB00002B/567